HE WAS DEMANDING MORE AND MORE OF HER....

She bristled. "Exactly what are you suggesting, Mr. Murphy?" She took two small steps away from him as if she feared contamination.

"A bargain."

Letty didn't say anything for a couple of moments, then swallowed hard and asked, "Exactly what kind of . . . 'bargain'?"

He smiled slowly and looked her over, allowing his gaze to linger over the fullness of her breasts and the subtle curve of her hips. He was sure to let his appreciation show in his eyes.

"One night. You and me together, all night. In exchange I'll accompany you into Zarcero."

SOONER OR LATER

Debbie Macomber

HarperTorch
An Imprint of HarperCollins*Publishers*

This is a work of fiction. Names, characters, places, and incidents are products of the author's imagination or are used fictitiously and are not to be construed as real. Any resemblance to actual events, locales, organizations, or persons, living or dead, is entirely coincidental.

HARPERTORCH
An Imprint of HarperCollins*Publishers*
10 East 53rd Street
New York, New York 10022-5299

Copyright © 1996 by Debbie Macomber
Cover photograph by Comstock
ISBN: 0-06-072733-0

First HarperTorch special paperback printing: April 2004
First HarperPaperbacks printing: June 1996

HarperCollins®, HarperTorch™, and ◆™ are trademarks of HarperCollins Publishers Inc.

Printed in the United States of America

Visit HarperTorch on the World Wide Web at www.harpercollins.com

To my friends who love the smell of chlorine in the morning as much as I do.

Rachel Williams, Audrey Rugh, Lorraine Reece, Joyce Hudson, Leta Taylor, Marjorie Johnson, Debbie Noble, Mary Cammin, Maria Houston, Janet Hane, Sue Felix, Mark Ryan, Jessie Truax, Greg Northcutt, Bill Irvine, Per Johnson, and Kathy Davis for watching over us all.

ACKNOWLEDGMENTS

Every now and again a writer is challenged with a hero like Murphy. The man drove me bananas in *Someday Soon* and refused to leave me alone until I promised him his own book. I knew from the beginning that it would take a special woman to win this chauvinist's heart. Soon Letty was born in my mind. A woman of grit and faith. A woman with a mission. The story came, but I struggled with the title. Then on New Year's Eve my husband got tickets for us to see a sixties musical review. Among those playing was Gary Puckett. He came on stage and sang one of his earlier hits. The lyrics leaped out–*sooner or later love is gonna get you*. My husband assumed I was overcome with memories when I stood up and cheered, but my excitement was because I'd found the perfect title. *Sooner or Later*. Murphy had challenged the fates and by heaven love got him! I hope you'll come to love him, too.

My gratitude to those who lent a helping hand along the way. My editor, Carolyn Marino, for her blue pen and her insights. To Susan Wiggs for critiquing the manuscript for me. Irene Goodman, my agent, who either pats me on the shoulder or kicks me in the butt, depending on what I need most. As always to Wayne for twenty-seven years of love and support. I don't know of any writer who's been blessed with more loyal readers. Your letters have touched my heart.

SOONER OR LATER

Prologue

A *woman's frantic scream* pierced Luke Madden's slumber. He bolted upright and shook his head, hoping to clear the sleepy fog from his brain.

The rumors had been rampant for weeks, filled with threats of a military coup, but the Zarcero government was handling the situation competently. Less than a week ago, Luke had personally been assured by President Cartago that there was no need for concern.

The screech of rapid-fire gunshots was followed by shrieks of horror and outrage.

Luke threw back the lone sheet and reached for his pants. The hair on the back of his neck stood straight out as the sound of booted feet slapped on the boardwalk outside his window.

No sooner had he yanked up the zipper than his door slammed open. A crazy-eyed soldier toting an Uzi stormed into Luke's bedroom, screaming at him in hysterical Spanish, demanding that he join the others in the compound.

The first thought that flashed into Luke's mind was that he was going to die.

Away from home. Away from his twin sister.

In that split second, he realized how desperately he longed to live. A mental image of Rosita, the brown-eyed beauty he loved and planned to marry, filtered into his thoughts as he rushed to follow the guerrilla's orders.

Chaos greeted him outside. Frightened, desperate women huddled in a circle by the fountain, protecting their children. Frantically Luke searched for Rosita and was relieved when he found her with the other women.

The lifeless body of Ramón Hermosa lay sprawled in a pool of blood outside the chapel doors. Mowed down by hate. Murdered in the name of progress. The dead man's open eyes stared blankly into the night.

Ramón. *Dear God, not Ramón.* Anger surged through Luke like an electric current. The kind old man was no threat to anyone.

"What is it you want?" Luke cried out, clenching his fists.

Three men, all heavily armed, approached him. One slammed the butt of his rifle against Luke's shoulder, shoving him closer to the women. Intense pain spiraled down his arm.

"What do you want?" Luke repeated, ignoring the danger to himself.

The three men parted when an officer approached.

Hate gleamed in their commander's eyes as he studied Luke. Luke could feel the other man's loathing as keenly as he'd once felt Rosita's love.

"I understand you are a friend of our president," the commander spat out. Slowly a sinister, evil smile edged up the sides of his mouth. "Or should I say *former* president."

"This is a mission," Luke explained, gesturing toward the church. "I have nothing to do with politics."

"You should have thought of that before you made friends with José Cartago. You will pay dearly for that friendship, *Señor.* Very dearly indeed."

He removed a polished pistol from his holster and pointed it at Luke's head.

"No, for the love of God, *no!*" Rosita screamed, and raced across the grounds. Sobbing, she threw herself at the commander's feet. "Please, I beg of you in the name of the Virgin Mother, I plead with you not to do this."

But it was too late, Luke realized. He was a dead man.

1

"I'm willing to pay you for your services."

"Let me see if I understand you correctly," Murphy said, eyeing the prim and oh-so-proper postmistress who held his mail hostage. "You want *me* to accompany you to Zarcero?"

The woman was nuts, Murphy decided. There were no two ways about it. Letty Madden, postmistress of Boothill, Texas, was a prime candidate for the loony bin.

She looked up at him from behind her scarred oak desk in her private office, her brown eyes as dark as bittersweet chocolate. This female-in-distress performance might weaken another man's defenses, but not Murphy's. He had no intention of interrupting a well-deserved rest for some woman with an itch up her butt, seeking adventure.

His opinion of the opposite sex had never been high,

and since his friends Cain and Mallory had both married, his attitude was even worse. It'd take more than the fluttering of this postmistress's eyelashes for him to traipse through some jungle on a wild-goose chase.

"You don't understand," she insisted.

Murphy understood all right; he just didn't happen to be interested in the job. Besides, the postmistress wouldn't earn enough money in two lifetimes to afford him or the services of Deliverance Company.

"It's my brother," she continued, and bit into her trembling lower lip.

A nice touch, Murphy mused skeptically, but it wouldn't change his mind.

"He's a missionary."

She actually managed to look as though she were on the verge of weeping. She was good, Murphy gave her that much. Sincerity all but oozed from her pores.

"Since the Zarceran government collapsed, no one in the State Department or CIA can tell me what's happened to him. The phone lines are down, and now the United States has severed diplomatic relations. The people in the State Department won't even talk to me anymore. But I refuse to forget my brother."

"I can't help you." He didn't mean to be rude, or heartless, but he simply wasn't interested. He'd already told her as much three times, but she'd apparently opted not to believe him.

This was the first of several errors on her part. Murphy was a man who meant what he said. If her brother was stupid enough to plant himself in a country on the verge of political collapse, then he deserved what he got.

"Please," she added with a soft, breathless quality to her voice, "won't you reconsider?"

Murphy heaved an impatient sigh. The last thing he'd expected when he stopped off to retrieve his mail was to be cornered by one of Boothill's most virtuous citizens.

"You can help me," she insisted, her voice elevating with entreaty. "It's just that you won't. It isn't as if I'm asking you to do this out of the kindness of your heart!"

Good thing, because Murphy's nature didn't lean toward the charitable.

"I said I'd pay you, and I meant it. I realize a man of your expertise doesn't come cheap, and—"

"My expertise?" No one in Boothill knew what he did for a living, and that was the way he wanted it.

"You don't honestly think I don't know what you are, do you?" Her chin came up a notch, as if he'd insulted her intelligence. "I'm not stupid, Mr. . Murphy. There are certain matters one cannot help but notice when sorting the mail. You're a soldier of fortune."

She said the words as though they made her mouth dirty. No doubt this lily white sister of a missionary had never sunk to such despicable levels before now. Murphy, lowlife that he was, loved it. He certainly didn't expect a decent, God-fearing woman like Letty Madden would encourage business dealings with the likes of him.

"I'll pay you," she offered again. "Anything you ask."

He snorted softly and purposely leveled his gaze at her breasts, wanting to shock her.

"I know all about Deliverance Company."

That caught Murphy's interest. "You do, do you?"

She stiffened. "Mr. Murphy, please, my brother is all I have. My parents . . . my father died four years ago and there's only Luke and me."

Murphy wasn't keen on delivering a few home truths, but it seemed necessary. "Listen, I'm sorry about your brother being in Zarcero. But nothing you say or do now is going to change the fact that the country's in chaos.

"If you're seeking my advice, then I'll give it. You'd be wasting your time, energy, and finances to look for your brother at this late date. The chances are he's been dead two weeks or more."

"No," she said with such vehemence that Murphy flinched. "Luke's my twin. I'd know if he were dead. I'd feel it here." She slapped her clenched fist over her heart, and her shoulders heaved with the strength of her conviction. "Believe me, Mr. Murphy, Luke's alive."

Murphy had no desire to argue with her. She could believe anything she damn well pleased, and if it comforted her to think her brother had survived the coup, so be it.

"Can I have my mail now?" he asked impatiently, and stretched out his arm.

Letty reluctantly handed him the few pieces. "Is there anything I can say or do to convince you to take on this assignment?" she asked, and boldly held his eyes.

"Not one damn thing." Now that he had what he'd come for, he turned and walked out the door. Before he left the post office, he glanced over his shoulder and experienced a twinge of regret when he saw her head bowed in defeat. He couldn't help feeling bad for her and her brother, but not enough that he'd sacrifice the first time he'd had free in months.

By the time Murphy arrived home twenty minutes later, his sympathy for the postmistress's plight had waned. He'd noticed her before, plenty of times. She was exactly the type of woman he avoided most. Those goody-goody, holier-than-thou ones were the worst.

Letty Madden was a pretty thing, or could be, if she'd ever stop apologizing for being a woman. She wore her long hair away from her face, as if pulling it tight enough against her head might erase any sign of wrinkles. The plain postal uniforms did nothing to enhance what nature had generously given her. If she wore any makeup, it would surprise him. She seemed downright afraid of her own femininity.

Murphy had no use for religion and even less use for women in general. Oh, they had their place, he'd be the first to admit, but that was generally atop a mattress, smelling of perfume and sex. He paid for their services and walked away free of any emotional entanglements.

He'd seen firsthand what a woman could do to mess up men's lives. In the last few years he'd lost his two best friends, and not to any bullet. No, the weapon that had ruined both Cain McClellan and Tim Mallory was far more deadly. Each had gotten hammered by the cockeyed emotion they called love.

At one time Deliverance Company had comprised

Cain, Mallory, Bailey, Jack Keller, and Murphy, a crack team of ex-military experts who'd pulled off some of the world's most daring rescue missions. But no more.

Murphy didn't need Cain or Mallory to teach him when it came to women. He'd learned everything he needed to know from his mother. The woman was both weak and pitiful. From the time he was ten, Murphy knew that he wanted nothing to do with the opposite sex. He may have only been a snot-nosed kid at the time, but his insight had served him well in the twenty-five years since.

Even Jack Keller, his best and most trusted friend, had been taken in by a woman's charms. His mistake had damn near cost him his life. Jack continued to carry the scars of his weakness, not that he'd learned his lesson, Murphy noted. Jack had come dangerously close to messing up more than one mission by not keeping his zipper closed. His friend had a weakness for a pretty face.

Murphy walked into his house ten miles outside of Boothill and slapped the mail on the kitchen counter. For all the hassle he'd gone through to get it, there wasn't anything more than a handful of bills and a few advertisements.

He opened the fridge, took out a cold beer, and headed for the porch.

The screen door slammed behind him as he slumped on the wicker chair and braced one booted foot against the post. The sun blared down hot and intense. Even the shimmering afternoon air seemed to protest the heat.

Boothill wasn't the end of the world, but a person could view it from there, and that suited Murphy just fine.

Smiling to himself, he took a long, deep swallow of the beer and wiped his forearm against his brow.

It didn't get any better than this.

2

Slim Watkins stepped into the post office at five minutes to five, right before closing time. The local rancher removed his hat and rotated the brim as he waited for Letty to acknowledge him.

She offered him a fragile smile and prayed he hadn't come to ask her to dinner. Her appetite had vanished when Murphy, her one last hope, had refused to help her. Not only was he not interested, but he'd barely given her a chance to tell him about Luke. Nor had he taken the time to hear her proposal. Letty didn't know what she was going to do now.

"Did you talk to him?" Slim asked anxiously. "The man you thought could help you?"

Slim was a decent, hardworking rancher. Although forty with one college-age son, he'd been Letty's most persistent suitor for the last couple of years. The pool of eligible young men had never been large in these parts and was fast evaporating.

"Letty?" he tried again when she didn't immediately respond.

"I talked to him."

"And?" Slim pressed. "Did he agree to accompany you to Zarcero?"

"No," she answered flatly.

A short, tense silence followed her announcement. "You aren't going alone, then, are you?"

"Of course I am," she insisted, irritated that he'd suggest otherwise. "I have to, don't you see? Luke's my brother."

"But I thought that man you talked to from the State Department advised you against making such a trip. He said there wasn't anything the United States could do if you got yourself in trouble."

"It doesn't matter what the State Department or anyone else advises me!" Letty cried. "I have to know what's happened to Luke. I don't have any other option. Luke would never leave me, and I refuse to abandon him."

The rancher lowered his head and slowly rotated the hat brim between his nimble fingers. "I'm going to worry about you, Letty, off in a foreign country, with no one there to protect you. You know I'd accompany you myself, but—"

"You have the ranch and your son. Billy might not live at home, but he still needs you."

Slim appeared relieved when she offered him a ready excuse.

"I'd go in a heartbeat if it wasn't for Billy."

Letty patted his forearm. "I know."

The rancher's eyes met hers. "How about dinner

tonight? I checked in at Rosie's and the special is Swiss steak. I know how you like Rosie's home cooking."

"Thanks, Slim, but not tonight," she said softly, knowing she was disappointing him. "I've got some thinking to do."

She had to find Luke. If she died in the process, so be it, but she refused to sit back and do nothing.

The house was dark but cool when Letty arrived home. She switched on the air conditioner and opened the top three buttons of her blouse, slipped off her shoes, and sat on the sofa. With her feet propped on the coffee table, she closed her eyes and let the cool air circulating the room revive her. A drop of perspiration slowly rolled from her neck toward the valley between her ample breasts. She pinched her lips, remembering how the mercenary's gaze had fallen to her breasts when she'd suggested paying him.

The man was dark and dangerous, and she'd been a fool to ask for his help. She should have known better, but she was desperate. He'd stood within inches of her, invading her space, filling up the tiny office with his presence. She could feel his heat, smell the uniquely masculine scent of him. The expression on his cold, dark face had been unreadable except when she'd offered to pay him. Then and only then had any expression leaked into his features, and he'd silently laughed at her.

Annoyed, she rose and in short order changed out of her uniform and into cotton pants and a sleeveless top. With a critical eye, she walked down the even rows of her herb garden, preferring to wait until the sun had set before she watered her precious plants.

Letty's grandmother, her namesake, had taught her about the medicinal properties of herbs. Letty had been an avid student until her grandmother's death when she was eleven. She'd grieved the death of Grammy more than she had the loss of her own mother.

Grammy had filled the shoes of Donna Madden soon after she'd abandoned her family and disappeared. Letty and Luke had only been five and far too young to comprehend what had happened. Over the course of years, rumors had reached Letty's tender ears about her mother's weaknesses. Stories of a woman addicted to alcohol and men.

After her mother's disappearance, their father, the local minister, had asked Grammy for help, so she'd moved in with the family.

Grammy was a grand southern woman who lacked neither grace nor charm. Whenever there was a death in the community, Grammy would visit the family home, stop the clocks, cover the mirrors with sheets, and place a cup of salt in the windowsill. More often than not Letty and Luke accompanied her on such trips. Letty never fully understood the purpose behind these rituals and didn't think to ask before Grammy's passing.

But when her father had laid his own mother to rest, Letty had raced home, and with tears streaming down her face, she'd reverently stopped the giant grandfather clock that tolled in the study and covered the bathroom mirror with a clean white sheet. Last, she'd dutifully set the salt in the kitchen window, then hurried back to the church, knowing her grandmother would have approved.

Letty had inherited her grandmother's green thumb, and her garden flourished year after year. She wasn't the healer her grandmother had been, but there were a number of home remedies she'd practiced on herself, her brother, and their father while he was alive.

The night before the news of the coup had reached Letty, she'd woken with her heart racing frantically, her head pounding. Instinctively she'd known something was terribly wrong with her twin. Many hours had passed before she'd heard that the government of Zarcero had fallen and guerrillas had taken over the capital. As the days progressed, news of atrocities committed against the people of Zarcero filled the television screen. Letty had watched in horror, praying her brother and his small, floundering group of followers had been spared.

The feeling that Luke was in trouble hadn't left Letty since that night. If anything, the sensation had intensified.

There was no help for it. She was going to Zarcero with or without help.

And it looked very much as if she'd be making the trip alone.

As luck would have it, two days later Murphy literally ran into Letty at the hardware store. He felt his backside bump against a soft, womanly figure and turned around, prepared to apologize. The words froze on his lips as his gaze slammed into Letty Madden's.

From her shocked expression, Murphy suspected their meeting had taken her by surprise as well.

"Good day, Mr. Murphy," she greeted him formally, as if they'd stumbled upon each other at a Sunday school picnic. Fat chance of that ever happening.

He nodded slightly and was ready to turn away when he noticed the contents of her shopping cart.

"I'm buying supplies for my trip into Zarcero," she informed him.

He picked up a flare and wondered if it was worth the effort to tell her that these were the last thing she was going to need.

"I thought flares might come in handy," she said, studying him.

Murphy tossed it back inside her cart. "Sure, if you want to alert the whole damn country that you've arrived."

"Oh, but I thought—" She stopped abruptly, clamping her mouth closed.

Murphy purchased what he needed and promptly left the store. At his best estimate Letty Madden would last fifteen minutes in Zarcero. If that.

He opened his truck door and was about to leave when she called out to him.

"Mr. Murphy . . ."

Groaning inwardly, Murphy climbed inside the cab. "What is it now?" he demanded, making sure she knew he resented the intrusion.

To her credit, she didn't cower the way some women would. "I won't keep you long." She stood on the sidewalk, looking uneasy but determined. The woman had mettle, he'd say that for her.

"When I approached you earlier, you didn't give me a chance to make my proposal."

"Any offer you could make wouldn't interest me." He didn't leave room for misunderstanding. Nothing she could propose would be enough to persuade him to join her in this suicide mission.

Her eyes held his. "I'm willing to pay you fifty thousand dollars to help me find my brother."

Murphy frowned, wondering where a woman like Letty Madden could come up with that kind of ready cash.

"My house is paid for, Mr. Murphy," she explained as though she'd read his mind. "It would be only a formality of signing a few papers at the bank for me to give you the cash in hand by tomorrow afternoon."

Damn it all, Murphy could feel himself weakening. It wasn't the money, either, but the woman. She was going to get herself killed for nothing.

He didn't figure he could stop her from going, but he wasn't going to encourage her. "There isn't enough money in the world to induce me to accompany you into Zarcero," he said smoothly, and started the ignition.

Her shoulders fell and she nodded, accepting his final word. "I apologize for detaining you. Have a good day, Mr. Murphy."

He didn't respond, merely put the truck in reverse and sped out of town, eager to make his escape.

"Damn fool woman," he muttered as he rode back to the house.

The light on his answering machine was blinking when Murphy walked into the kitchen. Only one person in the world outside of the good people of Boothill knew where he was: Jack Keller.

"How's the side?" Murphy asked when he reached his friend.

"It hurts like a son of a bitch," Jack muttered.

Murphy laughed. Jack had suffered two broken ribs from a confrontation with a runaway jeep during their last mission and had taken this time to recuperate in his condo. Jack preferred city life, but Murphy opted to stay away from people. The plains of Texas suited him just fine.

"I thought I'd check and see how things are going with you," Jack said.

If Murphy found any fault with his friend, it was that Jack was a social animal. The man simply didn't know how to relax. A week in Kansas City and Jack was bored, ready for new action.

"I'm fine," Murphy muttered. Damn, but he couldn't get that pesky Madden woman off his mind. Flares, she was buying flares to take into Zarcero. Talk about stupid.

Jack hesitated. "What's wrong?"

"Nothing," Murphy snapped.

"Well, something's troubling you. I can hear it in your voice."

Murphy didn't think it would do any harm to tell Jack about the postmistress. "I got a job offer," he said, and supplied the details.

"She's going to get herself killed," Jack announced flatly. Murphy didn't want to think about what would happen to Letty Madden when the rebel soldiers got hold of her. Odds were they'd torture her, rape her, and then take sadistic pleasure in killing her.

"What's she look like?" his friend asked next.

"What the hell does it matter?" Murphy barked. She was pretty and young, mid-twenties, by his estimate. Not that the guerrillas would care.

"Are you going to help her?"

Murphy's response was emphatic. "Not on your life."

"You know what it sounds like to me?" Jack said, and laughed lightly.

"I don't want to know."

"You need to get laid."

"What the hell?"

"You've been too long without a woman," Jack pronounced. "Otherwise this business with the postmistress wouldn't be bothering you so much. You've been living like a saint ever since you bought out Deliverance Company. Man, it's time to let down your hair and live a little."

"The last thing I need is a woman."

"Take my advice, Murphy, find yourself a hole-in-the-wall tavern, get good and drunk, and then let a woman take you home for the night. Trust me, you'll feel worlds better in the morning."

Sex was Jack's solution to everything. "My getting laid isn't going to stop the Madden dame from risking her damn fool neck," Murphy insisted.

"Maybe not, but you might not feel responsible for her death."

"I don't accept any responsibility for whatever happens to her."

Jack chuckled, that know-it-all laugh of his that caused Murphy's jaw to clench.

"What's so damn funny?"

"You," Jack returned evenly. "You're tempted to do it."

"The hell I am." It'd take a tornado to move him from his spread. He'd worked long and hard for this vacation, he deserved it, and he damn well was going to take it. He wasn't about to let an annoying post-mistress interfere with his plans. If she was hell-bent on getting herself killed, it wasn't his problem.

"Admit it, Murphy, you want her."

"It's time we ended this conversation."

Murphy went to replace the telephone receiver when he heard Jack laugh and shout, "Call me when you get back from Zarcero."

"I'll rot in hell first," he muttered, satisfied.

The restlessness that plagued Murphy the rest of that day and all of the next refused to go away. He tried all the things that normally calmed his spirit. He worked on the truck, rode his stallion across his land, and sat on the porch with a beer and a good book until the sun set. Nothing worked.

Again and again he reminded himself that Letty Madden wasn't his responsibility. As far as he was concerned, the woman was on her own.

Normally Murphy wasn't a man overly burdened by conscience. No one in his profession could be. He lived by his own rules and his own code of honor.

He didn't want to become involved. But if the postmistress insisted on rescuing her brother, which was laughable when he thought about it, death would come as a blessing. Miss Sunday School Teacher viewed him as crude and vulgar, but he was a pussycat compared to the horror that awaited her in Zarcero.

There had to be a way to get her to listen to reason and at the same time absolve him of any guilt.

The idea of how to do both came to him the following afternoon.

Murphy whistled as he drove into town, his mood greatly improved. In a manner of speaking, he decided, Jack was responsible. Murphy parked his truck outside of the post office and made his way inside.

Letty was selling stamps to an older gentleman, but her gaze was immediately drawn to his. He noted the surprise and hope filter into her eyes as he sauntered over to his box. Her look didn't waver as he took his own sweet time removing his mail. When the post office was empty he approached Letty.

"May I help you?" she asked, clearly struggling to maintain a crisp, professional voice.

"Are you still intent on traveling to Zarcero?" he asked briskly.

"Of course. My flight into Hojancha is already booked. I leave in two days."

"I've had a change of heart," he said, leaning indolently against the counter.

Her relief was evident. "I thought . . . I hoped the money might influence you. I'll stop off at the bank this afternoon and make the arrangements. If you want, I'll give you half up front and half when we return."

"We'll talk about the money later. There are other, more pressing concerns we should discuss first."

She blinked and stared at him as if unsure she'd heard him correctly. "Such as?"

"No money will change hands until—"

"You want it in securities? That might take some time, and I'm not sure—"

"I said we'll discuss the financial arrangement later," he said impatiently, louder this time.

"What is it you want?"

"You're a virgin, aren't you?" He spoke slowly, letting his words sink into that thick, stubborn skull of hers.

Her eyes went incredibly round, and she swallowed uncomfortably. "That's none of your business."

Murphy laughed coarsely. "That tells me everything I need to know. I'll overlook your lack of experience. Generally I prefer a woman seasoned in the art of lovemaking."

She bristled. "Exactly what are you suggesting, Mr. Murphy?" She took two small steps away from him as if she feared contamination.

"A bargain."

Letty didn't say anything for a couple of moments, then swallowed hard and asked, "Exactly what kind of . . . 'bargain'?"

He smiled slowly and looked her over, allowing his gaze to linger over the fullness of her breasts and the subtle curve of her hips. He was sure to let his appreciation show in his eyes.

"One night. You and me together, all night. In exchange I'll accompany you into Zarcero."

Her eyes widened to such proportions that he struggled to keep from laughing outright. To say she hesitated would have been an understatement.

"It's a take-it-or-leave-it offer," he said. She'd leave it. There wasn't a single doubt in Murphy's mind. If she decided to tackle this project on her own, then she would leave him with a clean conscience. He'd laid his cards on the table. Either she agreed or not; it was up to her.

Satisfied, he turned to go. He made it all the way to the door before she stopped him.

"Shaun . . . Mr. Murphy," she called out to him in a voice that trembled.

Shaun. No one called him Shaun. Few even knew his given name. He didn't like the sound of it on her lips. Didn't like the way her lilting voice cried out to him.

Confident, he turned back.

She smiled weakly. "Would tomorrow evening be convenient?"

3

The man was mad. That was the only possible explanation, Letty decided, for what he'd asked—no, demanded—of her.

He'd guessed correctly that she was a virgin. Her experience with men had been limited to a few chaste kisses shared with Slim, which surprisingly she'd enjoyed. Her awakening sexuality made Letty uncomfortable and slightly afraid.

Although she'd been raised by her father and with Luke, Letty wasn't accustomed to men. The boys in her class had thought of her as bookish and mousy. Deep down, Letty feared she might be weak like her mother, and she couldn't bear the thought. For years she'd done everything she could to ignore the female part of herself.

In an effort to pull herself together emotionally and physically, Letty gripped the dresser drawer with both hands and took in several deep, calming breaths. She had no choice; she needed Murphy. For protection, for guidance. For survival.

Once she found Luke, she could be rid of the mercenary. If the price for his help cost Letty her virginity, so be it. She'd gladly pay that and a hell of a lot more if it meant saving her brother.

She'd close her eyes, grit her teeth, and bear the humiliation. It should be over soon enough.

When the doorbell chimed, Letty quickly surveyed the scene. The dinner table was set, a bottle of wine was on ice, and the steaks were ready to be grilled.

She squared her shoulders before opening the door. The soldier of fortune stood on the other side of the screen. He looked none too pleased for a man who was about to receive the most precious gift she had to give. He studied the full length of her.

She was well aware how she looked. She'd dressed as if the temperature dipped below freezing instead of soaring in the mid-nineties. Letty knew her features were pale. The blush she'd added to her cheeks had failed to disguise her pallor. Her long-sleeved blouse was buttoned all the way to her chin, and the collar seemed to have a choke hold around her neck. The full-length skirt swirled to her feet, not giving so much as a glimpse of her slim ankles.

Silently she held the screen door open for him. He wore fatigues, she noted, as if he were already in the jungle. When he walked into her house, she realized he towered a good six inches above her five-foot-five frame, dwarfing her. She didn't remember him being so large earlier.

His gaze moved past her to the dining room table, and he frowned.

"I thought we'd have dinner first," she suggested timidly, hating the way her voice trembled.

"As you wish."

Letty's hands felt clammy. She rubbed them together and made an effort at conversation. It soon became apparent that Murphy wasn't interested in small talk.

"If you'd open the wine bottle, I'll put the steaks on the barbecue," she said into the silence. "I imagine you like yours rare."

"Very rare."

Letty didn't know how she'd manage to down a single bite of her dinner, but she'd face that when the time came. Her heart was racing already, and she felt light-headed and dizzy, and they hadn't made it to the bedroom yet.

While he dealt with the wine bottle, she carried the meat outside. The heat was stifling, and sweat beaded on her upper lip.

Murphy appeared a couple of minutes later, bringing her a wineglass.

"Thank you, Shaun." She called him by his first name in an effort to ease some of the tension between them. Since they'd be traveling together for a number of days, it'd help if they came to some sort of agreement.

"Call me Murphy." His voice was low, gravelly, and unfriendly, setting the tone for this meeting.

"All right . . . Murphy." The T-bone steaks sizzled as she placed them on the hot grill.

He studied her. Every move she made. His eyes

were like those of a hawk, watching its prey, ready for just the precise moment to pounce.

"Smile," he ordered sharply.

Her head came up. "I beg your pardon?"

"You heard me; I asked you to smile. You look like you expect me to skewer and roast you over that barbecue any minute now." He mocked her with that cocky grin of his.

With a determined effort, she managed a half-hearted smile. "There, is that better?"

"A little, but not much."

Letty focused her attention on the meat and flipped both steaks.

"You're overplaying the martyr bit," he offered next.

Her fingers tightened around the spatula, but she didn't take the bait.

"What's the matter, Letty, are you afraid you might enjoy it? It can be a pleasurable experience if you let it," he added.

She stopped herself from responding. She'd agreed to his terms and came to him of her own free will, but she considered him a cold-blooded bastard. But then he was exactly what she'd need in Zarcero in order to find Luke and get them out of the country alive.

"That's it, isn't it?" Murphy demanded gleefully. "You're afraid you might enjoy it."

She couldn't keep quiet a second longer. "I sincerely doubt that," she blurted out, forcing her voice to remain even.

His laugh was low and mocking. "There are ways of

making you want me. Trust me, before I'm finished, you'll beg me to take you."

He moved closer, so close she could feel his breath against her temple. She stiffened. It was all she could do to keep from backing away from him. By the sheer force of her will, she managed to hold her ground.

"Do all men possess this colossal ego?" she challenged. "Or is it just you? Do you honestly believe you're so irresistible that I'll beg you to make love to me?" She made his claim sound ridiculous. "All I can say is that you've been listening to women you pay for this sort of enjoyment."

"Are you suggesting I'm not paying you?" he taunted.

Letty blanched.

"Don't worry about it, sweetheart. Comfort yourself any way you wish. If you want to tell yourself you're doing this for Luke, for God, for country, then feel free. If you've convinced yourself you're making a noble sacrifice of your virginity, that's all right by me, too. Make it easy on yourself, it's no skin off my nose." He tapped his finger against her nose, and involuntarily she flinched. The small display of weakness appeared to amuse him.

He trailed his index finger down the side of her face, then idly took a meandering route downward over her shoulder and lower to the crest of her breast. He paused, like a cat toying with a mouse, leaving her to suffer the anticipation of him circling her nipple. In that moment, Letty almost hated him.

"Tell yourself anything you want," he whispered

seductively, "if it'll make the lovemaking easier for you. But we both know the truth, don't we?"

"I don't know what you're talking about."

He laughed, but the sound was devoid of amusement. "You've been wanting to be rid of your virginity for a good long time now, haven't you?"

She sucked in her breath, desperately afraid he spoke the truth. "No," she denied vehemently.

Then, without reason, he backed away from her and sipped his wine. "It doesn't matter, you've got the perfect excuse. You're doing it for good ole Luke. Just don't be shocked when you learn he's already dead."

"Don't say that," she shouted. "I told you earlier, Luke's alive. I know he is, as surely as I live and breathe, my brother's alive. Why would I agree to this if he wasn't?"

"That's the real question, don't you think?" he asked calmly.

Shaking violently, Letty hurriedly dished the steaks onto a platter and carried them back inside the house. Murphy followed, closing the back door. It shut with an ominous clang.

Disguising her distress behind a smiling facade, she set the platter in the center of the table, then brought out two salad bowls from the refrigerator.

"You can sit down now," she said, and took her place at the far end of the table, as if this were a festive dinner party. She waited while he took his chair before removing the brightly colored linen napkin and setting it in her lap.

He reached for his fork. She reached for hers and waited for him to sample the salad.

"Everything in the salad came out of my garden," she said proudly. "The dressing is an old family recipe. I hope you enjoy it."

He didn't comment, which was just as well, Letty decided. She held her breath and waited until he'd finished the salad before finding the courage to sample her own. Murphy acted as if this were a contest on how fast one could consume a meal. He'd sliced into his steak before she'd had more than two bites of her salad.

Letty Madden had nerve. Murphy would say that for her. He'd done his damnedest to ridicule, mock, and intimidate her. Yet for all intents and purposes it looked as if she actually intended to follow through with their agreement.

Damn it all to hell, this wasn't the way it was supposed to happen. He'd fully expected the virgin to fold. Okay, so it was going to take more than a few idle threats. He was prepared for that as well.

While she nibbled at her dinner, he took the opportunity to eat the best damn meal he'd had in weeks. Generally he didn't fuss much with food. His freezer was stocked full of frozen entrées, and he wasn't opposed to one of those military food packs meant for the field now and again. But a steak, grilled over an open fire, why, that was too good to let pass.

"How . . . is everything?" she asked.

"Good." If she was looking for him to gush all over himself complimenting her, then she had a long wait. These delay tactics of hers would be good for only so long. He had to hand it to her; thus far her strategy had worked.

He hadn't anticipated her fixing dinner. The way he figured, he'd arrive and five minutes later he'd have her backside plastered against the mattress. It was a hell of a lot longer than any of those rebel soldiers would give her if they got their hands on her. The thought didn't comfort him.

He finished long before she did, stood, and carried his plate into the kitchen.

"You ready?" he asked, looking down the hallway toward what was sure to be her bedroom.

She paled, a good sign, he figured.

"I . . . haven't finished with my meal. I'll only take a minute. Have another glass of wine, if you want. There's plenty."

"No thanks."

He could almost see the dread settle over her. With a dignity reserved for those who could afford it, she placed the napkin on the table and stood. Her steps were weighted with reluctance.

She led him to her bedroom and turned abruptly to face him. "If you don't mind, I'd like to brush my teeth."

He hesitated, then shrugged. "Fine, but sooner or later you're going to have to make good on your promise." While he waited, he sat on the edge of the mattress and unlaced his boots.

She took a long white nightgown into the bathroom with her. Her steps were slow, as if she were royalty walking to the guillotine.

"Let your hair down," he instructed.

She hesitated, then nodded.

By the time she returned, Murphy had stripped out of his fatigues and was under the sheets, his back braced against the headboard. He locked his hands behind his head, his elbows jutting out on either side.

"Nice," he said, studying her, and he meant it. She resembled Little Bo Peep in her long white gown. All she lacked to complete the picture was a long wooden staff and a few lambs traipsing behind her.

Her dark brown hair flowed halfway down the middle of her back in gentle waves. Her feet were bare. If she was hoping the portrayal of a fairy-tale character would persuade him not to touch her, she was wrong.

"Move closer to the bed," he instructed.

"Are you nude?" Her eyes shifted away from his torso.

He grinned slowly. "What do you think?"

She dragged in a deep breath, stiffened, and closed her eyes.

"Are you ready to abandon your brother already?"

"No," she insisted shakily. "A deal's a deal. You can do with me whatever you want."

"I intend to," he said, leaving no room for doubt.

"You're a bastard."

He laughed. "So I've been told."

She glanced over her shoulder. "Would you mind if I turned off the light first?"

"Leave it on."

A look of panic came over her, and she dashed from the bedroom. Murphy resisted the urge to laugh outright. He hadn't so much as touched her and already she was racing for the hills. He loved it. The poor, dowdy virgin was deathly afraid of a naked man.

To his surprise, she returned a moment later with the wine. She drank directly from the bottle herself, dipping her head back and liberally downing the alcohol. Amazed, Murphy watched.

"Getting drunk won't help," he told her.

"Don't be so sure." She pressed the back of her hand against her lips and wiped away the moisture. "Is there anything you want me to do?"

"Plenty," he assured her, "but we'll get to that soon enough."

She crumpled onto the edge of the bed as if her legs would no longer hold her. The gown shifted in the front, exposing the swell of her breasts. Murphy was intrigued. She had beautiful breasts, lush and full.

Keller was right: he had been too long without a woman. Letty Madden was beginning to look damn good.

"Kiss me," he ordered.

Her eyes appeared enormous as her gaze settled on his mouth. She hesitated, gulped down another swallow of wine, and shifted toward him.

He took the bottle from her hand and set it on the nightstand. "I promise not to bite." He clasped her firmly about the waist and dragged her across the top of the mattress until her torso was pressed against his. Her eyes were huge, her face deathly pale, and she held his look, waiting. Worrying.

He eased forward slightly and touched her mouth with his. He wasn't a cruel man, and despite himself, he almost felt sorry for her.

She didn't resist, but she was as stiff as cardboard.

"Relax," he ordered impatiently.

"I'm trying."

"Try harder." Then, because he was angry with himself for being gentle with her, he captured her head between his hands and yanked her mouth to his. The least she owed him for all his trouble was a decent kiss, although he strongly suspected he'd need to tutor her.

Again she held herself stiff and unyielding. Repeatedly he moved his mouth over hers, less gently this time, molding her lips, shaping them with his own. He felt the peaks of her breasts and battled the growing excitement that threatened to overtake him. Giving himself over to the sensation, he hungrily claimed her lips.

"Open your mouth," he muttered.

"I don't understand, how—"

He took advantage of her doubts by slipping his tongue between her lips and sweeping her mouth. She squirmed, objecting to the invasion, and he let her, although her silk-covered breasts stroking his chest were a torment all their own. Again to her credit, she didn't pull away.

"Like that?" she whispered huskily when he'd finished.

She was doing just fine. More than fine. If they continued like this, soon there'd be no turning back. "Yeah," he mumbled, sounding breathless.

"This part's not so bad."

This wasn't working the way Murphy had planned. He kissed her again, and this time her tongue shyly met his, welcoming his invasion. His breathing deepened, and he demanded more and more of her. To his surprise she freely wrapped her arms around his neck.

"You like this, do you?" He chuckled, wanting her to believe he remained unaffected. He was grateful for the blanket, which concealed his arousal. Her ability to excite him came as an unwelcome surprise. He hadn't counted on the frumpy postmistress having this strong an effect on him.

"What next?"

The only way his plan would work was if he made this as unpleasant for her as possible. "Strip."

She blinked as if she hadn't heard him correctly. "You want me to take off my nightgown?"

"That's what I said."

She looked toward the wall.

"Leave the light on," he insisted.

Ever so slowly, she climbed off the bed and stood directly in front of him. She was nervous and embarrassed as she slowly unfastened the buttons, taking her time with each one. Unfortunately she wasn't aware how much her hesitation enhanced his anticipation. With her eyes tightly closed, she slipped the material over one shoulder. She didn't seem to be prepared for the slick fabric to slither down her body and pool around her feet.

Murphy swallowed a gasp, shocked by her beauty. She was magnificent. Her breasts rose full and proud, her stomach was flat and smooth, and her hips were wide and inviting. With her hands clenched at her sides, she stood before him like a mythical goddess.

Kneeling on the mattress, he captured a nipple between his lips. She squeezed her eyes closed and whimpered softly as he continued to slide his moist tongue over her warm skin. She arched her back and bit into her lower lip.

Unable to wait any longer, he touched her breasts with his hands, bunching them together and squeezing them gently. Her nipples hardened beneath his touch, beading proudly. Her skin was soft, softer than anything he'd ever touched.

Nuzzling her neck with his lips, he ran his hands over her hips and buttocks, familiarizing himself with the silky feel of her. God help him, he'd never experienced anything quite like this, and he was the one with experience. Most of it had been with women far more practiced and skilled than this naive postmistress. Yet Murphy had rarely felt like this. Need clawed at his insides until it became a fierce kind of pain.

His finger touched the silky triangle of curls between the juncture of her thighs. She made a small sound.

"Open your legs for me." No longer did he sound like himself. His voice was husky with need.

"Please . . . let me turn off the light."

"No. Open your thighs," he said again, more forcefully this time.

"I can't."

He heard the anger in her voice, but it didn't sway him. Before another beat of his heart, she braced her feet a couple of inches apart.

"Very good," he praised her, and then, because he

wasn't sure what she expected him to do, he leaned forward and kissed her belly. Working his lips upward, he caught her nipple between his lips and sucked greedily. She swallowed a moan and he smiled to himself, pleased to note he wasn't the only one caught up in what they were doing.

He kissed her lips, subtly coaxing her responses, and then returned his mouth to her breasts. She gasped, and he took full advantage of her surprise to insert his finger inside her, delving between the soft folds of her femininity.

She tensed and started to struggle, but he braced his free hand against her waist.

"Relax," he whispered. "This isn't going to hurt."

Lightly he began to stroke her ultrasensitive flesh. It didn't take long before she was breathing hard.

"See? Didn't I tell you this would be good?"

Her eyes remained tightly shut. Murphy opened her legs farther apart with his hand and covered her mouth with his own.

His head spun and his control was close to snapping. Letty was soft and wet and on the verge of climaxing. She wasn't the only one deeply affected. Touching her like this was driving him wild.

His entire body was throbbing. Either they stopped right that minute or they raced full speed ahead. Murphy opened and closed his eyes in an effort to clear his thoughts. He felt as if he were sinking into a deep, dark pit.

It came to him then, what should have been abundantly clear from the first. Letty Madden wouldn't turn tail and run. Too much was at stake; she had no choice. She was his for the taking. Any hope of her backing out of their deal was lost, and frankly he was glad, because he wanted her. This stodgy, dull woman had turned the tables on him. He was so damned hot for her, he was close to losing it right then and there.

Not wasting any time, he caught her by the shoulders and brought her onto the mattress. Again he was amazed by her softness. She was smooth and sweet.

He kissed her, holding nothing back, then cursed under his breath when the room started to sway.

"What's wrong?" she asked.

"You. Me. Damn it, it's not supposed to be this good."

Fighting the need to rush, Murphy positioned himself between her legs, spreading them wide to accommodate his hips. When she felt his erection rubbing against her, she gasped and her eyes flew open.

"I'll go slow," he promised, forcing himself to remember she was a virgin.

"Murphy," she cried, "kiss me. It won't hurt so bad if you kiss me."

The room began to spin once more, only faster this time. He ignored the sensation and did as she asked, lowering his mouth to hers.

The kiss was wet and wild, as out of control as Murphy was starting to feel. The world began to tumble into a deep, dark precipice, taking him with it. He battled the sensation as long as he could.

He heard himself moan, felt Letty direct his mouth back to hers and kiss him. Damn, but she tasted good. All sweetness. The woman had given him one hell of a surprise.

He tried, God knew he tried. He reared back his head and pushed forward, but his aim was poor. He lowered his hand to his erection, to guide himself into her. She closed her eyes and turned her head, knowing there would be pain. He regretted bringing her pain. "I'll try not to hurt you," he whispered.

It was the last conscious thought Murphy remembered having.

The next time he opened his eyes, it was morning.

4

At first light, Letty slipped out of bed and dressed hurriedly. She dared not look Murphy in the eye for fear he'd know what she'd done. It had taken so long for the herb mixture to take effect that she'd begun to fear it never would. Since she hadn't concocted anything like that before, she wasn't entirely sure of its potency.

She'd thought—hoped, really—that there'd only be time for a few kisses and little else before he fell into a deep slumber.

She should have known he'd fight the effects. Instead he'd done far more than simply kiss her. Try as she might, she realized, she'd never forget her night with Murphy. She'd found pleasure in his arms, before and after.

In the middle of the night, she'd stirred to find herself trapped at his side. His arm was wrapped about her waist, her buttocks tightly tucked against his swollen manhood. By all that was decent, by all that was right she should have escaped him then and there. God forgive her, she hadn't. Even knowing what she did, Letty had closed her eyes and found a strange comfort and security in this mercenary's arms.

Before the herbs had taken effect, Murphy had mumbled that it wasn't supposed to happen this way. Once, he'd claimed it shouldn't be this good. The irony of the situation was that he'd voiced her own thoughts.

She felt that the kisses and the foreplay were something she'd need to endure in order for him to help her find Luke. The last thing she'd anticipated was pleasure. Her body had turned traitor on her. The warm sensation that had stolen over her had come as an unwelcome, unwanted surprise. Murphy was right, it shouldn't have been that good.

"What the hell happened?" he muttered from the other side of the bed.

"What do you mean?" she asked primly, fearing he'd guessed what she'd done.

He sat up and rubbed his face as if scrubbing awake his sleep-clogged mind. Letty was grateful to be completely dressed. She didn't trust him not to touch her again. Worse, she couldn't trust herself not to respond.

"Last night," he elaborated sourly.

"You know darn good and well what happened."

He glared at her, silent and knowing, as if reading her soul. Letty tensed, afraid he'd discovered the truth. The muscles along her shoulder blades tightened painfully.

Then he asked, "Did we . . . you know?"

It demanded every ounce of strength she possessed to look away. "I'd rather we didn't discuss last night."

"Like hell," he shouted, and then grimaced at the harsh sound of his own voice. "Just how much did I have to drink?" He reached for the wine bottle, and his brow folded into thick, irregular lines. "There was only this one bottle, wasn't there?"

"Our flight is scheduled to leave in four hours. I suggest we head for the airport as soon as you're dressed."

Her bags were already packed. She'd carefully considered each item. She had one suitcase, which she planned to leave in Hojancha, the country directly north of Zarcero. All she'd take into the country itself was a backpack. If they found Luke at the mission, they could be in and out in less than twenty-four hours. But if they had to break him out of some hell-hole jail, it would take longer. How much longer, she didn't know.

"You're not going with me," Murphy announced coldly.

"Oh no, you don't," she said, furious that he would try to change their plans now. "We have a deal, one for which I've paid dearly. You can't modify the agreement now."

Despite his nakedness, he threw aside the sheets.

Letty's eyes widened at the sight of the hard muscles of his chest, his lean hips and powerful thighs.

He bore countless scars on his shoulders and stomach. The worst disfigurement was on his left shoulder and looked to have been a bullet wound. She battled back the tenderness that came over her at the sight of his scars. He wasn't the type of man who would appreciate her sympathy.

In him she viewed both strength and beauty. Letty

was mesmerized and embarrassed. She could feel the color creep up her neck and bleed into her cheeks.

Murphy chuckled and appeared to enjoy her discomfort. "Come now, don't you think it's a bit late for the outraged virgin bit? You've seen it all before." He reached for his pants, and his dog tags jingled as he dressed without displaying any uneasiness.

"I'm going with you." She wouldn't take no for an answer. Not when she'd come this far. Luke needed her, and despite what Murphy might think, so did he. In the last two years Letty had been to Zarcero three times. In addition, she was fluent in Spanish. She knew the country and was familiar with the cities and some roads. There were people she knew whom she could trust. Friends who would tell her about Luke, who would help her locate her brother.

"I agreed to find your precious brother for you, and I will," Murphy muttered testily. "I'll keep my word, but I work alone. The last thing I need is a woman tagging along with me."

"This is a fine time for you to tell me that," she cried, furious that he would try to pull this on her now. "We agreed that *you* would *accompany me* to Zarcero for a price. You collected your fee in bed with me last night. You can't change the agreement now."

The coldness in his eyes sliced her to the quick, but Letty didn't so much as flinch. "I'm going with or without you."

He swore. "I know what I'm doing," he shouted. "You'll slow me down."

"I'll help you."

He swore again, louder this time.

"I'm going to Zarcero to find my brother." Unwilling to debate the issue further, she slipped the backpack over her shoulder and carried her lone suitcase outside. His truck was parked behind her car.

She set the suitcase in the truck bed and climbed inside the cab, waiting for Murphy to appear.

It didn't take him long. He soon joined her, slammed the pickup door, swore again, then started the engine. Once on the road, he drove like a man bent on getting himself arrested.

Although he'd been more than willing to vocalize his opinions earlier, he didn't mutter a word during the ninety-minute drive to the airport.

For her part, Letty was filled with questions. Since they were flying into the country of Hojancha, she wanted to know how Murphy intended to get into Zarcero now that the borders had been closed. No traffic was allowed into or out of the country.

In the plane that flew from Houston, they were seated next to each other. His massive shoulders rubbed against hers. Once they were airborne, he removed a map from his carry-on bag. She wanted to volunteer what information she had, but it was apparent that he was in no mood to listen to her, so she said nothing.

Closing her eyes, Letty pressed her head against the window and silently prayed his sour mood would improve. This trip was going to be difficult enough without the two of them constantly at odds.

She didn't expect Murphy to be good company, but it would help if they could be civil to one another. She'd make the best of it, she decided, despite his attitude.

While pretending to be asleep, she studied him as she hadn't before. Her life and that of her brother rested in this man's hands. By no stretch of the imagination would she call him handsome. Everything about the man was intense. If she were to describe him—say, to Luke or one of her friends from church—she'd claim the mercenary possessed battered good looks. Nothing about him was gentle or soft. He was paid to kill, to inflict hate and death and pain upon others.

It came to her then, this contrast she'd discovered, this dark side he flaunted to the world. She'd experienced none of it during their night together. With her he'd been gentle and caring. With her he'd sought to give instead of take.

At first his words had been cruel and demeaning, but his hands and his mouth had displayed a fierce kind of tenderness that had rocked her very core. Shocked her. By the time he'd readied her for lovemaking and guided her onto the bed, she'd wanted him desperately.

It hurt her pride to admit that, but it was God's own truth. Had the herbs not taken effect at that precise moment, she would have given herself to him eagerly.

As it was, she'd been left feeling deeply disappointed and at the same time relieved. She'd been lucky for a woman who'd made a deal with the devil himself.

Damned lucky.

Murphy had made some stupid mistakes in his time, he realized, but this outdid them all. What he needed was to have his head examined. Now he was trapped.

He'd agreed to an assignment he fully considered to be a wild-goose chase. He didn't doubt for a minute Luke Madden's fate. The missionary was long dead.

Even now he didn't fully understand why he'd involved himself in this craziness. It wasn't often he misread people. His life depended on skill and intuition. He could have sworn the minute he went to touch his reticent virgin, she'd swoon. Either that or clench her principles against her plump breasts and run for high ground. It hadn't happened.

To be on the safe side, he'd come to her with a contingency plan. He was a soldier and well aware of the importance of strategy. On the rare possibility of her submitting to his lovemaking, Murphy had decided to leave her virginity intact and renegotiate their deal.

Instead he'd ended up taking her. He wasn't proud of the fact, but there was no going back now. He wasn't a weak man—unlike Jack Keller, who was often a victim of his own desires, especially those of the flesh. To Murphy's way of thinking, women were to be tolerated and used when the opportunity arose. Nothing more. Yet he'd fallen prey to his own physical desires and bedded Letty Madden.

Everytime he glanced her way, something he tried to avoid, he was left to wonder. For reasons he couldn't explain, his memory had gone patchy on him. He remembered everything that led up to the point when he'd actually committed the deed. It worried him.

It could have been the wine, or was it Letty herself he found so potent? Murphy wasn't sure he'd like the answer.

He found that reading her was damn near impossible. Each time he'd broached the subject of their lovemaking, she'd clammed up like an oyster hiding a pearl. God in heaven, he wished he could remember. Now, however, the deed was done, and he had no out. Because of his weakness he was stuck escorting Letty Madden into Zarcero.

The plane landed in Hojancha City at five that afternoon, Texas time. After clearing customs, which meant walking past a guard asleep at his desk, Murphy led the way into the busy terminal.

The inside of the airport had been uncomfortably warm, but the heat outside hit him like a sandblaster. It was like this for him the first few hours in the tropics. The heat, the stench, overpowered him. Depending on the time of day and the year, he sometimes found it difficult to breathe.

His clothes clung to him. Texas in summer wasn't exactly a Garden of Eden, but the tropics were something else. The heat could drain away a man's strength in a matter of hours. He glanced at Letty, wondering how she would adjust, and cursed under his breath at the thought of her tagging along after him through the jungle.

Letty scurried behind him, holding on to her luggage with both hands. Since she'd insisted on bringing along a suitcase, she could damn well carry it herself, Murphy decided.

"We'll be staying in a hotel for the night, won't we?"

"No." As far as he was concerned, the less she knew of his plans the better.

Murphy scanned the crowd, searching for Ramirez, his contact. Ramirez would deliver the weapons and put him in touch with men who'd provide him means across the border into Zarcero. No easy feat, according to what he'd learned. Both would be pricey. Not that he cared; he wasn't the one footing the bill.

"I'll need someplace safe where I can keep my suitcase."

"Did you bring along any valuables?" he asked, glancing over his shoulder. She was doing her best to keep pace with him and not succeeding.

"No, of course not."

At least she was smart enough not to carry cash. "What's inside?"

"Clothes for Luke and a few other medical supplies he might need."

Without hesitation, Murphy took the heavy suitcase out of her hand. He set it on the first available space he could find, flipped open the lock, and tossed a fresh set of clothes over his shoulder.

"What are you doing?" Letty shouted, scrambling to grab the shirt and slacks. Unfortunately a beggar reached them first.

"Murphy," she cried, her voice trembling with outrage.

He ignored her as he continued to discard the contents, including the medical supplies too bulky for her backpack. As far as he could see, there wasn't a damn thing either of them would need. Within seconds a crowd had gathered, scrambling for the clean clothes, creating a commotion behind him.

"You can't do that," Letty cried again. "Those things are for Luke."

She might have entered the fray herself if he hadn't

stuffed the empty suitcase into the closest trash can. Two toothless old men battled for that.

"Why . . . what about Luke?" Letty looked as if she were about to burst into tears.

"Let's get something straight right now," Murphy barked. "If you come into Zarcero with me, you do exactly what I say without question. The minute you contradict or argue with me, the whole deal's off. Understand?"

A rapid transformation came over her as she straightened her shoulders and nodded. "It would be crazy to pay you this ridiculous fee if I didn't bow to your expertise," she agreed, but glanced longingly at the clothes that had once belonged to her brother. "I'll trust you to supply whatever Luke needs when we locate him."

Murphy resisted the urge to remind her Luke was already dead. Far be it for him to burst her bubble. If she chose to believe her brother remained alive, it was her problem.

"We wait over there."

Together they crossed the street. Traffic buzzed past with little regard for safety. Rotting garbage was heaped up against the curb, the stench bad enough to make him want to gag. Murphy saw a rat crawl over it and wondered if Letty had seen it, too. As if she'd read his mind, she glanced at him and grimaced.

"You can wait in a clean hotel while I go into Zarcero if you want," he suggested, hoping she'd see the wisdom of his offer.

As he suspected she would, Letty rejected him with a hard shake of her head.

Murphy groaned inwardly. This was supposed to be his vacation, a little R & R before going back into the field. Instead he'd allowed himself to be outmaneuvered by the sister of a dead missionary. He just hoped Jack had the decency not to tell the others about the mess he'd gotten himself finagled into.

A jeep careened around the corner, and Murphy recognized Ramirez. He'd worked with the dark-skinned contact a couple of years earlier. Not only was Ramirez capable of providing the necessary supplies, his information was generally accurate.

The contact slammed on the brakes in front of the curb and smiled at Murphy, revealing a row of brown teeth. Without further delay, Murphy tossed his duffel bag into the back of the jeep and leaped into the front seat. Letty had a bit of difficulty and wasn't completely inside when Ramirez stepped on the gas and drove off. From his peripheral vision, Murphy saw Letty fall face first into the back, and he laughed silently. To her credit, she didn't cry out or complain, although he was certain her feathers had been ruffled.

"Who's the woman?" Ramirez asked in Spanish.

"No one important," he returned.

"What's she doing here?"

Murphy wasn't in the mood for long explanations. "You don't want to know."

Ramirez frowned. "Is she trouble?"

"No," he returned with a deep sigh, "just a royal pain in the ass."

5

Jack Keller played back the message on his answering machine twice, certain he'd missed something. It was Murphy's voice all right, but Keller had a difficult time believing what his friend was saying.

He'd done it. By heaven, Murphy had actually agreed to escort the do-gooder's sister into Zarcero. Keller wouldn't have believed it if he hadn't heard it with his own ears. His fellow mercenary didn't sound any too pleased about it, either. From the background noise, he must have phoned from the airport.

Ignoring the pain in his ribs, Keller sat back, folded his hands behind his head, and propped his feet on the ottoman. He couldn't help wondering what had brought on this bout of altruism. Jack grinned, knowing full well Murphy's feelings about this assignment. Either this postmistress had more money than God or she'd fed Murphy one hell of a line. But that didn't add up, either.

If this woman had that kind of wealth, she wouldn't be working for the post office. As for someone—particularly a woman—suckering Murphy into doing something he didn't want, well, Keller had yet to see that happen. Women weren't a big temptation for Murphy. He disapproved of any type of distraction. Murphy claimed he'd saved Jack's sorry ass more than once by keeping his pants zipped.

Unfortunately, Keller had learned his lesson the hard way. He'd been set up by a pretty señorita a couple of years back and damn near had the bejesus beat out of him as a result. It'd taken nearly six months for him to heal, and he'd carry the scars of that encounter all of his life. Since then he'd stringently followed Murphy's lead. A mission was a mission.

Kansas, however, was a different story. He liked to brag about his sexual exploits, and to be fair, he'd had his share of women. He'd never quite figured out what it was about him that attracted them. One look in the mirror confirmed he wasn't calendar material. He suspected it was his blue eyes. Women appeared to have a thing about blue eyes. Sinatra would testify to that. Brad Pitt, too.

For reasons he didn't want to examine too closely, Marcie Alexander came to mind. He'd been in town close to three weeks now and he'd yet to call on Marcie. Ever-welcoming Marcie. He could go six months or longer without contacting her, and the minute she saw him all was forgiven.

He couldn't remember where he'd met the blonde. Probably some bar. The hairdresser had a heart of pure gold. Unfortunately everyone knew it and took advantage of her generosity, Keller included. It shamed him when he thought about the way he'd used her over the years.

He'd arrive unannounced on her doorstep, and she'd take him in like a stray tomcat, feed him, pet him, make love to him, and expect damn little in return. Generally that was what she got.

She never questioned the lies he fed her, and there'd been some real doozies. Once she even bailed him out of jail. Now that he thought about it, he wasn't entirely sure he'd reimbursed her.

What he liked best about Marcie was that she never hassled him. Not with questions. Not with demands. She gave and he took. But then he figured he wasn't the only recipient of her generous nature. Marcie was the kind of woman a man used.

He'd been in town a while now, and he could have gotten laid every night of the week if he'd wanted. Trouble was, he didn't feel like paying for what most women would give away free. He'd never experienced much trouble convincing a lady to spread her thighs. What he didn't like was the expectation that went with it.

Just the other night he'd gone home with a stacked blonde, and after the usual tap dance to the bedroom, he'd spent the night. The next morning she'd asked if he'd fix her toilet for her. For the love of heaven, her toilet, and then she'd gotten all bent out of shape when he'd refused. Apparently she'd felt that since she'd pumped him dry, he owed her.

The more he thought about it, the more inclined he was to contact Marcie. He could use a little of her tender, loving care. She'd never been particularly beautiful, but what she lacked in looks was more than compensated for by her body. His mouth watered just thinking about her breasts. Lush and full, they were probably the finest specimens he'd ever laid eyes on, and he'd seen more than his fair share.

He loved it when they were in bed together and he'd be flat on his back and Marcie would lean over him. He'd play with her nipples, tease her unmercifully with his tongue until she'd whimper and whine. Only then would he give her what they both craved. Heaven almighty, the woman knew how to satisfy him, and she wasn't looking for him to work on her toilet afterward, either.

The decision made, Keller headed out the front door. If he timed it right, he'd arrive at Marcie's beauty shop before she closed down for the night.

By the time he started his car, Keller was wondering if he'd hold out long enough to make it over to her place. The way he felt right then, the chair in the lunch room in the back of the shop would suit him just fine.

Keller sighed with relief when he turned onto her street and saw Marcie's shop. A lot of things had changed in nine months, and he'd half feared she might have gone out of business.

He parked on the street, stopped off at the flower shop a couple of doors down, and picked up a bouquet of spring flowers. The roses were prettier, but a lot more expensive. Marcie wouldn't know the difference and certainly wouldn't care.

The bell above the door chimed when he entered

the shop. He was greeted with the faint acrid scent of perm solution. A young blond woman behind the counter eyed him with open curiosity.

"I'm looking for Marcie," he announced, flashing the girl an easy smile. His timing couldn't have been more perfect. There seemed to be a lull in business.

The girl ran her finger down the appointment book. "Are you scheduled?"

"I'm an old friend," Keller explained. "If she's in, I'd like to surprise her."

"She's here." The girl gestured with her head for him to go on back.

By then Keller was so eager, he nearly trotted to the rear of the shop. He pulled back the makeshift curtain and gifted Marcie with a smile potent enough to melt glacial ice.

"Hello, dahlin'."

She sat at the table, her feet propped up by a chair, eating popcorn. Her eyes widened with surprise mingled with delight when she saw who it was. "Johnny."

Another sin. Keller had never gotten around to telling her his name was Jack. What the hell, Johnny was close enough.

"You look fabulous." He told her that everytime he saw her, especially after a lengthy absence, only this time it was true. She'd done something different with her hair. It was shorter, curlier, blonder. He'd miss burying his hands into the thick, waist-deep length, but this style suited her much better.

She opened her mouth, but nothing came out.

He set the flowers on the table and reached for her,

lifting her out of the chair. Before she could protest, and he knew she wouldn't, he had her in his arms.

Her mouth was as sweet as he remembered. She tasted good, damn good. Better than anyone in a hell of a long time. She smelled faintly of lilacs instead of stale barroom smoke, as fresh and clean as summer itself.

One kiss didn't come anywhere close to satisfying him. Before she could tell him how much she'd missed him, he had her backed against the wall with his tongue halfway down her throat. She squirmed against him, her eagerness stroking his pride and his manhood. Soon he was so damned hard, his erection throbbed against the metal teeth of his zipper. This was even better than he expected. For the life of him, Keller couldn't remember why he'd waited so long to contact her.

"In a minute, baby," he whispered between deep kisses. He wanted to see and taste her breasts before he gave them what they both wanted.

He had three buttons of her pink uniform unfastened before he heard her.

"No, Johnny."

He was sure he'd misunderstood. "No?" He must be hearing things. Her body was telling him one thing and her lips another.

"It's been nine months since I last saw you."

"I told you before, baby, I travel for business."

She closed her eyes and breathed hard and heavy. "Then what's this?"

He slipped his hand inside her uniform and sighed audibly when he cupped her breast. Her nipple pearled instantly. "Pleasure, sweetheart, pure pleasure." He kissed her again before she could say anything more. When he finished, they were both breathing hard.

"This isn't such a good idea," she said. Again her body claimed it was the best idea either of them had had in a hell of a long time.

"I've missed you." To prove how much, he gripped her hand and placed it over his erection. "See?" he whispered.

"I don't think you heard me," she said, and it was clear she wanted him as much as he did her. "This isn't a good idea."

"Marcie, what's wrong?" He nuzzled her neck, sucking and licking, doing all the things she enjoyed most. At least he thought it was Marcie who enjoyed this kind of love play. Faces tended to blend together in his mind.

"I'm not the same person I was before."

Keller groaned and lifted his head reluctantly. "You got married?"

"No . . . ."

Relieved, he kissed her again, deeper this time, persuading her in ways words never would.

"Johnny . . ." She sounded as if she were about to weep.

"You're engaged?"

"No."

Kissing away her protests, he bunched her breasts with both hands. It took him far longer than it should have to realize there wasn't as much there as had been previously. Slowly he lifted his head, and his eyes found hers.

"I had breast reduction surgery." She answered the question before he could ask.

Personally Keller couldn't understand why she'd go and do anything so silly. He wanted to tell her that, but she started talking as if she intended never to stop.

"You can't flitter in and out of my life any longer. I've never been anything more than a convenience to you, Johnny. You're here one day and gone the next. You never let me know when you're coming or, worse, when you're leaving. The last time—" She stopped abruptly and seemed to strengthen her resolve before she said, "I refuse to be used any longer."

"Use you? Me? Honey, that's not true." He put on a hurt look, but that didn't seem to faze her.

"A bouquet of flowers isn't enough to make up for nine months of silence."

"But I've already explained—"

"You've barged in and out of my life for the last time," she said, cutting him off. "It'd be better for the both of us if you left now." Her eyes flashed with conviction.

"Fine, if that's the way you feel." He had half a mind to remind her there was plenty of what she gave away.

She lowered her head. "Good-bye, Johnny."

He turned around, intent on walking out the door, letting her think it was no skin off his nose. They'd had some fun together, could still, but she wasn't willing. So be it. He jerked back the cloth curtain and happened to glance back. Marcie stood with her shoulder braced against the door, her head lowered and her bottom lip trembling.

"Do I owe you any money?" he asked.

"No."

Hell if he could remember if he did or didn't. "Good-bye, Marcie," he said softly. With that he left the beauty salon.

An hour later he sat in a bar, feeling more than a little melancholy. He didn't know what the world was coming to these days. He hadn't had a cigarette in three years, but he needed one now. After downing the last of his beer, he walked outside.

A whore, dressed in leather pants and a halter top, leaned against the side of the building. Catching sight of him, she offered a coy smile.

"Looking for a good time, honey?" she asked.

It was a sad commentary that Keller had to think about the answer. Sure, he'd been after a good time, but he'd wanted it with Marcie.

"I don't know," he said, playing her game. "What are you offering?"

With her hand planted against the swell of her hips, she sidled toward him, her cherry lips easing into a sultry smile. "I'll give you anything your little heart desires," she whispered, then laughed softly, "and then some."

"What is this, a slow night?"

"You want it slow, you got it slow."

For the life of him, Keller couldn't dredge up the enthusiasm. All he could think about was Marcie and the feel of her as her sweet body had rubbed against him.

"Another time," he said.

"Hey, you're missing out on the best time of your life."

Keller doubted that. The best time had been nine months ago with Marcie. He wouldn't be any kind of man not to know she'd wanted him. Damn, he'd like to know what had gotten into her.

Marcie. By heaven, he'd have her again just as soon as he figured out a way to change her mind.

6

He was alive, although he wasn't sure why. After repeated interrogations and torture, Luke Madden would have welcomed anything that would relieve the agony of the past two weeks. Even death.

He tried to find a place in his heart to forgive the men who abused his body and tormented his soul. With regret, he admitted that forgiveness had become more of a struggle than dealing with the crippling pain.

From the look in the soldiers' eyes, Luke realized they found pleasure in his suffering. Pleasure in the power they held over him.

Once he figured out their game, he did his utmost to keep from crying out, refusing to give their demented souls the satisfaction they sought. Consequently they beat him harder, tortured him longer, in an effort to break his spirit and steal from him what remained of his dignity. That, too, along with everything else, lay in shambles at his feet. He had no will to continue.

Even now, Luke didn't understand the beatings. He was a missionary, a man of God. Despite evidence to the contrary, his captors believed his mission in Zarcero involved far more than preaching the gospel. They assumed he'd been a confidant of President Cartago. While it was true that he'd known and admired Zarcero's president, he'd never been an associate. From what Luke had gleaned, Cartago had managed to hide a large portion of the country's treasury before his death. Why his captors assumed he would know anything about that, Luke could only guess.

"Luke?" Rosita's voice came to him like a siren's song, soft and lilting, tender and healing.

With effort he raised his head from the thin mattress and tried to open his eyes, but they were swollen shut. After the interrogation, when the pain burned in his gut and racked his soul, he found comfort in thinking about Rosita. How beautiful she was, how gentle and kind.

"Rosita?" He prayed as he'd never prayed before that she hadn't been taken, and in the same breath, the same heartbeat, he thanked God for the one last opportunity to see her.

"I'm here. Don't fear, it's safe, no one knows."

"A guard . . . someone might find you."

"My uncle is a guard," she whispered. "He arranged it so I could see you."

The risk she took far outweighed any benefit. Luke

couldn't bear thinking about what would happen if she were discovered. His beautiful Rosita had risked her life for him.

Luke heard the key that opened the cell door.

"Oh, Luke, what have they done to you?" Emotion rocked her voice. How he wished he could have spared her this.

Luke knew that his swollen eyes were the least of his injuries. His figured that he had several broken ribs, along with any number of internal injuries. His fingernails had long since been ripped off, and he suspected a muscle in his leg had been torn.

Whispering in Spanish, Rosita gently brushed the hair from his brow, her fingers trembling with tenderness and love. He felt her anguish as keenly as his own.

With her arm supporting his neck, she elevated his head and pressed a cup to his lips. Luke drank thirstily, gratefully.

When he'd finished, she bent forward and whispered close to his ear, "We will free you soon. Hector and the others have a plan, and—"

"No, Rosita, no." He wouldn't survive much longer, of this he was certain. Another beating like the one that afternoon would surely kill him. He didn't understand even now why he was alive. The future held more pain; death would come as a welcome release, more of a friend than an enemy.

"Please, my love, be strong, hang on just a little longer," she whispered frantically.

"No." He refused to allow his friends to put their lives at risk in an effort to save him. "It's too late for me."

"No, you must be strong. Soon, very soon, you will be free."

"Rosita, I can't . . . forgive me, but no." With every ounce of strength he possessed, he pleaded with her.

He must have lost consciousness because the next thing he knew she was gone. Perhaps it had been a hallucination; he prayed it was. It would be far better that she not see him like this. His heart swelled with love and regret for the life they might have once shared. It was too late for them, much too late.

With thoughts of Rosita lingering in his mind, Luke felt weighted down with a great sadness. He hadn't the strength to continue or the will to go on. He prayed Rosita would forgive him. Rosita and his sister.

Thoughts of Letty crowded his head. They'd always been close, he and Letty. His death would devastate her, and for that he was truly sorry. He knew his twin as well as he knew his own heart. With that knowledge came the understanding that Letty wouldn't want him to suffer any longer.

7

Letty stood under the shade of a low-hung roof as the sun beat down upon the parched land like a giant hammer. Heat shimmered in the early afternoon, the sun so bright it nearly blinded her.

She was joined under the thatched roof by a young mother, who held an infant of about six months. The woman eyed Letty wearily and appeared to be waiting for one of the men arguing with Murphy on the other side of the road.

Letty focused her attention on Murphy and Ramirez while they haggled with the wiry, dark-skinned man and an older gentleman. Their raised, excited voices stirred the hot afternoon air. Letty could make out only an intermittent word, just enough to catch the gist of the disagreement, which had to do with money. Her Spanish was excellent, but the men all seemed to be talking at once, heatedly disagreeing with one another.

Murphy objected loudest. From what she could make out, the two men claimed that the danger had greatly increased and the price for guiding him and Letty across the Hojancha border into Zarcero had doubled.

Once, briefly, Ramirez glanced across the dirt road toward Letty, as if to let her know she was the real reason for their trouble. She stiffened her spine and glared right back, unwilling to let him intimidate her. Since she was the one financing this venture, he had no reason to complain.

From Murphy's stance, Letty could see he wasn't the least bit pleased with this turn of events. Not once did he look her way. She could have keeled over in a dead faint before he'd take the trouble to recognize her. If then.

Since they'd boarded the plane in Texas he'd gone out of his way to make it abundantly clear that he didn't want her with him. It went without saying that he considered her presence on this trip nothing but a damn nuisance.

Letty removed her hat and wiped the perspiration from her brow with the back of her forearm. The backpack cut into her shoulder blades and she shifted the thick straps, hoping to relieve the pressure. Her khaki shirt was drenched with sweat, but she'd die before she'd complain about the heat or anything else.

The previous night and a good portion of the morning had been spent being tossed about like a sack of potatoes in the back of Ramirez's jeep. She couldn't be sure what Murphy had told the other man, but she strongly suspected he'd offered him a bonus if he could find a way to be rid of her. The jeep's journey across Hojancha was worse than any carnival ride she'd taken.

When they'd arrived in this village, Murphy had ordered her out of the jeep like a drill sergeant talking to a raw recruit. Her legs had felt weak, but she'd managed to climb down.

When the wiry man and his friend arrived, Murphy had insisted she wait for him across the dirt roadway. It seemed to Letty that he could have used her help with the negotiations. But in an effort to keep the peace, she'd done as he asked without arguing. She did note, however, that Murphy was forced to rely on Ramirez more than once to translate for him. She could have done just as well.

Irritated and frustrated, Letty paced the shaded area and waited for the men to resolve the money issue. As far as she was concerned, it didn't matter what it cost. They had to get into Zarcero without being discovered.

A weak, pitiful cry cut into her thoughts. Letty turned to find the clean-scrubbed young mother attempting to comfort the infant in her arms by feeding her a bottle. A second frail sob racked the sick baby, and the woman's eyes filled with tears that she struggled to hold back.

Letty had been so caught up in her own troubles that she hadn't given the mother and child more than an indifferent glance.

"Is the baby ill?" Letty asked gently in Spanish.

The woman glanced up, her eyes riddled with worry and tears, but she didn't respond.

Letty pressed the back of her hand against the infant's forehead. The baby burned with fever.

The woman closed her arms more securely around her child and nodded.

Letty asked a number of questions and learned the other woman's name was Anna and the baby's Margherita.

Letty slipped the backpack off her shoulder and knelt on the dirt floor. Not knowing in what condition they'd find Luke, she'd brought along a variety of herb creams, tinctures, and ointments. Surely she could find something that would help reduce the baby's fever.

"I'm not a doctor," Letty explained as she drew out a small plastic bottle. She explained that the liquid had been made from Chinese honeysuckle, often called jin yin. "I know about herbs, and two small drops of this added to juice or sweetened water will help the baby's fever."

Anna's eyes widened as if she weren't sure she should trust Letty.

"You must reduce her fever," Letty implored, realizing she could offer Anna no reassurances. This woman knew nothing of her.

Weighing the decision carefully, Anna handed Letty her baby's bottle. Using an eye dropper, Letty added two tiny drops of the tincture to the water.

With a damp cloth, she moistened the infant's face and chest. Sitting side by side, the two women cooled the baby. Temporarily comfortable, the infant sucked her bottle dry.

"Ramón is Margherita's father," she said, glaring at the wiry fellow standing next to Murphy.

"Your husband?"

Quickly Anna lowered her eyes. "No." Her shoulders stiffened as she raised her head, her look strong and proud. "I came because I hoped Ramón would help me find a doctor for Margherita. When I told him I was pregnant, he said a baby was my responsibility, not his. I loved him. I gave my heart to a man with no soul." Leaning slightly closer, Anna gently pressed her hand over Letty's arm. "He is a man who makes many promises and delivers few. Learn from my mistake. Do not trust him."

Across the road, Murphy looked all the more disgruntled. Ramirez's face was red from arguing, and he shook his head repeatedly.

"I must get into Zarcero," Letty whispered, confiding in Anna.

Her face and eyes revealed her dismay. "No, señorita, Zarcero is a dangerous place for you and your man."

"My brother is there."

Anna's expressive face revealed her apprehension. "It isn't possible. The soldiers won't let you cross the border," she insisted.

"I know. Ramón was supposed to help us."

"Ramón?" Her dark eyes widened all the more, contrasting with the white peasant blouse and flowing skirt. "No," she said with conviction, and shook her head. "Do not put your faith in him, señorita."

"My brother is a good man," Letty returned. "He needs my help."

"A good person like you?" she asked, her hand gripping the tincture bottle.

Letty smiled. She wasn't as good as Luke, not nearly as generous or forgiving. He'd always been there for her, and she refused to abandon him now.

"Like my brother," she agreed meekly.

"I will help you," Anna promised.

"But how?"

Anna glanced over her shoulder and lowered her voice. "Wait here and I will bring my uncle."

"Your uncle?" In Zarcero, Letty had found, every citizen of the country seemed related in one way or another.

Anna smiled for the first time. "He is a man who knows many things."

She slipped away. Discouraged, Letty sat down in the dirt. No more than a minute had passed when Murphy, in a display of anger, stalked across the roadway. Slapping his hat against his thigh, Ramirez stormed to the jeep and drove off.

Joining Letty in the shade, Murphy slumped down next to her and draped his wrists over his knees. "I don't trust that son of a bitch. He'd sell his grandmother's liver without giving the matter a second thought."

"Ramón?" she asked casually.

He pinned her with his glare. "How'd you know his name?"

"How could I have missed it? You were arguing loud enough to alert the Canadian Mounties."

Murphy ran his hand along the back of his neck. "Getting into Zarcero isn't going to be any picnic."

"I didn't expect it would."

"Ramirez suggests we wait a couple of days. . . ."

"No," she responded emphatically, "we don't have that kind of time."

"Listen, I don't like this any better than you do. It's a pain in the ass, but we don't have a choice."

"I might have found someone who can help," she said.

If she hadn't garnered his full attention earlier, Letty had it now.

"What do you mean?"

"The young woman who was here earlier told me about her uncle. Apparently he has connections."

"An uncle? We're supposed to trust some girl's uncle?"

"I'd rather put my life in his hands than rely on your man. I'd like to remind you, I'm paying top dollar for your expertise. The next time we need someone, I suggest you check out their credentials."

To her surprise, Murphy tossed back his head and laughed out loud. "You want me to check their credentials? Now I know why I let you come along. For comic relief."

She ignored his humor, especially since it was at her expense.

Fifteen minutes later Anna returned with her uncle. The old man looked to be in his seventies. He was barely able to walk, his gait was slow and measured. A large straw hat shaded his face from the sun.

"I'm Carlos," he whispered in a voice that sounded surprisingly young. "I understand you are on an important mission?"

"Yes," Letty responded eagerly.

Murphy said nothing, but his eyes rounded with surprise when he realized she was fluent in Spanish.

"Come, my niece has been remiss in not offering you refreshments."

Encouraged, Letty stood and brushed the dirt from her backside.

The older gentleman's eyes bored into her. "Margherita is sleeping comfortably for the first time in two days."

Murphy scowled and glanced at Letty, not understanding. Letty didn't bother to enlighten him. If Murphy learned of her knowledge with herbs, he might put two and two together. It wouldn't take much for him to figure out the cause of his memory lapse.

Once inside the old man's dilapidated house, Carlos offered them canned juice. Before the old man could serve the refreshment, Murphy pulled him aside and started asking questions. Once again he ignored Letty as if she had no interest in the discussion.

The two men spoke in a low murmur. She noticed that Murphy did most of the talking. His body language told her that he found the terms to be more to his liking, and he nodded a couple of times.

Only once did he glance her way. He frowned before responding to Carlos's inquiry.

Letty was tired of being left out of the conversation, particularly one that pertained to her and rescuing Luke. She was strongly tempted to speak her mind, but soon the two men appeared to come to some agreement.

Carlos nodded and left, leaving Letty and Murphy alone in the tiny house.

"What's happening?" she asked.

"Carlos has a boat by the river. He's agreed to smuggle us into Zarcero himself. He's known and trusted, and even if he is stopped and questioned, the rebels aren't likely to search the boat." He hesitated and studied her as if seeing her with fresh eyes. "But if we are stopped, we need to be prepared. Do you know anything about guns?"

She swallowed uncomfortably. "Some." Damn little if the truth be known, but she was afraid to admit it.

"Well, you're about to get a crash course. If you're going into Zarcero, then you'd better damn well know how to take care of yourself."

"That's why I have you," she argued.

Apparently her answer didn't please him because he reached behind him and produced a deadly-looking handgun and laid it across his palm. "Either you learn how to fire this or you stay here and wait for me."

He walked out of the house, leaving her the option to follow him or sulk alone inside. Given no choice, she scurried after him. Murphy would like nothing better than to leave her behind.

Letty didn't know how long they walked; it seemed like forever. In reality, they'd probably gone a mile. The Hojancha countryside, like that of Zarcero, was unsurpassingly beautiful and variable. The air, cooler now, was soft and sweet as they traipsed across the parched grass.

By the time Murphy stopped, her legs ached and her breath stung her lungs, but she managed to keep up with his murderous pace.

Tucking a white piece of paper in the low-lying arms of a Cenizero tree, Murphy stated matter-of-factly, "We don't leave for Zarcero until you can fire a bullet into this."

"You've got to be joking."

One cold glance told her he wasn't.

"This isn't what I'm paying you for." She hated guns and couldn't imagine actually having to fire one, let alone kill another human being. She'd rather die herself.

Unfortunately Murphy gave her no option. It was either learn to handle the pistol or wait while he went into Zarcero for Luke.

"Give me the pistol," she demanded, determined to learn how to use it, just to spite Murphy.

8

The moon cast a reflective glow across the smooth waters of the Colon River, which separated Hojancha from Zarcero. Carlos's small engine echoed in the night like a rusty buzz saw. Letty wondered how it was that no one could hear their approach.

Hidden under the tarp, she lay tense and stiff after holding still for so many hours. Murphy, disguised in clothes borrowed from a native fisherman, sat next to Carlos in a boat little bigger than a dinghy. It amazed her that the vessel had been able to keep from sinking with the three of them, plus their supplies.

Letty would have liked to point out the unfairness of such an arrangement—her under the tarp, Murphy not—but she knew before she protested that it would do no good. When Murphy set his mind to something, it took an act of God to convince him otherwise.

In an effort to ward off the stench of rotting fish,

she alternately held her breath and closed her eyes, neither of which helped. She would have given just about anything to escape in the luxury of sleep. The night before she'd spent in the back of a jeep, being jostled around like a popcorn seed in hot grease. She could no more have slept during their road trip than leapt over the moon.

Murphy hadn't gotten any more rest than she, and she wondered how he fared. He gave no indication that it had affected him in any way, but for all she knew he might routinely go without sleep just to prove how tough he was.

"It isn't wise to take the woman with you," Letty heard Carlos say. She had to strain to hear Murphy's response.

"It isn't my choice."

"What is so important in Zarcero that you would risk your lives?"

"The less you know, old man, the better," Murphy returned without emotion.

The boat engine slowed to a crawl. "She is a good woman."

Murphy snorted.

In other circumstances Letty might have felt guilty for having duped Murphy into accompanying her to Zarcero, but not after his insulting proposition. As far as she was concerned, he got what he deserved.

It troubled her the way her mind continued to return, like a homing pigeon, to their lone night together. It had been a momentary lapse in judgment. She wasn't perfect, but she wasn't like her mother either, selling herself and her family for the pleasure she found in the arms of another man.

The episode wouldn't be repeated, of that she was confident.

The boat engine died completely, and Letty stirred beneath the tarp. Turning her face toward the narrow opening, she angled upward to catch a whiff of cool, fresh air.

"Are we there?" she whispered.

"I told you to keep quiet," Murphy answered impatiently.

"I want out from under here."

"All in good time." He pressed his booted foot against her rump. "Don't move a muscle, understand?"

"The area is said to be crawling with rebel troops," Carlos warned. "Stay off the main roads."

Not waiting another moment, fearing Murphy wasn't to be trusted not to leave her behind, Letty peeled back the tarp and sat upright. Even in the thick night, she felt Murphy's displeasure.

The rowboat butted gently against the bank.

Murphy grabbed Letty's upper arm and helped her to her feet. "Be as quiet as you can, understand?" he demanded.

"I wasn't planning to break into song."

Murphy leaped onto the riverbank and left Letty to make her own way out of the boat while he dealt with the equipment.

Carlos handed him the necessities collected from Ramirez earlier.

"Be very careful, my friends," Carlos warned before he made his way back to the helm and artfully steered the dinghy away from the bank. "I will search each night for the signal for your return."

"Thank you," Letty whispered back, and waved.

"Come on," Murphy urged, "remember what Carlos said."

The old man had said plenty, most of it in an effort to dissuade Letty from going into Zarcero. After a while she had paid little attention.

"Come on, we've got a long walk."

"I won't hold you up," she said, determined she'd keel over before she gave him the satisfaction. Carlos had given them the name of a friend, someone they could trust, who would put them up for the night.

After strapping the supplies onto his back, Murphy started walking. Letty hurriedly slung her backpack over her shoulder and followed. Neither spoke.

In other circumstances Letty would have paused to admire the heavens. A smattering of stars littered the night with tiny beacons of light. After the crushing heat of the day, the cool breeze came as a welcome relief.

Murphy didn't give her time to stargaze. She quickened her pace in order to keep up with him and was soon winded, but she didn't complain. Regulating her breathing, she kept her steps in line with his.

They rested once, and only then because Murphy thought he might have heard something. He held out his hand, pressed his finger to his lips, and stopped dead in his tracks. The moments seemed interminable. The night spoke to them in snippets of sounds. A bird's call echoed like crickets, or perhaps monkeys, and the breeze whispered through the thick foliage. Letty smelled orchids. The texture of this country her brother loved so dearly wrapped itself around her.

After what seemed a lifetime, they continued walk-

ing. It came to her that this was the first time she was
truly alone with Murphy. Her survival and that of her
brother rested squarely on his shoulders. The realiza-
tion brought home the fact that she knew very little
about this man. Not much more than his name and
post office box. True, she'd sorted his mail for a number of years, such as it was. A few bills now and again,
magazines, most with a military orientation. What she
knew about him wouldn't fill an envelope, and yet
she'd trusted him with her life.

When the farmhouse Carlos had mentioned came
into sight, Letty sagged with relief. The straps from
the backpack dug into her shoulders, and her calves
ached from walking at Murphy's killing pace.

"Wait here," Murphy ordered in the imperious tone
he used with her. He guided her under the protection
of a large tree.

"Where are you going?" she asked.

"I can't and won't explain my motives everytime I
ask you to do something," he snapped. "I'll be back as
soon as I can."

She opened her mouth to argue and knew it would
be useless.

Carlos had already told them his cousin would see to
their needs. If it had been up to her, she would have
walked up to the farmer's front door, knocked politely,
and explained who she was. But not Murphy. He apparently felt it was necessary to break in like a criminal.

Unfortunately the moonlight wasn't bright enough
for her to see where he'd gone. The man all but disappeared into the shadows. Either that or she'd viewed
too many James Bond movies.

With her back braced against the tree trunk, Letty sat. She must have drifted off to sleep, because the next thing she knew, Murphy had returned.

"We'll spend the night in the barn," he whispered.

She rubbed the sleep from her face and nodded. Anything with the word "sleep" in it appealed to her.

"There's a small catch."

She raised questioning eyes to him.

"We stay together."

She frowned, not understanding the problem since she thought that was why she'd hired him.

"In other words, we sleep next to each other."

9

Men baffled and exasperated Marcie Alexander. She stood in the room in the back of her beauty shop and mulled over her life to this point.

For her first thirty-one years the only place she found herself capable of communicating with the opposite sex was in bed. Well, she was finished with that, finished with having her friends marry and start a family while she waited on the sidelines, and for what? To get passed over again and again.

She'd never had a problem attracting a man. At certain times in her life she'd dated three or four at a time. But instead of feeling wanted and charmed, she felt more like an air traffic controller.

Finding men had always been a snap, especially the needy kind. From the time she was sixteen and lost her virginity in the backseat of a car at a drive-in movie during *Raging Bull*, she'd maintained steady relationships with the opposite sex. Unfortunately her relationships rarely lasted more than a month or two at a stretch.

As the years progressed, Marcie had learned a painful lesson. Men flattered her, courted her, borrowed money from her—which they seldom repaid—and then promptly deserted her. The pattern rarely changed. She'd fallen in and out of love so often, it had all become a revolving door.

Men flocked to her. Mostly penniless ones with problems for her to solve. She specialized in rescue operations. For years she was convinced that all these poor, misunderstood men really needed was the love of a good woman.

In her search for a husband, Marcie had gone so far as to take out a loan in order for Danny, the man of the hour, to hire an attorney so he could get a divorce. It was understood that once he was free from his battle-ax of a wife, he'd marry her. It took Marcie two months to learn he'd never been married. The money had paid for a weekend in Vegas with another woman. It had taken her sixteen months to pay back the bank.

What hurt most was that a couple of her beauty school friends had been married twice. They'd already started families with two different men while Marcie had yet to snag even one husband.

Every time she saw another one of her friends with a baby and a doting husband, her heart ached. She wanted it all. A husband, a gentle, kind man who would love her to distraction. One man enough to keep her satisfied in life and in bed.

Heaven would testify that she'd done her best to

land herself a lifetime mate. But in her long, often tumultuous search, Marcie had met only one such candidate. Johnny.

She was crazy about him the minute she laid eyes on him in the Pour House, a local bar. Her mistake, she realized, was sleeping with him too soon. Way too soon.

He'd gone home with her on some phony excuse and, against her better judgment, stayed the night. Hard as she tried, Marcie couldn't make herself regret it. Sex with Johnny had been incredible. Probably the best of her entire life.

The following morning, after he'd left her, Marcie feared she'd never hear from him again. She'd nearly wept tears of joy when he showed up on her doorstep a month later. She'd already decided that, if given a second chance with him, she wouldn't make the same mistake. She'd been waiting all her life for a man like Johnny, and come hell or high water she was going to find a way to marry him.

Unfortunately Johnny made her weak, and before she'd realized what was happening, they were back in the bedroom again. This time he stayed the entire weekend. Nothing interrupted them. Not televised football. Not phone calls. Nothing. He didn't even want her to cook, had insisted on ordering out and paying for it himself. When he left her that time, Marcie was so completely exhausted she'd had to stay home from work for two days.

If ever there was a man capable of keeping her happy, it was Johnny. It went without saying that if she wanted to marry him, she'd need to play her cards right, and that meant careful planning.

She was well aware that becoming intimate before forging an emotional bond was a tactical error. Johnny had to want her for more than her body. Marcie knew it, yet she'd allowed herself to be manipulated right back into bed. Mainly because he was such an incredible lover.

As time progressed he stopped by more and more often, but rarely for longer than two or three days. Sometimes he'd show up unexpectedly at the shop and every now and again at her apartment. He wouldn't believe it if she told him, so she never did, but she hadn't been to bed with another man since they'd met.

In their times together, she noted that he rarely spoke about himself. But then they seldom talked other than superficially, which was fine. The trust would come in time. If she had to pick up snatches of his life here and there, that was okay with her, too. She was a patient woman.

What made Johnny special was that he proved to be an unselfish lover, inventive and generous. A fair portion of her previous lovers had been sexual brontosauruses. The type who considered lovemaking to consist of ripping off her clothes, throwing her down on the bed, completing the act while grunting as though in the midst of a cardiac arrest, then rolling over and promptly falling asleep.

The men Marcie had loved generally knew little about foreplay. This was where Johnny excelled. No one needed to tell her he was a rare breed. She'd been around long enough to appreciate a lover with a slow touch. One who titillated her verbally, who seduced her with words before he so much as kissed her.

It amazed Marcie how well he read her moods. There were times when she was too desperate for him to wade through the long, slow process of being undressed and adored as he stripped away each piece of clothing.

Johnny gauged her mood without her having to say a word. He'd smile, his mouth soft and sexy, then quickly dispense with the preliminaries. Before long he had her pinned against the wall, her skirt up around her waist. By the time he finished she was breathless and limp with satisfaction.

After she'd been seeing him fairly frequently, there'd been a lull. Several months passed without a word. At first she suspected he might be married. But having fallen into that trap before, she'd come to recognize the signs. Not Johnny. He was a free spirit, a salesman whose job often took him away for weeks on end.

It killed her not to question him, but if he wasn't willing to tell her of his own volition, then she didn't ask. To the best of her knowledge there was no faster way to get rid of a potential husband than to make demands on him. From her experience, if she mentioned the word "commitment," she might as well hold open the front door as he raced past. Mow a man down with questions and chances were the relationship wouldn't rebound.

Marcie had made far too many mistakes in her life to fall prey to those traps. She wanted Johnny and was willing to be patient.

After a lengthy silence, Marcie figured she'd lost him for good. That was when she'd taken a long hard look at her life. Frankly, she hadn't liked what she'd seen, so she'd made some basic changes. Cleaned up her act, so to speak.

The first thing she'd decided was that she wouldn't go to bed with a man again until there was a ring on her finger. When she'd first made the decision, it had sounded drastic even to her own ears. She'd enjoyed an active, healthy sex life from the time she was a teenager. But to her surprise, she found she rather enjoyed being celibate.

Clothes shopping took an entirely different slant. No longer did she judge an outfit by how sexy a man would find her or how seductive she looked. She purchased clothes that felt good, clothes that made her feel good about herself.

Once she looked at herself differently, she learned to view men by more than how much they needed her. She was no longer interested in rescue operations. The money and emotional energy she saved made her feel years younger.

She wanted to marry Johnny, but if she couldn't have him, then she had no option but to move on to greener pastures. So she'd gone on a campaign to find herself a husband. One who didn't frequent a bar.

A sign of exactly how serious she was came the day she applied for and received a library card. Because she hadn't paid nearly enough attention in school, her reading skills weren't what they should have been. She started out borrowing books on tape. That satisfied her for a while, but shortly afterward she progressed to reading the books by herself. Especially the self-help ones.

It wasn't long before she recognized that she was a woman who loved too much.

Too much. Too often. Too soon.

Now, just when she believed she was about to achieve her goal and meet someone decent, Johnny popped back into her life. Well, she wasn't the same woman he'd left behind. Besides, there was Clifford. She'd been dating him for two months, which was something of a record. It was certainly the longest time she'd gone out with a man without going to bed with him.

Clifford Cramden owned a plumbing company, played on the local softball team, and hadn't once asked for a loan. Well, he had run out of check blanks that once, but he'd repaid her promptly. He wasn't a bad kisser. Their petting had gotten heavy a couple of times, but he'd always put an end to the foreplay before it got out of hand. Only once had he suggested spending the night. Marcie had gently rejected the idea, and he hadn't pressed her. He wouldn't be any kind of man, she decided, if she didn't tempt him sexually.

They were at the point in their dating where Marcie felt free to talk about "their relationship." For the first time in her life, she was on first base, and she wasn't about to let a weekend fling with Johnny ruin that.

It sounded good when she reasoned it out. Johnny was in town briefly, looking for a good time, and she was a good-time girl. Or had been.

If ever a woman stood at the crossroads, it was Marcie. The minute Johnny had walked into her back room she'd seen the need flash in his eyes. Heaven help her, she'd wanted him too. That she'd been able to refuse him confirmed how much she'd changed.

Johnny would be back. Marcie would bet her last dollar on that. He wasn't used to losing, wasn't accustomed to not having what he wanted, when he wanted it. Next time, she suspected, he'd come with a whole lot more than a bouquet of cheap flowers.

"Marcie."

"In here," she answered, calling over her shoulder.

"Someone's come to see you."

Something in Samantha's voice alerted her that it wasn't one of her LOLs. Marcie worked wonders with older women's hair. Her little old ladies loved her, and she showered them with attention.

"Who?" she asked. She knew her schedule, and she was finished for the day. From the inflection in Samantha's voice, she guessed it was a man. Probably Johnny.

"Come and see."

She came out from the back, wiping her hands dry on a towel, praying for the strength to resist him. If ever a man could push her buttons, it was this salesman.

She saw the huge teddy bear first.

"Hi, sweetheart." Clifford's head appeared from behind the stuffed animal. His grin stretched wide.

"Clifford." Her relief was so great, she nearly succumbed to tears.

"Just a little something special so you'll know how much I love you."

10

He should be asleep, Murphy thought darkly. He would be, too, if the little hellion next to him hadn't irritated him to this extent.

Carlos's friend had generously put them up for the night, a risky proposition for a man who jeopardized his life doing a favor. After all, he and Letty were strangers, and this man owed them nothing, least of all his hospitality.

Murphy was the one who'd insisted they stay in the barn. From the look Miss Holier-Than-Thou had given the stall, one would think she'd expected him to locate a Hilton Hotel just for her comfort. Concierge level!

What irked him was that he was even in Zarcero. All he'd been looking for when he'd traveled to Texas was a little rest and relaxation. Instead he was risking his ass for a man already dead because this woman was convinced her brother was alive.

As best Murphy could figure it, there'd obviously

been a lapse in his sanity. He'd spent less than two days with Letty Madden and couldn't imagine enduring that many more.

Even asleep she irritated him. The pristine postmistress lived in fear that he'd take advantage of her. Well, Murphy had news for her. He'd rather become a monk than lay a finger on her.

Her problem, he decided, was that the woman didn't know what she wanted herself. Her mouth said one thing and her body another.

He doubted she'd be that forthright or honest about her own needs. She batted her eyes at him, moistened her lips, and tempted him beyond what any red-blooded man should be asked to endure.

One night with her had only created a need for more, but he wasn't game. This woman was trouble. Big trouble.

She'd have to strip naked and beg him to make love to her before he'd so much as touch her again. Even then, he'd need to think twice.

The outraged virgin could— He stopped. Letty was no longer a virgin. She'd surrendered that to him in exchange for his help.

Regret settled squarely, heavily, on his shoulders. Regret and guilt. He was uncomfortable with both emotions. Uncomfortable and unfamiliar.

Murphy wished to hell he could remember what had happened between them, but try as he might, the memory was lost.

Letty slept soundly at his side. They shared a common blanket, which she'd insisted they place on top of the straw instead of using it for warmth.

Her deep, even breathing lulled him into a state of semiwakefulness. With his hand tucked behind his head, he lay on his back and forced his body to relax.

It'd be light in another couple of hours. He'd prefer to travel at night. Both Carlos and Juan, the farmer, had warned him about guerrillas who roamed the countryside. Murphy wished he had the luxury of waiting, but he needed a vehicle and there wasn't exactly a used-car lot for him to choose from.

Without a means of transportation, it would take them several days to find their way into San Paulo, the capital. From what Letty had told him, Luke's mission was situated in Managna, less than ten miles outside of the capital.

San Paulo was located in the central part of the country, in a lush green valley. No matter which route he took, they had to get through the dense mountains.

His best chance, he decided, was to make his way into the nearest village and steal a jeep, preferably one from the army. Thievery didn't bother him while on an assignment, especially when he was able to abscond with the adversary's property.

Letty rolled from her back onto her side, facing him. Apparently she was cold, because she snuggled up against him tighter than a miser's budget. He was still figuring out how to ease himself away from her when she pressed her head against his shoulder, using him as a pillow.

With anyone else he might have shared his body's warmth, but he wasn't about to be accused of anything untoward with her. The woman was under the misconception that he lusted after her every minute of the day and night. Well, it'd be a cold day in hell before he'd give her that satisfaction.

Murphy squeezed his eyes closed, determined to ignore her close proximity. He'd partially succeeded when she moaned. He frowned, wondering if he'd imagined it.

Then she did it again, louder this time, as if she were in a great deal of pain. Murphy waited, unsure what he should do. Her head rolled from side to side, and a low, almost wailing sound slid from her lips.

"Letty," he whispered, not wanting to startle her awake. But he couldn't very well have her raise a commotion. A woman's scream had a way of echoing through the night. The last thing they needed was for her to send out an announcement of their arrival to a rebel outpost.

No sooner had the thought entered his head than Letty bolted upright and let loose with a bloodcurdling cry that roused the chickens and just about everything else.

Rarely had Murphy moved faster. He had her flipped onto her back with his hand planted over her mouth before another second passed.

Her frantic eyes flew open and met his in the dim moonlight. What happened next surprised him even more than her scream. She released a soft sob and wrapped her arms around his neck as if she intended never to let go. Next she buried her face in his neck and began to sob.

"Letty?" He'd experienced just about everything in his lifetime, but he hadn't a clue on how to comfort a crying woman. "What is it?"

"A dream." Her hold tightened, and she trembled in his arms.

"There's nothing to worry about—everything's fine," he said as matter-of-factly as he could.

"No. No, it isn't. My brother's in terrible pain."

He should have known the dream involved her brother. "It was a dream, Letty. You don't know what condition Luke's in."

"But I do. I saw him."

"Saw him?" The least he could do was humor her. Murphy didn't go for this so-called telepathy between her and Luke that she'd attempted to feed him. Something about a mental connection. Okay, so they were twins. But Luke was a man and she was a woman. He'd read that that sort of thing happened with identical twins, but even then he wasn't entirely sure he bought it.

"He's been tortured."

That part Murphy could believe. If the missionary hadn't been murdered outright, there was every possibility he'd been taken in for questioning. What Letty's brother could possibly have to disclose remained a mystery.

Letty felt incredibly soft and vulnerable in his arms. Almost against his will, he found himself stroking her hair away from her face.

"We've got to find him."

"We will," he said as if he believed it were possible.

Letty sighed audibly, releasing her warm breath against the skin at the hollow of his throat.

"Promise me," she insisted. "Promise me we won't leave Zarcero without finding Luke."

He couldn't do that. "Letty, be reasonable."

"Please, we've got to rescue him."

Murphy said nothing. He wasn't being cruel, just realistic. He'd like to give her all the reassurances in the world, but he couldn't, not this time.

Not that he opposed lying to a woman in bed. He'd done it plenty of times. He simply told a woman what she wanted to hear and saved himself grief.

But he couldn't make himself do it with Letty.

"Luke's going to die unless we rescue him." Her words trembled from her moist lips. Murphy felt the action of her mouth against his skin and the slick feel of her tears as they rolled down her cheeks.

"You don't understand," she said. "Luke's dying."

Murphy struggled, not knowing what to say.

"Promise me."

Instead of comforting her, his silence agitated her, and she moaned softly, her pain and grief overwhelming her.

"All right, all right," he whispered against her hair. "You have my word of honor. No matter what it takes, we'll get Luke out of here."

"Thank you. Thank you," she repeated again and again until her voice faded completely.

Murphy didn't know how long he continued to hold her. Long after she'd returned to sleep. Much longer than was necessary.

He'd find her brother for her. Dead or alive. If nothing else, Murphy was a man of his word.

11

Letty woke with her head nestled against Murphy's shoulder and his arm tucked protectively about her. She felt both cozy and shielded from harm until she remembered her dream.

A sense of urgency filled her, and she rolled away from Murphy and sat up. She tried to think, tried to remember the dream. Luke, poor Luke, had called out to her to tell her he wanted to die because the pain was too much to endure any longer.

She sensed that he was already close to death. They had to get to Managna and find him before it was too late.

Brushing the wild array of hair from her face, she recalled the way she'd clung to Murphy last night and pleaded with him to find her brother. And he'd given his word. From the hesitant reluctance in his voice, she'd known he would rather have ignored her fears, but in the end he'd vowed they wouldn't leave Zarcero without finding Luke.

The man was an enigma. In the two full days that they'd been together, he'd been impatient and sometimes cruel. Yet last night he'd taken her in his arms and agreed to rescue Luke, even if it meant putting his own life at risk. Letty simply didn't understand him, but then she suspected that no one really did.

She felt his movement at her side as he stirred. He didn't look at her, and she sure as heaven didn't glance at him. The scene from the night before mortified her now.

"We need to get out of here," he muttered, "the sooner the better."

Letty realized Murphy was concerned about putting Carlos's friend in danger, and she shared his fears.

"How far from San Paulo are we?"

"A hundred miles, maybe more. There's a village close by. I'll get us a car there."

It went without saying that he'd have to steal it. Letty never would have believed she'd condone such an action, but she did. Her heart sagged with relief. With a vehicle and a bit of luck, they could reach San Paulo and Luke before the end of the day.

Murphy left her for a short time while he scouted out the surrounding countryside. She used the minutes effectively and was packed, ready and eager to leave the protection of the barn, when he returned.

He held open the door for her. Sunlight spilled into the cool, dim interior of the outbuilding, heralding another picture-perfect day in Zarcero.

They left the farmyard and walked through a field of tall grass, avoiding the road. For the better part of two hours they traveled without communicating.

Murphy seemed aware of every sound and stopped abruptly a couple of times. He pressed his finger over his lips and waited before proceeding.

When they came to a grove of large Guanacaste trees, Murphy stopped and reached for his canteen. He drank first, then handed it to Letty. The water tasted terrible. She'd seen Murphy add a capsule to it and knew it must have been some form of purification pill. It was difficult for Letty to estimate how far they'd traveled. It felt like five miles or farther, but she couldn't really say.

Murphy wasn't any friendlier than he had been earlier, which disappointed her, following his promise from the night before.

A conversationalist Murphy wasn't.

He seemed to have reached a decision, because he sat down near a tree. Without a word he unfolded a map, pressed it down upon the ground, and studied it intently.

"How much farther is it to the village?" she asked.

He didn't look up. "Not far." He refolded the map carefully and placed it inside his knapsack. He stood, and Letty reluctantly came to her feet.

"I want you to stay here."

"Why?"

He answered by removing the pistol from his shoulder holster and handing it to her.

She stared at it, almost afraid it would explode in her palm. "What's this for?"

"I want you to keep it with you from here on out. Understand?"

"But—"

"Do you want to find your brother or not?"

"Of course, but—"

"Then do as I ask." His eyes cut her to the quick. "You probably couldn't hit the broad side of a barn, but it's the only security I have to offer you."

"What should I do while you're away?"

"Wait quietly," he suggested impatiently.

He started to walk away, but a terrifying thought came to her. "Murphy?" she called out.

He glanced over his shoulder, looking none too pleased with her.

She implored him with her eyes, nervous and more than a little afraid. "What if . . . what will happen if you don't come back?"

A slow, easy smile claimed his face as if he found her question comical. "I'll be back."

She nodded and offered him a shaky smile of her own. "Okay."

Holding on to the gun with both hands, she glanced around her suspiciously, wondering if there might be guerrillas hiding in the bush, ready to attack her the minute Murphy was out of sight.

She started to call out to him a second time, but he was gone. He'd virtually disappeared from one moment to the next. Vanished like a puff of smoke.

Truly alone, Letty walked the circumference of the grove and glanced at her wristwatch. Murphy had been away all of five minutes and already she was worried.

She shifted the pistol from one hand to the other,

wondering if she was actually capable of killing another human being. And doubted it.

As far as she was concerned, Murphy's lessons on firing the .45 had been for naught. Apparently it made him feel better leaving her with some form of self-defense, despite the fact she found it useless.

By five o'clock, nine hours after he'd left, Letty forced herself to stop looking at her watch. Murphy had been gone far longer than she'd expected.

He could have been captured. Could have been killed.

He had no means of letting her know his predicament. True, he'd given her specific instructions to remain right where she was, but just exactly how long was she supposed to wait? Nine hours seemed far too long.

As unpleasant as it was, she had to accept the possibility that he would never return. True, he was an expert at what he did, but that didn't make him invulnerable.

The chance existed that he'd met up with a group of guerrillas and been taken captive himself. Perhaps he'd been caught attempting to hot-wire a vehicle and thrown in jail by the local authorities.

Fearing the worst, Letty wondered what she should do. If anything.

The option of retracing her steps and going back to the farmhouse presented itself, but she didn't want to backtrack. Not after her nightmare. If she intended to reach Luke in time, it meant making her way into San Paulo or Managna, and she couldn't do that waiting days on end for Murphy. Especially if he was no longer able to come for her.

On the other hand, Murphy had been specific about her following orders. She'd never seen a man so hardheaded or unreasonable. Just exactly what was she supposed to do?

The decision was made for her several minutes later when gunfire sounded in the distance.

Murphy was in trouble. She could sense it. Not in the same way she knew Luke was in trouble. This time it was woman's intuition.

She had to find a way to save him.

Praying she was doing the right thing, Letty reached for her backpack and placed it on her shoulders. With the gun clenched in her hand, she headed in the same direction she'd seen Murphy go.

12

Jack Keller decided to let Marcie wait and wonder. Her cool reception had come as something of a shock. In the beginning he'd been angry, but he'd since changed his tune. Actually, he understood.

It'd been months since they'd last seen each other, and a woman had her pride. Things changed. People changed. He'd left her without a word. She had every right to be displeased with him, but he intended to make it up to her. Once he'd soothed her ruffled feathers, things could go back to the way they'd always been between them.

Marcie was a sensual woman, and it was rare to find one as uninhibited and generous in bed as she was. It was even more rare that she'd never asked or hinted for anything in return for her favors.

This time when he stopped off to see her, he brought long-stemmed roses. Floral shop ones that came in a box with a fancy silk ribbon, not a cheap bouquet comprising carnations and a few other common flowers.

He dressed up, too. Not a suit and tie, but in a shirt fresh from the cleaners and pressed slacks. If he'd been more certain of his reception, he would have phoned first.

When he arrived at her apartment he found her car parked at the curb. He smiled. One thing about Marcie, she was consistent. As he recalled, she wasn't keen on a lot of change. Keller liked that. She'd lived in the same apartment for ten years and drove the same car she'd had when they'd first met.

He rang the doorbell and waited. He half expected her to answer, wearing her robe and little else. As he remembered, when she arrived home she habitually changed out of her uniform and into something more comfortable. He definitely approved of her choice.

To his surprise, she answered wearing white shorts and a high-necked, sleeveless blouse. "Johnny." Her voice was decidedly even, and he couldn't tell if she was pleased or not to see him.

"I came to apologize for the other day," he said, looking and sounding contrite. "You must think me a Neanderthal to come on to you the way I did."

She stood on the other side of the screen door, her hand on the knob as if she weren't sure she should let him in.

Keller decided a little underhanded persuasion just might be necessary. "I would have contacted you sooner, but I was in an accident." It was necessary to stretch the truth now and again, although he didn't make a habit of it.

"An accident?" Her pretty eyes widened with concern.

"I'd really like to talk to you, Marcie. Nothing more, I promise." He raised both hands in a gesture of surrender.

She hesitated.

"Please," he added with a sincerity few could refuse.

His plan worked; she unlatched the screen door.

"It's good to see you," he said as he walked into the apartment. He made it sound as if he were damn lucky to be alive.

To Keller's surprise, he found the interior of her apartment markedly different. The furniture was the same, but everything else had changed. The drapes were bright, the windows sparkled. A knitting basket filled with yarn was next to the chair. Several magazines were fanned out across the top of the coffee table.

Without waiting for an invitation, he sat down. Again he made it look as if it were a trial for him to remain upright for any length of time, which wasn't far from true. His ribs had been killing him for weeks.

He set the box of roses on the coffee table and all but collapsed against the back of the sofa.

"What happened?" she asked.

Keller hid a smile at the gentle concern in her voice. "Car accident," he whispered. He thought to tell her there was a metal plate in his head but feared that was carrying the story a bit too far. "If you don't mind, I'd prefer not to talk about it."

"Of course." Her warm, caring voice was a balm after her earlier rebuff.

A moment of strained silence passed between them. Everything was going as planned, except that Marcie remained standing on the far side of the room almost as if she feared what would happen if she sat next to him. Keller wished she would. If he had the chance to kiss her once or twice, they might get past this awkwardness. All she really needed was a little gentle persuasion.

She seemed to be waiting for him to say something, so Keller brought up the first thing that came to mind. "The reason I stopped by, other than to apologize for the other day, was to personally thank you for bailing me out of jail."

"It's all right, Johnny."

"I'd like to show you how much I appreciate our friendship, Marcie. I don't know what I would have done without you." Several months back he'd been foolish and gotten himself arrested in a bar fight. Charges had later been dismissed, but Keller had been stuck in the clinker and would have spent the night if it hadn't been for Marcie. Normally he would have done the time, but Murphy had needed him, and he'd had a plane to catch.

"You don't owe me any money," she claimed as he withdrew his wallet. "You must have forgotten with the accident and all."

"You're sure?"

"Oh, yes. A cashier's check arrived a week later."

"Good." She'd reassured him of that earlier, but wanting to make sure she'd been reimbursed put him in a good light.

Again he confronted a short, awkward silence.

"You're looking wonderful." That was no exaggeration. Marcie did look good. Better than he remembered. "What's different?"

"A lot of things."

He leaned forward, bracing his elbows against his knees. "I don't suppose you have something to drink?" As he recalled, Marcie kept a full liquor cabinet.

"Coffee?"

At first he thought she was joking, but it was clear she wasn't. "Sure."

"Sugar and cream?"

"Just black."

She walked out of the living room, and he was left to twiddle his thumbs. Keller waited a moment and then followed her into the compact kitchen.

Marcie was busy assembling a pot and glanced over her shoulder when he entered.

"Johnny," she said, and seemed nervous as she continued in a hurried, rushed voice. "There's something you should know. I'm seeing someone else now."

So that was it. Well, it didn't come as any real surprise.

"He's real good to me."

"In other words he doesn't disappear for months at a time."

She shrugged, as if his disappearances had never really concerned her.

"I'm happy for you, sweetheart." Keller wanted to shove his fist down the other man's throat, but he didn't let Marcie know that.

"You are?" She visibly relaxed.

Keller nodded. "You deserve the best."

The coffeepot made a gurgling sound, and the dark liquid drained into the glass pot. Marcie turned and opened the cupboard doors and reached for two cups.

Keller moved behind her, pressing his body intimately against her backside. "Let me do that for you," he whispered. She was soft, warm, and womanly. Her buttocks cushioned him as if she'd been custom-made just for him. Normally he wasn't a jealous man, but Keller felt a flare of the ugly green monster just thinking about Marcie in bed with another man. The emotion came as an unwelcome surprise.

Gradually he eased himself away from her and brought down two ceramic mugs. "Tell me about your new boyfriend," he encouraged. The more he knew, the better he could undermine the other man.

He noticed that Marcie's hand shook ever so slightly as she poured the freshly brewed coffee. Keller smiled inwardly. She'd enjoyed the brief intimacy as much as he had. She didn't like it, but she couldn't deny it.

"His name is Clifford Cramden and he's a plumber."

"A plumber." Something was wrong. The Marcie he remembered would be bored to tears with a man named Clifford Cramden. It didn't add up.

"Is he the jealous type?" Keller asked, helping himself to a kitchen chair.

"Clifford?" She raised questioning eyes to his. "I don't know. I've never given him any reason to be jealous."

No reason to be jealous? Marcie?

"Do you think he'd mind if I took you to dinner to thank you for your bailing me out of jail?"

"That's not necessary."

"It's the least I can do," Keller insisted, sounding as sincere as he could. "If you think it would help, I'll contact your boyfriend myself and explain. The last thing I'd want is a misunderstanding between you two."

Marcie lowered her lashes, and it was clear she was tempted.

"The Cattleman's Place," he said, mentioning the most expensive steakhouse in town.

Her pretty eyes met his. "I've always wanted to have dinner there."

It was on the tip of his tongue to tell her that a plumber wasn't likely to be able to afford it.

"How about it, Marcie? Tomorrow night. I'll pick you up at six."

She closed her eyes, shook her head, and answered hurriedly. "I can't."

"The next night, then," he pressed, unwilling to drop it. "If that doesn't work, then you choose the day and time."

A long moment passed before she spoke. "Saturday?" The lone word was breathless, as if she weren't sure even now if she should.

"Saturday it is," he said cheerfully, feeling as if he'd won a decisive battle. "I'll be by for you at six."

"Just between friends," she said, her eyes holding his.

"Of course," he lied. But then friends made the very best lovers.

13

Night had settled over Zarcero, and Letty would have been lost completely if not for the village lights that gleamed in the distance like small beacons, guiding her. She made her way down the steep incline into the town as carefully as she could, fearing she might lose her balance with each step. Intermittent bursts of gunfire could be heard in the distance.

The moon and stars offered little in the way of illumination. As she drew closer to the town, she heard boisterous music and singing. It took a bit more time for her to make out the words of the raunchy song, and she blushed as she translated them. Apparently the civil unrest hadn't disturbed the civilians as much as she'd assumed.

Once she reached the outskirts of the town, Letty hid, to assess her options. She'd been traveling four or five hours at this point and had seen no trace of Murphy.

He'd come for a vehicle and apparently hadn't succeeded, which meant he'd probably been captured.
She'd steal a car first and then find him. Although she
knew next to nothing about cars and engines, she did
hope that with a bit of patience and a hairpin in the
ignition switch, she might coax an engine to life. She'd
heard a credit card could open a locked door, and if
that was true, then surely a hairpin could start a car.

A number of vehicles would surely be parked outside the cantina. But stealing one of those and driving
away undetected would be next to impossible. She
had no choice but to scout around.

Flattening herself against the side of an adobe
building, Letty silently made her way down a deserted
alley. Sweat broke out across her brow as she feared
discovery. Perhaps she should wait . . . . After a
moment she decided against it. She'd already wasted
an entire day, fruitlessly anticipating Murphy's return.
She tried not to think what had happened to him or
what those gunshots had meant.

The thought he might have been killed produced a
tightness in her chest, and she banished the worry
from her mind. She'd go after Luke first, she decided,
then return for Murphy.

Once she'd had the opportunity to scout out the
town, she'd weigh her options, make her choices, and
move.

The entire village appeared to be deserted except
for the cantina. The music was growing louder and
more boisterous.

Eventually she was able to maneuver herself
between two buildings and look out onto the main

road that ran in front of the local bar. From the laughter and good cheer, one would never guess the country was in chaos.

As Letty suspected, six or seven jeeps and a variety of dilapidated American cars thirty years or older were parked in front of the bar. Thus far they were the only vehicles she'd seen.

The people inside didn't seem to have a care in the world. The doors were wide open, and tables spilled into the streets. A number of women paraded around in tight-fitting skirts and low, elastic-style blouses. Some delivered drinks, others brazenly touted their wares and openly invited attention.

Out of the corner of her eye, Letty watched as a soldier grabbed a woman's waist and dragged her onto his lap. The young waitress squealed with delight before he slammed his mouth over hers. Soon the two were all over one another. The woman squirmed in the soldier's lap and straddled his hips. Panting, she threw back her head, and he buried his face in her ample bosom. His hands cupped her full breasts as he licked and sucked at her neck.

Letty was mesmerized, unable to make herself look away. The two were all but making love in full view of the entire cantina. Letty's mouth felt dry, and she couldn't understand why she found such a blatant display of sexual activity so fascinating.

All at once it came to her.

That wasn't a soldier with the waitress. It was Murphy.

The shock was enough to make Letty's knees go out on her. With her back against the building, she slid to the ground until her buttocks landed in the hard dirt.

Murphy. The dirty son of a bastard had left her to wait in the hot sun for hours on end while he was making love to a . . . a floozy.

Rarely had Letty been more furious. All this time she'd fretted and stewed, certain he'd been captured or worse. The afternoon had been hell, worrying about him.

She'd risked her life in an effort to find out what had happened to him. Anything might have befallen her as she'd made her way into the village. Not that Murphy would have cared. He'd have been grateful to have her out from under his hair.

She'd made a drastic mistake trusting Murphy. The man had no morals. No decency. She hoped he died a slow, painful death. She relished the thought of him suffering.

Her anger was enough to motivate her into action. Whereas before she'd been almost afraid to breathe for fear of discovery, now she moved freely from one building to the next, being sure to remain in the shadows. She was careful, very careful, but not stupid.

Still uncertain about the odds of successfully stealing a jeep, she made her way to the far side of town, thinking that she'd hide in the church until the wee hours of the morning. By then the soldiers would be too drunk to realize what she was doing.

As she neared the church, she heard the soft, almost soundless approach of someone behind her. Her blood ran cold. Fear was an amazing thing, she realized. Never had her thought processes been more clear.

She waited until he was almost upon her before

whirling around, thinking she would startle her stalker.

To her shock Murphy stood almost directly behind her.

"Murphy?" She nearly shouted his name in her surprise.

He clamped his hand over her mouth and shoved her against the side of the church. "Just what the bloody hell do you think you're doing?"

One aspect of soldiering Murphy had learned early in his career was that emotion was as much an enemy as a gun-toting revolutionary. Murphy went into a mission with no feelings, did what he was paid to do, and got the hell out in the most expedient manner possible. In all his years with Deliverance Company, he'd lived by those rules.

Then he'd joined forces with one Letty Madden.

Everything changed the minute he agreed to accompany the postmistress to Zarcero. She caused him to see red faster than anyone or anything he'd ever known.

This latest escapade of hers, slipping down a dark alley in enemy territory, sticking out like a sore thumb, was a prime example. It didn't matter how much the rebels had drunk, they were still soldiers. It was only a matter of time before she'd be discovered.

Murphy had carefully bided his time, waiting for nightfall to make his move. He'd sat on the fringes of the cantina, in a "borrowed" rebel uniform, gathering valuable information. By the time he'd joined the rowdy assembly, most of the soldiers were three sheets to the wind. Carlotta, the shapely woman in his arms, had provided the perfect camouflage while he'd learned what he needed.

Then out of nowhere Letty appeared, as obvious as a bull in a china shop. He'd damn near gone ballistic right then and there. She was fortunate he hadn't done more than shove her up against the side of a building.

She struggled and bit down on the fleshy part of his hand between his thumb and index finger. Hard. Murphy swallowed a yelp and pinched her jaw until she released him. Despite the pain, he continued to hold her captive.

"Just what the hell are you trying to do, get us both killed?" he demanded. "I told you to wait for me." As soon as he could reason clearly, he'd deal with the fact that she'd disobeyed a direct order.

She pressed her hand against his chest and shoved, but he didn't budge.

"You dirty son of a—" She bit off the last word and glared at him with eyes that would have quelled a lesser man.

"Me?" he muttered, not understanding her fury. "Listen, little sister, let's get something straight right here and now. When I give an order it's to be obeyed."

"You've given me your last order, buster." She squirmed against him and would have done him injury had he not escaped her knee.

Her fury caught Murphy off guard. What the hell did she have to be so mad about? It took him far longer than it should have to realize Letty had seen him with Carlotta. The waitress had been all over him, hawking her goods, looking for a few extra dollars on the side.

"Let me go," she insisted, her chest heaving. At another time, Murphy might have enjoyed having her squirm against him. But not when it put them both at risk.

"Shut up before you get us both killed," he said none too gently.

Murphy relaxed his grip on her wrists, but only slightly. They needed to clear the air. Unfortunately they couldn't do it in the alley with rebel soldiers partying across the street.

"I'll release you if you promise not to speak." He waited for her acquiescence, which she gave grudgingly with one sharp nod of her head.

Satisfied, Murphy wrapped his hand around her upper arm and half dragged her out the back side of the alley. He led the way out of the village, not stopping until he was confident they wouldn't be heard.

"I will not tolerate insubordination," he said heatedly, the haze of his own anger only now beginning to fade.

"You won't have to," she returned calmly. "You're fired."

He was confident he'd misunderstood her. "Fired?"

"I'll find Luke without you."

Murphy couldn't help it, he muffled a laugh. "Really?"

"I absolve you from your duty." She dismissed him with a dramatic wave of her hand, in an action befitting royalty.

"Just how far do you think you'll actually get before you're discovered?"

"Farther than I did today. How long did you intend to leave me baking in the sun while you and that . . . that woman were—"

"That woman kept me from being discovered." Letty seemed to conveniently forget he'd placed himself in considerable risk on her behalf.

"I know exactly what that woman did for you," Letty spat, disgust dripping from every word.

Murphy didn't need this, not after the day he'd had. If she wanted him off the mission, it was fine by him. As far as he could see, it was a waste of time anyway. "Great," he returned. "Wonderful. I couldn't be more pleased." He turned and started to walk away.

His mind buzzed with fury and outrage. After all he'd been through, this was the thanks he got. The woman was a candidate for a mental hospital. For that matter, so was he for ever having agreed to escort her to Zarcero.

Well, he was finished. He washed his hands of her and her do-good brother. He didn't need this kind of grief.

He hadn't taken two steps when she stopped him.

"Wait."

It didn't take her long to come to her senses, he noted, mildly pleased. She needed him, and rehiring him wasn't going to be as easy as she seemed to think. He'd set a number of things straight. First off, she couldn't follow the simplest instructions. One thing he wouldn't tolerate was insubordination. Not from anyone, much less a fickle-hearted woman.

He turned around to discover Letty kneeling on the ground, digging through her backpack. "I won't be needing this," she said, retrieving the .45. She held it between two fingers as if it were something dead she'd rather not touch.

His weapon. She'd flustered him to the point he'd forgotten his single most valuable survival tool, the very one he'd voluntarily left behind for her protection.

"Before you go," she said, shoulders squared, "I want you to know I think you're the most unprincipled, unscrupulous, immoral man I've ever met."

Murphy hitched his eyebrows up a notch and chuckled softly. "You mean to say it's taken you this long to discover that?"

She was seething.

Murphy loved it. He'd done his duty, gone the extra mile. Extra mile, hell, he'd gone a whole lot farther than that. Letty Madden was on her own, and he couldn't be more pleased.

He tucked the gun inside his belt. "Good luck finding your brother."

"I don't need luck," she said, righteousness echoing like thunder from her lips. "God is with me."

"If that's the case, I don't know why you ever felt you needed me," Murphy returned without malice.

"Frankly, I don't either."

With wide, determined strides, Murphy continued up the steep incline that led away from the small village. Without trouble he should be able to make his way back to the farmhouse that night. In the morning he'd talk to Juan and signal for Carlos. If everything went smoothly, he'd be in Boothill in two days' time.

14

For reasons Luke would probably never know, the beatings had stopped. The pain was manageable now, and with this unexpected reprieve came the will to continue. For the first time since his capture, he found the strength to live.

In the back of his mind, a hazy remembrance of Rosita's visit haunted him. Had it been real? He no longer knew. For whatever reason, God had allowed her to come to him, whether in body or spirit, he didn't know. Whichever form, Luke was grateful.

Try as he might, he didn't recall what she'd said, if indeed she had actually visited him.

All he remembered was that in the worst of his pain, when the agony had been more than he could bear, she'd been there, smoothing his hair from his brow, whispering reassurances. He'd felt her love and her courage as powerfully as if she'd dressed his physical injuries.

Luke's heart swelled with love for the beautiful woman and the future he'd planned with her as his wife.

When he'd been assigned Zarcero, Luke had been confident the Lord had sent him to the troubled Central American country for a specific reason. He'd been in Zarcero almost two years before he'd discovered what God had wanted to teach him.

Love.

Not for the gentle peasants who made up a large part of his ministry. His heart had been prepared to love and encourage them for years beforehand. That they had accepted and loved him in return had come as a bonus. The people of Zarcero had been both generous and gracious from the first.

No, what God had sent him to Zarcero to learn was about the love a man has for a woman. What his parents might have shared at one time but had lost.

Luke couldn't remember the first time he'd met Rosita. It wasn't her beauty that stood out in his mind, although she was more lovely than words could adequately express.

Each morning she walked her younger brother and sister to the mission school on her way to work at the market. He must have greeted her a hundred times before he truly noticed her the way a man notices a woman.

This sudden awareness had taken him by surprise. Luke had dedicated his life to God's work, and after his own parents' miserable marriage, he'd decided to remain single.

Mission work was frequently demanding, and he

didn't want to be forced to make the often difficult choice between the needs of his congregation and those of a family.

Paul Madden had never completely recovered from the loss of his wife. He'd lived with doubts and regrets the remainder of his days.

Luke's father had loved his wife heart and soul, and when she'd abandoned him with two children for another man, he'd accepted the blame as if he were the one solely at fault. If only he'd been a better husband instead of a good minister. If only he'd paid more attention to his wife and less to his congregation. He'd never forgiven himself. Never remarried. Never chanced love a second time.

Luke had vowed not to make the same mistake. Naturally he'd been tempted to fall in love. He was as human as the next man, and susceptible to the attention of attractive young women. There'd been any number who'd caught his eye.

But never anyone like Rosita. She was good and kind, gentle and caring. He noticed how the people of Managna loved her. Anyone who knew her couldn't help being affected by her goodness and delicate beauty.

It had taken months for him to pay her heed, but the same wasn't true for Rosita. She claimed her younger brother and sister were fully capable of finding their own way to school. With love shining from her eyes, she took pleasure in reminding him that he was probably the most obtuse man in the universe.

Luke didn't doubt it.

It took him months to actually get around to asking her out. The night of their dinner, he was a nervous wreck. He was twenty-seven years old and felt as though he were seventeen all over again.

When he stopped off at Rosita's house, his tongue seemed glued to the roof of his mouth. He chatted amicably with her father, patted the top of her sister's head, and joked with her brother. Then Rosita came out, wearing a lovely white dress with a flowing skirt and red belt. His heart hitchhiked straight to his knees.

Later that evening, when Luke brought her back to her family, he was convinced he was the worst dinner companion she'd ever known. Their meal had been a disaster, and he'd been the one at fault.

True, nerves had played a part in his uneasiness, but more than that Luke realized that he loved this woman. His sentiments had long since been decided. This wasn't high school or college, where he'd found himself fleetingly attracted to the opposite sex. This was love and the real world.

He hadn't come to Zarcero looking for a wife or the responsibilities of a family. He'd charted his course, confident he was doing the right thing. Then God in His almighty wisdom had hurled a wrench into his picture-perfect blueprint.

Instead of rejoicing in this wonder, instead of thanking God for this unexpected gift, Luke had decided he wanted nothing to do with love. Love would hinder his work. Loving Rosita would handicap his efforts with the people of Zarcero. Love would distract him from his purpose.

Luke decided he wanted none of it. In time, whatever physical attraction he felt for the beautiful young woman would fade.

It didn't.

Instead it grew and blossomed without so much as a touch or a kiss.

Luke wrote his sister, asked for prayers for a deep, inner struggle without telling her exactly what it was he battled. As close as he was to Letty, he feared she would never understand.

When it came to love and marriage, he and Letty appeared to be of the same mind. She'd shown no more inclination toward the married state than he did himself.

Finally, after avoiding Rosita for two months, he inadvertently ran into her while visiting an elderly widow, Mrs. Esparza.

To his shock and hers, Rosita answered the door. She'd been reading to the sickly ninety-four-year-old, and for the first time in days Mrs. Esparza was sleeping comfortably.

Luke was inclined to leave quickly, avoid temptation. A disciplined man by nature, he made his excuses, promised to return later, and headed out the front door.

For reasons he never understood, before he walked out, he turned and looked back at Rosita. He discovered her sitting by the old woman's bed, her head bowed and her eyes bright with tears.

When he questioned her about the emotion, she blushed and claimed dust had gotten in her eyes. Once more Luke turned to leave. And couldn't.

All at once he was tired of fighting what he wanted most. Tired of pretending he was strong. Tired of ignoring his heart.

That was the afternoon Luke learned the lessons God had been struggling to teach him. The lessons he had rejected. The lessons of love.

Luke was a man. But he'd been trying to live the life of a saint, with his head buried in the sand, ignoring the man God meant him to be. It had taken this slap alongside of his head to accept and appreciate the human side of his nature.

The physical part of him had been ignored and repressed for so long that when he set it free, it nearly carried him straight over a cliff.

From that day forward Luke knew it was either preach one thing and live another or marry Rosita. Two weeks before the army overtook the government, Luke had asked Rosita to be his wife and she'd agreed.

He'd known asking her to share his life and his ministry was what God intended from the minute he'd found the courage to pop the question.

He'd hungered for the day he and Rosita could be married. Silently he'd vowed to find a balance in his life, to continue his work with the mission and at the same time be a good husband and father.

Luke opened his eyes and looked around the bare jail cell, and with renewed strength he prayed for the future.

That evening, when a plate of unpalatable food was shoved into the cell, Luke forced himself to swallow a few bites. Then, because he needed to say it aloud, he sat at the end of his bunk, raised his eyes to heaven, and whispered.

"I want to live."

15

Anger was an unfamiliar and uncomfortable emotion to Letty. She sat on the dark hillside and trembled with outrage after Murphy's departure.

The sight of him with that . . . woman, burying his face in her breasts, kissing and sucking her neck, was enough to make Letty physically ill. Her stomach burned every time she thought about it.

She was well rid of him. Clearly she had misplaced her trust. It was a painful and expensive lesson, but one best learned now. Murphy had already delayed her an entire day. Who was to say how much more time he would have wasted while he entertained himself with that hussy.

Undoubtedly he considered her a fool for having dismissed him. The decision had been made in the heat of anger, but that didn't mean she was without resources.

The church steeple silhouetted the moonlit sky. Although Luke had been in Zarcero only a little over two years, he was well known and loved in the religious community. All she needed was to contact another minister or priest, and they would lead her to her brother.

Careful to avoid detection, Letty made her way toward the Catholic church. The street was dark and silent in front of the hundred-year-old structure. Tall, thick doors marked the entrance.

Letty studied the street a long time, fearing that the moment she moved into the open, she'd be caught. Her concern was unjustified. Murphy had apparently paraded around all day in that silly looking uniform and no one had noticed him.

Drawing in a deep breath, she walked out of the shadows and stepped smartly toward the church. By the time she'd made it up the few short church steps, her heart felt as if it were about to explode inside her chest

To her relief, she found that the building wasn't locked. The moment she applied pressure, the thick wooden door creaked open.

She stepped into the vestibule and heard an eerie clicking sound. Blinded by the light, she raised her hand to shade her eyes.

The first thing she noticed was that the pews were missing. Instead the church was filled with desks. And soldiers. Lots of soldiers.

The strange clicking noise she'd heard earlier was the sound of rifles.

Letty froze. The barrels of a dozen guns were pointed at her heart. This place no longer served as

a house of God; it was a command center for rebel
soldiers.

The farther he walked, the angrier Murphy became.
Soon he found himself swearing, first under his
breath and then louder, until he had to restrain himself from shouting. But even that didn't make him feel
better.

And he knew why.

Despite the fact Letty had fired him. Despite the
fact he cursed the day he'd ever laid eyes on her.
Despite his better judgment, he was going back.

He couldn't think of a single reason why he should,
except his conscience. If anything happened to her,
and it would—the woman was not only stupid, she
was as naive as they came—he'd never be able to live
with himself.

In addition, there was the small problem of his
promise. He'd assured her, again knowing he'd regret
it, that he'd find her brother.

While it was true he'd have a hell of a better chance
rescuing Luke Madden without Letty, in good conscience he couldn't leave her behind to an uncertain
fate.

As much as he'd like to do exactly that.

The woman exasperated him. She was God's revenge
against a life of not giving a damn.

As he made his way back to the village, Murphy
brought his emotions under control. He was going to
need his wits about him. He'd have to deal with the
rebels, true, but he'd managed to stay alive in these

types of situations for years. He excelled in the art of disguise, of blending into the background. The unknown element, what gave him the greatest concern, wasn't the rebels. It was Letty.

It would be just like her to give them both away the minute she laid eyes on him. The woman didn't possess a nickel's worth of common sense.

As he reentered the town, he noted that the music continued to blare from the cantina. The festivities had yet to wind down and wouldn't, he suspected, until the wee hours of the morning.

He walked down the street with purpose, as if he were under important orders. No one stopped to question him, and he doubted that they would.

He paused as he neared the far end of the main street. The last structure left on the block was an old church. He almost discounted it, almost looked past the obvious.

Lights on at this time of night? In a church?

Something was very wrong.

Letty was forced into a chair, and her arms were tied behind her. She glared up at the rebel leader, whose name was Captain Norte, and refused to allow him to see her fear.

"How did you get into Siguierres?" he demanded in broken English.

She told him the truth. "I walked." She said it without emotion, without sarcasm.

He backhanded her across the face. Blood filled her mouth, and she blinked up at him, shocked and stunned by his violence. He looked as if he'd relish hitting her again.

"Put her in jail. Let her cool her heels with the rats for the time being and see if that loosens her tongue," he instructed two guards.

Her hands were untied, and with a soldier at each side she was half lifted from the chair and escorted out the front door. The cool air felt good against her burning, stinging face. She moved her lips carefully. She'd never known a slap could be so painful.

The two men at her side spoke in whispers. At first Letty couldn't make out what they were saying, then she understood that they'd agreed not to take her directly to the jail. They intended to have a little fun with her themselves first.

"No," she said, jerking her elbows first one way and then another. She spoke rapidly in Spanish, telling them that their captain would be greatly displeased when he learned what they'd done. She reminded them that officers expected their orders to be carried out without question and that their captain had ordered them to escort her to the jail.

Desperate now, she told them that if they were to rebuild their country, they must do so with honor. Not with despicable acts of violence against innocent women.

She spoke fast, reasoned hard, and with each frantic plea she realized she might as well have saved her breath. The two weren't about to be cheated out of their pleasure.

They dragged her kicking and screaming behind a building and threw her down upon the hard ground.

She fell against her backpack, and the wind was knocked out of her.

One man held her shoulders, pinning them to the ground. It took both men to restrain her. They allowed her to kick and writhe until her energy was spent before the larger of the two men knelt and ripped open her blouse.

Letty closed her eyes, refusing to look at him. She nearly gagged at the rough feel of his hands over her smooth skin. She kicked and bucked with renewed effort, but to no avail. Soon he straddled her legs and began to unfasten the snap of her jeans.

When the man holding her shoulders urged the other to hurry, Letty started to sob, her ability to fight, to resist, nearly depleted.

The first man positioned himself atop her, his weight crushing her to the ground.

At that precise moment the night exploded around them. The ground trembled, and a blast rocked the entire town. Flames shot into the sky, followed by a low rumble that grew in intensity.

"The fuel dump!" one of the men shouted in terror. He released her and ran. The soldier atop her was only momentarily fazed. Using his forearm for leverage, he rammed his arm across her throat, cutting off her oxygen supply. Her struggles ceased as a new, immediate need took over. She needed to breathe.

Just when Letty thought she was about to pass out for lack of air, the pressure was gone. The rebel went limp. His arm fell from her throat and she gasped, drawing in a deep, fresh breath of air. He was propelled away from her, his eyes frozen open, an expression of shocked horror on his face.

Sobbing, she looked up at her savior, certain what she saw must be an apparition.

Murphy leaned forward and offered her his hand. "Come on," he shouted, "we've got to get out of here, and fast."

For the life of her, she couldn't move. Not giving her the option, he reached down and brought her to her feet. Impatiently he swept her into his arms. The next thing Letty knew, she was tossed in the front seat of a jeep with its engine running.

Within seconds they were barreling out of town, leaving a huge dust trail in their wake.

Murphy continued at a dangerous pace. It was all Letty could do to keep from being hurled onto the road.

By the time he slowed down, reaction had set in and Letty was trembling from head to foot with a chill that came from the inside out.

Murphy glanced at her. "You all right?"

She answered him by slamming her fist against his upper arm and sobbing, "You came back. . . ."

"Well, don't thank me or anything."

She wrapped her arms around herself as the cold, brutal reality of what had nearly happened refused to let go.

"Answer me," Murphy snapped. "Are you okay?"

She closed her eyes and nodded.

"You sure?"

"Yes, damn it, I'm sure."

"It's going to be all right," Murphy said with surprising tenderness.

Letty had dealt with his anger, his harshness, his unfriendliness. She didn't know how to deal with his gentleness. She brushed the tears from her face and sniffled.

"Thank you," she whispered.

16

As Marcie sat at an elegant linen-covered table next to Johnny, the irony didn't escape her. This was their first real date, yet they'd been enthusiastic lovers for almost two years. They'd shared fabulous sex, good times, and fast-food meals, but they'd never gone out. Not in the traditional sense.

Occasionally Johnny brought her gifts, inexpensive baubles and trinkets, as a means of thanking her. Of paying her, she realized sadly, reluctantly. Until recently she'd never looked upon his presents as payment, but it was long past time to be honest.

The stuffed teddy bear Clifford had brought her represented the first time a man had ever given her anything without her sleeping with him first.

Up to this point ninety-five percent of her communication with Johnny had taken place between silk sheets. She knew very little about him and his life. He was a physical man with physical needs, and those needs had dominated each brief rendezvous.

Although she'd agreed to this dinner date, she wasn't sure that she was doing the right thing. Because she felt guilty, she'd casually mentioned the outing to Clifford, making light of it. An old friend, in town for a day or two. Hoped he didn't mind.

Sometimes it was difficult to know what Clifford actually thought about things. His one failing, if she could call it that, was his interminable politeness.

While Marcie was certain he wasn't pleased, Clifford had chivalrously told her to have her dinner with Johnny and to enjoy herself. He'd be talking to her again soon. The conversation had ended with that.

"Have you decided what you'd like to order?" Johnny asked, setting aside his menu.

Marcie couldn't believe the prices. A single meal at the Cattleman's would pay for her weekly supply of groceries. "The small filet?" she said questioningly.

He grinned broadly, as if she'd made the only intelligent choice on the entire menu.

It surprised Marcie how nervous she was. Not because she was with Johnny; he was an easy person to talk to, when they took time to talk. But she wasn't accustomed to sitting in an ultrafancy restaurant where the waiters wore tuxedos. Nor had she eaten anyplace where the flatware comprised more than two spoons.

"Did you have any problems explaining our date to Clifford?" he asked as if he were sincerely concerned.

"Clifford's not the jealous type."

Johnny reached for the wine menu. "He sounds like a decent sort."

"He's very good to me." Better than anyone.

The waiter arrived, and in gentlemanly fashion, Johnny ordered for her and then requested a bottle of expensive French wine, a Bordeaux.

As the meal progressed they chatted comfortably. Generally when a man asked her out, Marcie was subjected to a long, self-serving monologue. At times she'd wonder if these men feared that she didn't have a brain, or an opinion. In the end she'd decided that they were afraid of what she'd say. They came to her, she suspected, to recover from the weenie roasting they'd suffered at the hands of the feminists.

The men in Marcie's illustrious dating career endlessly touted themselves in an attempt to impress her, to reveal how fascinating or intelligent or wonderful they were. Mostly what they really wanted was to get her into the sack as quickly as possible with the least amount of fuss and prove what a magnificent lover they were. And often weren't.

By the time she'd reached her late twenties, Marcie had learned a lot about the dating scene. She realized that single men often felt an unmarried woman her age was desperate to find a husband. While it was true Marcie wanted a husband and children, her standards were higher than just any man with a pair of sperm-producing testicles. She longed for companionship, shared goals, and the dirtiest word of all. One that caused fearless men to run screaming into the night. Commitment.

Marcie didn't need the wine to relax. By the time

the steaks arrived, she was as happy as she could ever remember. Johnny was both intelligent and generous.

In comparison, Clifford, dear, dear Clifford, seemed stodgy and a little dull. His idea of a fun evening was a night at the movies and a shared bucket of popcorn. Clifford was the salt of the earth, and Johnny was the spice of life. Unfortunately her diet had been bland for a long time, and she was ready for a taste of cayenne.

Marcie had known the minute Johnny walked into her beauty salon that she wanted him, but until their dinner date she hadn't realized how much.

Subtly he altered the course of their conversation, reminding her of how fabulous the lovemaking had always been between them. His deep blue eyes sparkled with devilment as he continued to speak of the raw excitement they'd experienced in each other.

His voice was low and seductive, coaxing. Marcie felt as if she were slowly being drawn into a vortex, trapped in the memories. Soon she was a willing, eager victim, adding her own remembrances.

His eyes bored into hers relentlessly as he regarded her with a look of wonder, as though she were the only woman alive with which he'd shared this incredible marvel.

Marcie battled the fluttery beat of her heart. Johnny slowly extended his arm to her and opened his hand. His meaning was unmistakable. He wanted her. Needed her. Was going crazy without her.

Marcie experienced a bevy of contradictory feelings. She'd come so far, learned so much; but then Johnny had always made her weak.

"Marcie . . ." Her name was a soft plea that fell from his lips. A way of saying he'd go mad without her. Marcie needed to be needed, wanted to be wanted.

Her love, her body, would ease his pain, would heal his suffering, would soothe away his troubles. He'd come to her. Only her.

In the morning, she reminded herself, she'd feel like a fool, used and abused. But the promise of pleasure outweighed any threat of remorse.

Slowly she placed her hand in his. Johnny closed his eyes and sighed, as though his relief and gratitude were great. Clasping his fingers around hers, he carried her hand under the table. With his eyes holding hers prisoner, he pressed her palm against the hard bulge in his crotch and grinned.

The oxygen fled her lungs as she flexed her long nails over the strength of his erection.

Johnny heightened the anticipation for them both by insisting upon dessert, then coffee, lingering over each. His eyes filled with promise, he paid the bill and left a generous tip.

By the time the valet had brought around the car, Marcie was breathless with anticipation. The only indication Johnny gave that he was as eager for her was the speed with which he drove back to her apartment.

Neither spoke.

Marcie didn't make the pretense of inviting him inside for coffee, and he didn't ask. He parked the car, got out, and followed her to her front door.

The minute they were inside, he turned her into his arms. Their first kisses were filled with hot urgency.

He ravaged her mouth until she had to break away in order to breathe. Soon, however, the blistering, sweet fire altered as the fierce edge of their hunger abated.

His mouth and hands were unbelievably erotic as he explored her body, familiarizing himself with her breasts, hips, buttocks. He removed her sweater and bra, then sucked greedily from each of her nipples while lowering the zipper to her skirt. He was like a boy given free rein in a candy store, unable to decide which delicacy to sample first.

It didn't take him long to decide, and soon he elicited a series of soft, impatient moans. Their bodies writhed against one another, burning with need, until they threatened to burst spontaneously into flames.

Marcie helped him discard his own clothes. Between wet, wild kisses she steered him into her bedroom. Johnny picked her up and gently laid her across the top of her mattress.

As he had over dessert and coffee, he prolonged the anticipation, using his hands and his mouth until she was sobbing with need, wanting him with a desperation that made her fear she was going out of her mind.

"In time," he promised with a husky whisper. "We have all night, dahlin', all night."

Impatient, Marcie held out her arms to him. Inadvertently her head hit something soft and fuzzy.

Johnny reached for the teddy bear and tossed it off the bed.

The teddy bear. Clifford's gift. The one he'd given to remind her how much he loved her. The only gift she'd ever received from a man who didn't expect payment in return.

Johnny might as well have poured a bucket of ice water over her head.

He went to kiss her, but she jerked her head away. "I can't do this."

Johnny went stock-still. "Can't do what?"

"Make love with you."

"Sweetheart, it's a little late for regrets. We're already making love." He laughed good-naturedly, as if this were all a bad joke, but one he was willing to overlook.

While she possessed the strength, Marcie rolled off the bed. Unsteady on her feet, she walked to her closet and hurriedly donned her robe. "You got a cigarette?" she asked shakily. She'd given up the habit, but she needed a smoke now, worse than any time since she'd quit.

"A cigarette?" Johnny sat at the end of her bed and scratched his head. "Don't we generally wait until afterward for that?"

"I don't smoke anymore," she whispered, then realized she'd been the one to make the request. "I do sometimes when I'm under a lot of stress."

Johnny plowed all ten fingers though his hair. "I'm apparently missing something here. Maybe you could clue me in? What the hell just happened?"

"It's a long story." Remembering that she might have an old pack of Salems around, Marcie walked over to her dresser and searched through the top drawer until she found a cigarette.

Her hands shook so hard, she had trouble lighting up. She inhaled deeply, blew the smoke at the ceiling, and then coughed until she thought she'd heave her guts out.

She went into the bathroom and tossed the lit cigarette into the toilet.

"Marcie, sweetheart, tell me what's wrong?"

"You have every right to be angry," she said, walking back into the room and retrieving the teddy bear. She held it against her abdomen like a shield.

"I'm not mad," he said gently, "just confused."

"It's Clifford."

"Clifford," Johnny repeated as if he weren't quite sure he remembered the name. "Your new boy-friend?"

"Right." She nodded once, profoundly. "He's never asked anything of me." Her gaze skirted back to the bed. "He's been kind and good—"

"I'll be good to you, too, sweetheart." His words were heavy with insinuation. "Give me a chance to show you exactly how good it can be."

"It's not that kind of good," she said, and realized she was doing a poor job of explaining herself. She swept the hair away from her face. "Clifford doesn't ask anything of me," she said bluntly.

Johnny's eyes rounded with offense. "Hey, I didn't buy you dinner because—"

"I know. I know," she interrupted. "I don't know how to explain it. He's kind and steady and—"

"You're still talking about Clifford, right?"

"Right. I can't hurt him like this because you turn me on." She continued to clench the stuffed animal against her middle.

Johnny didn't respond.

"You have every right to be furious. I wouldn't blame you if you walked out that door and never saw me again. It'd probably be best for both of us if you did."

Again Johnny didn't say anything. Buck naked, he stood and retrieved his clothes.

"How about putting on a pot of coffee," he suggested.

"Coffee?"

"Make it strong, all right? Real strong."

She nodded.

Then he headed for her bathroom. "You don't mind if I use your shower, do you?"

"Not at all." Johnny was closing the door when she realized she hadn't told him about the problem with the hot-water knob.

"Don't worry about it," he muttered after she explained, rubbing a hand down his face. "I won't be using the hot water."

17

Murphy parked the jeep on the side of a rut-filled dirt road and studied the map. He'd managed to stay off the main thoroughfares, but he wasn't fool enough to presume they'd made a clean escape.

Blowing up the fuel dump had created the diversion he'd needed in order to rescue Letty, but it wasn't something Captain Norte was likely to forget or forgive. Captain Norte, however, was the least of his worries.

Murphy's neck was on the chopping block, and consequently Letty's was too. But the good captain and his band of murderous cutthroats had to find him first, which was something Murphy intended to make damned difficult.

Once he'd found his bearings, he folded the map and replaced it inside his knapsack.

Letty slept fitfully at his side. It had taken several

hours for her to fall asleep. She'd curled up and ridden in stone silence until pure exhaustion had taken hold.

Murphy's experience with comforting women was limited. He didn't know what to say to ease her mind, so he'd said next to nothing. Mainly he heaped the blame for the near rape upon his own shoulders, and he cursed himself for ever having left her. In his defense, he reminded himself that Letty had been unreasonable and stupid and he'd responded in kind.

He didn't calculate how long he'd been away. Not long, thirty, forty minutes. In that time she'd managed to walk waist deep into a pile full of shit.

Murphy refused to continue to beat himself up. The ordeal was over, the soldier who'd attacked her was dead, and he and Letty were miles away from Siguierres.

Letty stirred, sat up, and rubbed her hand along the back of her neck in an effort to work out the kinks. "How long have I been asleep?"

"A couple of hours."

He felt her stare and her hesitation.

"I . . . I was wrong," she said.

Murphy shifted the gear into first. "Which time?"

"I should have waited like you instructed. It was a mistake to go after you. It's just that ten hours can be a terribly long time when one is waiting. I heard gunshots and I didn't know what had happened to you and . . . It doesn't matter now. I made a mistake. It was all my fault and . . ." She let the rest fade away.

"As I recalled, you fired me," he remarked stiffly.

"I shouldn't have done that, either."

"True." He wasn't going to argue about the obvious. She'd learned her lesson the hard way. "What are you prepared to offer me to come back?"

She closed her arms protectively around her torso.

"Don't worry, the terms will be different this time."

"What do you want?"

He noted the apprehension in her voice.

"One thing, and one thing only." He held up his index finger for emphasis. "You will do what I say, when I say, without question. If you disobey an order again, it's over. Understand?"

She nodded.

"Good. Now that that's clear, let's find your brother and get the hell out of here."

The road was filled with ruts large enough to swallow small animals. They were far enough off the beaten path that Murphy didn't worry about being detected. He slowed to a crawl in order to manipulate the vehicle around problem areas.

He worried about Letty. He didn't like a lot of chatter on a mission and up to this point had discouraged conversation. Although she'd abided by his unwritten demand, he'd felt her eagerness to ask questions. Not this day. Her silence was a good indication of how badly the attack had shaken her.

"You hungry?" he asked after a while.

"A little."

"We'll stop soon." If he was a different kind of man, he'd take her in his arms. Tenderness was as foreign to him as comforting distraught women. Besides, he was fairly certain that the last thing Letty needed or wanted was a man's touch. Murphy frowned. Much

more of this and he'd turn into one of those men
seeking to find their inner child.

"Would it be possible for me to have a bath?" she
asked after a while.

A bath? Judas H. Priest, what did she expect? They
weren't likely to run across a luxury spa in the jungle.

As he remembered from the map, there was a small
lake close by, and he told her so.

The higher the elevation, the more lush the vegetation, and they'd been climbing steadily since leaving
Hojancha. The terrain was dramatically different
from the hot, dry area they'd left two days earlier.

Murphy found a decent spot to park the jeep, and
while Letty nibbled at breakfast, he made a half-mile
circle around the lake to be sure they hadn't plopped
themselves down in the middle of a rebel-infested
area.

"Go ahead and take your bath," he said when he
returned. He removed his hat and wiped the sweat
from his brow with the back of his arm.

Letty hesitated. "Is there a chance anyone will be
watching me?"

"No one human," he answered confidently.

She thanked him with a weak smile and walked
behind a low-lying bush to remove her clothes.

Murphy climbed inside the jeep, scooted the seat
back as far as it would go, and tried to sleep. He'd
been up the better part of thirty hours and felt it.

He heard water splash as Letty stepped into the
lake. A picture of her body formed in his mind, and
he struggled valiantly to banish it. To no avail.

Try as he might, he couldn't expel the mental image

of her lush breasts and her milky white skin from his mind. Sweat broke out across his brow.

"Murphy . . ."

Her cursed under his breath. "What now?" he answered gruffly.

"I'm sorry to bother you, but do you happen to have any soap?"

The next thing he knew, she'd be asking about face cream and deodorant. He bit back the sarcastic question and reached for his knapsack.

"Just a minute," he said with a decided lack of enthusiasm.

"Thank you. I really do hate to bother you."

He'd just bet she did. Murphy located the soap and walked over to the water's edge. It lapped lazily against the sandy shore, inviting. Birds chirped merrily nearby. He was pleased someone was happy.

Letty had squatted down in about three feet of crystal blue water so all that showed was her neck and creamy white shoulders. It was enough. His jaw clenched at the angry-looking bruise her blouse had covered. The acid in his stomach burned along with his hate for the men who had inflicted those bruises.

"I'll catch the soap if you throw it," she volunteered, and lifted her hands out of the water. In doing so, she inadvertently exposed the top half of her generous breasts.

Murphy heaved the small soap bar in her direction, turned abruptly, and headed back toward the jeep.

"The water's wonderful."

He grumbled some nonsensical reply under his breath. He was in no mood for her chatter.

"You should come in yourself," she offered next. "I'll be out of your way in no time."

The temptation was strong, far stronger than it should have been. Murphy knew better, but he was hot and overly tired and in need of something. Exactly what remained a mystery.

Before he could question the wisdom of his action, he sat down in the sand and removed his boots. He peeled off his clothes in record time, leaving on his briefs, and walked out to meet her.

Letty's eyes rounded with each step he advanced toward her. "I thought you'd wait until I'd finished," she mumbled.

"I decided not to." He wasn't entirely sure what she expected him to do. Once he was waist deep, Murphy dove headfirst into the cool water and swam below the surface until his lungs felt as if they would burst.

Damn, but it felt good.

He turned around and found Letty exactly where he'd left her. "Do you want the soap?" she asked timidly, her back to him.

"Yeah." He swam toward her and stopped a respectable distance away, offering her a semblance of privacy. His feet touched the bottom and he stood. The water lapped at his chest.

Letty held on to the soap bar as if it were gold. "Murphy?"

The emotion in her voice caught him off guard. "Yeah?"

Her throat worked convulsively, as if she were trying to swallow something too big to go down her esophagus. "I . . . need to say something."

"Now?"

"Yes," she cried, half laughing, half weeping, "now, while I still have the courage."

A woman's mind was a mystery to Murphy. Why she'd choose this precise moment, when they were both near nude, for this tête-à-tête made no sense to him.

"I want to thank you for saving me from those soldiers." Each word appeared to be a struggle for her to enunciate.

His inclination was to make light of his role. He'd been hired to protect her, to get her in and out of the country as quickly and as safely as he could. She seemed to conveniently forget that none of this would have happened if they'd both done as they should. It was a lesson well learned.

She swabbed at the moisture on her face. "Could you . . . would you mind very much holding me for a moment?" she asked brokenly.

Before he could react, Letty was in his embrace, clinging to him as if he were a rope dangling over the edge of a cliff. Her arms circled his neck, and she buried her face in his shoulder, sobbing softly.

"I was so frightened."

"I know, I know." Unsure what else to say or do, Murphy gently patted her slender back, doing his best not to notice how soft her skin was.

"If you hadn't come when you did—"

"It's over now."

"He meant to kill me," she said with conviction. "He was going to rape me and then strangle me. He pressed his arm against my throat and I couldn't breathe."

"It's over, honey."

She clung to him, her skin cool and slick, her body nestling against him. Murphy wasn't made of stone. He couldn't ignore the way her breasts teased his chest any more than he could ignore her legs rubbing against his.

Gritting his teeth, he wrapped his arms around Letty's waist and held her firmly, securely, in his arms. What she needed was his strength, his protection, his confidence. That was what she sought.

"Come on," he whispered, and used his jaw to caress the side of her head. "We need to get out of here."

She nodded and wiped the tears from her eyes. "Friends?" she asked.

The question was one he preferred not to answer.

Raising her head, Letty met his eyes. "Friends?" she asked a second time.

Letty Madden and him. Not likely. His friends were few. Carefully chosen. He was a hired gun, and he didn't want her painting him as her personal knight in shining armor because he'd killed the bastard about to rape her.

"No thanks, sweetheart. I got all the friends I can handle." He knew, even as he spoke, that his words would insult and offend her, but that couldn't be helped. They'd come to Zarcero to do a job. When it was finished he'd be out of her life and she'd be out of his.

Letty's head snapped back, and she glared at him. "You're a nasty son of a bitch, aren't you?"

"Yes." He wouldn't deny it. "You'd best not forget it."

He stalked toward the shore. "It's time to get back on the road," he said evenly. "We leave in five minutes."

Letty plowed out of the water, making more noise than a Sherman tank, sloshing and kicking, venting her frustration like a woman scorned.

Murphy quickly donned his clothes and had a hell of a time hiding his smile.

His amusement quickly faded when he realized they were being watched. He didn't know where or who was out there. Not yet. Over the years he'd developed a sixth sense about such matters.

"Letty . . ." He kept his voice low and calm.

She ignored him.

"Without being obvious, walk over to me."

Something in his voice must have alerted her to the danger. She picked up her clothes and walked directly to his side. "Someone's out there," she whispered.

He grinned. "Yeah, I know."

18

Jack Keller returned to his condominium around two in the morning. He let himself inside, tossed the keys on an end table, and strolled aimlessly through his living room while rubbing the back of his neck. His night certainly had taken an unexpected turn. He'd had Marcie in the palm of his hand, whimpering for what they both wanted, and then whammo, the next thing he knew she was asking for a cigarette and listing Clifford's sterling traits.

Jack should have been angry. A woman couldn't lead a man to the point of no return and then call it quits. But Marcie had done exactly that. Naturally he'd been frustrated. It'd taken ten minutes under an ice-cold shower to cool his libido. The disappointment had been as sharp as his frustration. Damn it, he wanted her. It'd taken half a pot of strong coffee to clear his head.

Even now he wasn't entirely certain he understood about Marcie and Clifford. He was fairly certain she wasn't in love with the plumber. Marcie wanted *him*, and that wasn't his ego talking, either. He loved the way her eyes lit up when she saw him. His touch flustered and fascinated her. She was both sensual and honest, a rare combination in a woman, he'd discovered. It distressed him to realize that if he didn't act soon, he was going to lose her. Not to any fast-talking shyster, either, but to a plumber.

Jack openly admitted that he'd underestimated Marcie. She deserved far more credit than he'd given her. He had assumed he'd easily be able to manipulate her into bed. Dinner, a little sweet talk. A kiss. Hell, it hadn't even taken that much. By the time their meal had arrived they could hardly stay in their chairs for want of each other. All that had changed, however, shortly after they'd arrived back at her place.

Right up to the moment Marcie had rolled away from him, Jack had thought it'd be a snap to have her. Not so, but then he always had enjoyed a challenge. It stirred his blood. Marcie was a hell of a woman, in bed and out, and it'd do him well to remember that.

His mind was filled with thoughts of Marcie and the pleasure that awaited them. Jack was determined to have her. Hell, just how difficult could it be? No woman in her right mind would choose a plumber named Clifford over him. Women needed excitement, pleasure, adventure, and he offered all three.

Okay, okay, Clifford had won round one, but the championship fight had only just begun. Jack fully expected to gain the prize, and frankly he didn't expect it to take much longer. A little subtle planning, and he'd close in for the kill.

He got excited just thinking about it.

Too keyed up to sleep, he turned on the television and plopped himself down in front of the boob tube. No sooner had he finished a complete surf of the channels than his doorbell chimed long and loud.

"What the hell?" he muttered, glancing at his watch. People generally didn't make social calls this time of the morning.

His peephole revealed two clean-cut men standing on the other side of his door. They might have been twins if one hadn't towered a good six inches over the other. The two had "the law" written all over them. Officious. Pompous. Self-important. Both looked as if they were struggling to hold in a fart.

The taller of the two impatiently pressed the buzzer a second time.

The temptation not to respond appealed to Jack. He was already short-tempered, and having to deal with a couple of tight-ass federal agents didn't rate high on his list of ways to pass the wee hours of the morning.

On second thought, he had to concede that their temperaments wouldn't improve if he left them sitting on his porch all night. Forcing himself to disguise his irritation, Jack opened the door.

"We're sorry to bother you this time of night," the shorter man said. He pulled identification from inside his suit jacket and flipped it open. Ken Kemper. CIA. The second man, Barry Moser, showed his identification as well.

Unimpressed, Jack folded his arms and leaned against the door frame. And waited. "What do you want with me?"

"We need to ask you a few questions."

"Now?" Jack asked. He pointedly looked at his watch, stating silently that he had better things to do with his time. After all, he had company. *Nick at Night* was waiting for him.

"We can do it here, or we can take you downtown," Barry suggested, his voice monotone, making it sound as if it made no difference to him. "The choice is yours."

The fact that Jack had supposedly been given a choice when he had none didn't escape him. Sighing loudly, he made a sweeping gesture toward the living room. "Make yourselves at home, *gentlemen,*" he said.

The two agents walked across the room and then like robots simultaneously sat on the sofa.

Jack reluctantly reached for the controller and turned off the television.

"I understand you're a friend of a man who goes by the name of Murphy."

Jack rubbed his jaw and played dumb. "Murphy?"

"Let's skip the bullshit," Kemper said impatiently. "We know all about you and Murphy and Deliverance Company."

"We're not here about covert activities," Moser added.

Jack just bet. "Then what do you want?"

"Where's Murphy?"

"I don't know," Jack told them, which was true enough. The last time he'd heard anything at all had been that phone message, in which he'd learned that Murphy was headed toward Zarcero with the Madden woman. He hadn't seemed any too pleased about it, either.

"You don't know where Murphy is?" Ken Pompous asked a second time.

"Did you check Boothill, Texas?" Jack asked.

"He's missing," Moser, the one with the tighter of the two asses, replied. "By sheer coincidence, so is Letty Madden."

"Letty who?" Jack asked, continuing to play dumb. At this point it wasn't difficult. He was getting slow in his old age, and careless. Stupid mistakes. He'd learned the hard way that mistakes cost lives. It was apparent the two men had been sitting outside his condominium waiting for his return. And he hadn't noticed.

"Letty Madden," Barry repeated. "She's Boothill's postmistress."

"Never heard of her."

The two men exchanged knowing looks, but they didn't challenge him.

"Don't you find it the least bit curious that these two people both disappeared at the same time?"

Jack didn't respond for several tense moments. "Do you think Murphy kidnapped her? If that's the case, shouldn't the FBI be handling the case?"

Both men ignored his suggestion. "Have you ever heard of Zarcero?" Ken asked next.

Jack pretended to roll the name around in his mind. Then, like a schoolboy who'd done his homework, he replied, "It's the country in Central America that's going through all that political upheaval, isn't it?"

"Letty's brother, Luke Madden, served as a missionary in Zarcero."

Both men appeared to wait for some kind of reaction to this. Jack gave them none.

"From what we've been able to learn, Ms. Madden is determined to locate her brother. Determined enough to ignore the advice of her country and go after her brother herself."

"Is that a crime?"

"It depends on what she does about it."

Jack stifled a yawn, swallowing it loudly, and hoped the two took the hint. They weren't going to get any information from him. Even if he had some to offer, he wouldn't share confidences with the likes of them.

"What's all this got to do with Murphy?" he asked, pretending to find their conversation taxing.

Neither agent seemed particularly interested in answering him. Apparently they preferred to be the ones asking questions.

"We believe Ms. Madden may have hired your friend to help her locate her brother."

"Really?" Jack arched his eyebrows as if to suggest this was news to him. "Do you really think a postmistress could afford Deliverance Company's services?"

"Not Deliverance Company," Kemper, the shorter one, informed him primly. "We believe she hired Murphy."

"Why would she do something like that when all she need do is contact the helpful people employed by the State Department? Surely the State Department would be able to assist a worried postmistress hoping to locate her long-lost brother. All you people need do is apply a few sanctions and a little diplomatic leverage, and Luke Madden will be coming home singing the praises of a democracy. Hallelujah, brothers," he sang, raising his arms above his head and waving his hands.

Neither man appeared to find his antics amusing. "Have you ever heard of Siguierres?" Kemper asked, scooting forward on the cushion, narrowing the distance between them.

"Siguierres," Jack repeated, and shook his head in complete honesty.

"We've received word of an explosion."

"A fuel storage tank," the second agent supplied.

"The work is suspiciously like that of your friend Murphy."

"Is that right?" Jack swallowed a grin and lazily leaned against the chair's cushion. He cupped the back of his head, his elbows fanning out on each side of his face.

"We don't know if your buddy's in contact with you or not," Ken said stiffly, and stood. Barry followed. "But if you are, we have a bit of information for him."

"What makes you think Murphy would contact me?"

"Birds of a feather, perhaps," the taller agent suggested.

"For all I know, Murphy could be sport-fishing in the Gulf of Mexico." Jack shrugged as if to say his friend's whereabouts remained a mystery to him.

"If you do hear from Murphy, tell him he's in over his head this time."

"Just a minute," Jack said, and leaped out of the chair.

He rushed to a side table, where he withdrew a pad and a pen. "What was that again? I want to make sure I got it right. Far be it from me to miscommunicate this important missive. *In over his head?* Is that what you wanted me to tell him? Anything else, fellows?"

Both men glared at him and then wordlessly walked out of the apartment.

Jack followed and closed the door, struggling not to laugh outright. It certainly sounded as if his pal were up to his old tricks. Briefly Jack wondered what kind of mess Murphy had gotten himself into. From the sound of it, he was taking care of matters nicely.

19

"Don't move," Murphy instructed Letty in an urgent whisper. He crouched behind the jeep himself. "Don't even breathe."

She nodded as her muscles tightened warily. Her heart was lodged in her throat. Even the birds in the trees seemed to have quieted. The stillness that fell over the area took on an eerie quality.

Murphy reached for his weapon and carefully took aim.

Hunkered down against the four-wheel drive, Letty tried to think clearly. Her senses fine-tuned, she heard every noise as if it were announced over a public broadcasting system. A scarlet macaw flew from one tree to the next, its brilliantly colored wings flapping against a backdrop of blue sky and lush green jungle. Birds called, their cries loud and discordant in the sudden silence. Thick green leaves wavered and weaved in the breeze, stirring the fresh morning air. The day was indescribably beautiful. And deadly. The sounds fit together like intricate puzzle pieces, creating a graphic picture in her mind. Except for one distinct sound: hushed voices.

Letty froze with fear. She didn't move, didn't breathe, didn't make a sound. Murphy was poised beside her. He'd heard the same thing she had and leveled his pistol in that direction. She studied him and knew that he was calculating their chances of escaping, weighing their alternatives. It was either flight or fight.

If they were caught, Letty was well aware of what would happen to her. She'd received a foretaste of that the night before. Although her mind was hazy with fear, she had the presence of mind to murmur a silent prayer. If she was to die, she preferred to go quickly. She wasn't afraid of death as much as the process of dying.

The flicker of hope that they might escape faded as she studied their situation. They were trapped by the lake and had nowhere to go. Each soldier, and there was no telling how many there were, would be heavily armed. Murphy would hold them off as long as he could, but there was only so much one man could do. She was useless to him and, consequently, herself.

Her throat went dry, making it impossible to swallow. She thought about Luke and her father. Grammy. Surprisingly her mind was sharp, clear, alert.

All at once a muffled sob broke the tense silence. Like that of a small child. One terrified and lost.

"Murphy," she whispered, making a clumsy effort

to dress. Somehow she managed to slip the dress over her head and insert her arms into the short sleeves. "It's a child."

"I heard." But he kept his gun poised and ready. "Come out," he shouted in Spanish.

Letty rolled her eyes. The poor thing was terrified. Murphy's gruff voice wasn't going to encourage anyone into the open.

"We mean you no harm," she added on a gentler tone, again in Spanish. "You're safe."

No sooner had she spoken than a bronze-skinned girl of about twelve appeared, a baby propped against her hip. She walked into the clearing, barefoot, her dress in rags. Her large brown eyes sought out Letty, her look empty, weary, afraid.

"Sweet Jesus," Murphy whispered when four other children, who looked to be between the ages of five and ten, stood, revealing themselves one by one.

They were terrified, Letty noted, trembling, shaking, huddling together, uncertain of what awaited them.

Murphy barked a number of questions, but they appeared to be too frightened to answer.

Letty moved from behind the jeep while Murphy slipped into his pants and followed.

"Where are your parents?" Letty gently asked the oldest girl.

The youngest boy, who was about five, started to sob, and the girl who held the baby placed a protective hand on his shoulder. "We don't know."

"What are your names?" Murphy demanded.

Letty glowered at him. The children were frightened enough without him shouting orders at them. The oldest, the girl, introduced herself as Maria and her brothers as Vincente, Esteban, Rico, Dario, and the baby, Pablo.

"The soldiers came," Vincente explained, his dark eyes bright with weary defiance. "Early in the morning, they stormed into our village. Our mother woke us and helped us escape out the window . . . . She told us to run and hide in the jungle, and we did."

"Then we heard the guns."

"After the soldiers left," Maria whispered, her eyes glazed over with the horror of what had happened, "we returned and everyone in the village was gone."

"All the houses were empty."

"Except for Carlos and Juan and Ernesto. They were dead." Vincente, who was no more than eleven, stiffened his shoulders as if to say had he been there he would have helped save the men. What struck Letty was the way in which the youth mentioned the three dead men. He made it sound as if soldiers routinely plundered the village, as if the happenings were an everyday occurrence.

"We buried them as best we could," Maria whispered, comforting her baby brother by bouncing him gently on her hip.

"Everyone was gone?" Letty repeated. "Where would the soldiers possibly take them?" She looked to Murphy for answers. He'd been through this sort of thing countless times, unlike her. He'd know what to say and do. Expectantly, the children turned to him as well.

He shrugged as if he were as much in the dark

about all this as they were. "Generally they're only interested in the men."

"For what reason?" Letty asked, before she realized he couldn't possibly answer. Whatever the answer, it was sure to distress the youngsters.

"When did this happen?" Murphy asked, ignoring her inquisitiveness.

"Three days ago."

"Three days," Letty cried. No wonder the children looked so wretched. "You must be starving." Without waiting for Murphy's approval, she took the baby from the girl's arms and cradled him against her side. "When was the last time the baby had anything to eat?"

At the mention of food the children gathered around her like small chicks fleeing a storm. Letty half expected Murphy to disapprove, but he didn't. Nor did he complain when she dug through their own meager supplies.

The children ate like animals, stuffing the food into their mouths and tucking what they couldn't manage just then inside their pockets. Letty's heart ached as she watched them. She wished she had more to give them. When they'd finished, the six thanked her with wan, pitiful smiles.

Murphy continued to ply the youngsters with questions, extracting as much information as he could. Again and again he interrogated the family, until she glared at him, silently reminding him that these poor children had suffered enough.

She took them aside and helped them wash. While she combed their hair, she mulled over what they should do. It wasn't possible to take the six with them into San Paulo; the risk would be too great. But her first priority had to be Luke. She wanted to discuss the matter with Murphy, but he was sitting apart from her and the children, studying the map.

"Vincente," Murphy called after a few moments.

The next time Letty glanced in his direction, he'd squatted down in the sand. Maria and the four boys huddled around him while Letty gave the toddler a sponge bath. She watched as the girl found a stick and drew a diagram in the sand. Now and again she nodded and answered Murphy's questions. The boys added details.

Busy as she was washing the baby, Letty couldn't make out what the exchange was about. But she did learn that the children were lost. They'd been walking for days, seeking their grandmother's village, and had somehow gone hopelessly astray.

"Our mother told us to go to our grandmother's," Maria said, fighting back tears. "*Abuela* will know what to do."

Letty rose and walked over to place an arm around the girl's thin shoulders and smooth the hair from her brow. Not even a teenager and already the girl carried the heavy burden of caring for her five younger brothers.

"Everything will be fine," Letty whispered, praying it was true.

The girl smiled weakly and nodded.

The minute Letty was able to separate herself from the children, she confronted Murphy. The baby rode her hip as if he'd spent the majority of his life there.

"What are we going to do?" she asked. "We can't take the children with us. It's much too dangerous."

His eyes held hers. "I agree."

"Nor can we leave them here." The small family was hopelessly lost, half starved, and terribly frightened.

"Luke . . . I don't think he's going to last much longer." She wanted Murphy to supply the answers, to reassure her, but he did none of that.

"This is your call," he said evenly.

"My call," she repeated, wanting to weep with the agony of it. Her brother's life hung in the balance. But she couldn't just abandon six children.

Murphy stared at her. "You ready?"

"Ready?" Letty glanced toward the children. He gave her little enough time to make the most important decision of her life.

"We can't sit around here and debate the issue all day. Decide."

She leveled her face to the sky, letting the sun warm her. Hardly aware of what she was doing, she closed her arms protectively around the toddler. All at once he felt incredibly heavy.

Murphy glared at her. "What's your call?"

"Luke's my brother," she cried. Then her gaze fell upon the five small boys, Maria's brothers. The weight of the girl's responsibility made her far older than her years. The twelve-year-old was left to see to their very survival.

"Fine, we go without them," Murphy said, and started toward the jeep.

"Wait." Letty bit into her lower lip. She couldn't do it.

Murphy paused.

"We'll take the children to their grandmother's village," she whispered.

"You're the boss." A slight movement of his mouth might have been an approving grin, but it was difficult for Letty to tell with Murphy. He was quite possibly the most complex man she'd ever known.

Murphy estimated that Questo, the village the children had been trying to find, was approximately fifteen miles from the lake. However, with the roads in the condition they were, Letty feared it would take them the better part of a day. That meant delaying their arrival into San Paulo.

"This was what Luke would want me to do," she mumbled as she climbed into the jeep. She knew this to be true, but it hadn't made the decision any easier, convinced as she was that Luke was close to death. But she couldn't leave the children to an uncertain future. Not when it was within her power to help them.

Murphy helped the two smallest boys inside the jeep. He crowded them between Letty and Maria. The older boys rode on the hood, hanging on to the windshield, and pointed the direction from which they'd traveled.

Exhausted, the baby slept in Letty's arms. She found it strangely comforting to hold the toddler. His head was nestled close to her heart, his chubby fist pressed to her breast. Although she loved children, Letty hadn't given much thought to being a mother. She suspected her hesitancy had a great deal to do with her own mother and her parents' failed marriage.

A ready excuse was that she hadn't found the right man.

There was always Slim, of course. He'd proposed to her on a semiannual basis and was profoundly patient with her. She'd always told herself that she would marry sooner or later, but she was in no rush.

Unbidden, her gaze scooted to Murphy. Letty didn't know how he was able to drive with two small boys poised on the jeep's hood, but he managed admirably. The poor little ragamuffins looked self-important to be riding in such a choice location.

Murphy must have sensed her scrutiny because he glanced in her direction. He didn't smile. She suspected he wasn't the kind of man who often did, but in his own way he told her he approved of her choice.

Without explanation, she experienced a rush of warmth. A feeling of peace and rightness. Of tenderness. She was with this man, a paid soldier, in the thick jungles of Zarcero with a baby in her arms, and she'd never felt more right. She kissed the child's chubby cheek, smiled softly at Murphy, and looked away. He'd openly disliked her, rejected her friendship, and maintained a wide emotional distance from her and just about everyone else. Yet he was an honorable man. He'd come back for her, even after she'd fired him. He'd held her, comforted her.

Murphy might not choose to have her as his friend, but she was beginning to think of him in those terms. He quite possibly was the best friend she'd ever had.

The back roads were in deplorable condition, and the jeep pitched and heaved its way along the rough-strewn path. At this rate, the thirty-mile distance would take the majority of the day and possibly part of the night.

They stopped to rest late in the afternoon, when the sun was directly overhead and the heat was at its worst. The children were exhausted and cranky. The eight of them shared a meal meant for two adults, then lay down in the shade of a sprawling tree. Letty stretched out in the cool grass with the children, who promptly fell asleep.

Murphy sat apart from her and the others, his back propped against the tree trunk. His rifle rested atop his bent knees.

Again, Letty found herself scrutinizing him, fascinated by every aspect of his personality. He was gruff and impatient and at times surprisingly caring.

She didn't view him as handsome. He was too rugged, too hard, for that. With several days' growth of beard, he resembled the roughest kind of redneck. A Texas specialty. Perhaps that was the reason he'd chosen Texas as his home.

"When was the last time you slept?" she asked, sitting up.

"I forget."

She stood and moved toward him. "If you want, I'll stand watch and you can rest."

"I appreciate the offer, but no thanks."

"How much longer do you think it'll take before we reach Questo?"

"Four, possibly five hours. It would be almost faster to walk."

She sank onto the grass across from him and crossed her ankles. "Why Texas?"

"Texas?"

"Why did you choose to live in Texas when you could live anywhere in the world?"

His gaze left hers, and when he spoke it was with reluctance. "Because it's home."

"You were born and raised in Boothill?" This surprised her. Having lived there most of her life, she thought she knew everyone.

"No."

"But you bought that piece of property."

Again it was a long time before he answered. "Those thousand acres belonged to my grandfather several years back," he murmured, almost as if he were uncertain he should tell her that much.

"Mr. Whitehead?"

He shook his head. "Long before Whitehead. My grandfather lost the farm during the Depression, sometime in the early thirties. I wanted to buy it back for him, which I imagine is fairly illogical since he's been dead now far more years than I can remember."

"It isn't unreasonable in the least. I, for one, am grateful to your grandfather, otherwise I'd never have found you. Once we get Luke safely out of Zarcero, he'll be grateful, too."

"Don't jump the gun, we haven't found him yet."

"But we will," she said with absolute confidence.

"Your top button's unfastened," Murphy said, gesturing toward her dress.

"It is?" She looked down and noted the small V created by the opening. She'd purposely left it unbuttoned, allowing the breeze to cool her.

"When I first met you, you'd have had that thing fastened all the way to your nose."

"That's ridiculous."

He didn't answer, but she knew he spoke the truth. She'd lowered her guard with him. With herself.

"It's too hot to keep it buttoned," she said, hoping the explanation would satisfy him. She should have known better.

"No hotter than Boothill in August."

She pinched her lips together, and to her surprise he laughed outright.

"What, might I ask, is so funny?"

"You. Damn it, woman, we've been lovers. Loosen up a bit, will you?"

She blinked rapidly, furious with him for announcing such a thing in front of the children, even if they were sleeping. "I'd like to remind you," she said, seething with indignation, "that our one and only night together was the fee I paid for your services and nothing more."

Murphy picked a blade of grass and chewed on it casually. She could tell that her reaction to his gibe had amused him. Frankly, she didn't take kindly to being the brunt of his jokes.

"You could be a hell of a woman if you gave yourself half a chance."

"You mean if I lifted my skirts to you or any other randy man who took a liking to me?" she tossed out angrily.

"No," he snapped back. "One man. What the hell's wrong with you, anyway? I saw you cuddling that baby. You're a natural. You should have been married long before now, raising a houseful of your own kids."

"I don't care to discuss with you the manner in which I choose to live my life."

"With anyone, I'd imagine." He spoke casually, chewing on the grass as if he hadn't a care in the world.

Murphy had ruined everything. She'd been enjoying this moment of tranquillity, this peaceful interlude, and he'd purposely set out to rattle her. And succeeded. She wanted to stand up and slap him, but that was what he expected of her. Quite possibly, it was what he wanted. Out of pure stubbornness, she stayed exactly where she was.

"How was it?" His voice dropped to a seductive level, warm and yet strangely weary. "The lovemaking between us?"

Letty could feel the heat rising up her neck, like floodwaters racing toward a levee. "Let me assure you, Mr. Murphy, what we experienced wasn't lovemaking, it was sex."

"Fine, how was the sex?"

Apparently he had no interest in arguing semantics. Hardly aware of what she was doing, Letty started uprooting the grass at her sides by the handful. Her breathing grew deep and slightly labored.

Murphy chuckled softly. "That good, was it?"

"I beg your pardon?"

"Look at you. You're getting all hot and bothered just thinking about it." He appeared to be highly entertained by her discomfort.

"Do you mind if we change the subject?" she said primly.

"Why? I'm perfectly content with the way our discussion is going. You enjoyed yourself. Hell, sweetheart, there isn't anything wrong with that. For the record, so did I."

Her eyes met his. "You did?"

"What I remember of it." He scratched the side of his head and frowned. "I usually don't have a memory problem. Either you were the finest piece of ass I've had in years or it was so incredibly bad, I've blocked it from my mind."

Letty had had all she could take. She roared to her feet and balled her hands into tight fists at her sides. "You're the most disgusting, vulgar man I've ever known. Every time I start to believe you're capable of being noble and good, you go out of your way to prove otherwise."

His smile faded. "It'd serve you well to remember that."

"Don't worry, I will."

20

Marcie, *dressed in white cotton* pants and a blue sailor top, watched outside her living room window for Clifford's truck. He was picking her up on his way to the baseball game that evening and was due any minute.

When he'd phoned earlier, she'd heard the hesitation in his voice, as if he expected her to tell him something he didn't want to hear. She promised to be ready on time. And she was. Physically. But mentally was an entirely different story. This was the first time since she'd started dating Clifford that she wasn't pleased to see him.

Marcie needed time to sort through what had happened with Johnny and her feelings for him. She'd expected him to be angry, cutting him off the way she had. Naturally he hadn't been overly pleased, but he hadn't yelled at her, either. Instead they'd sat at her kitchen table and talked everything out. She told him about Clifford, and he'd listened and understood.

Then, before he'd left, he'd kissed her gently. The kiss itself had been almost brotherly, but not quite. It had lasted too long to be considered a show of affection between friends. With the kiss had come the hint of a promise. That was what had kept her awake most of the night: the promise. And when Johnny made a promise, verbal or otherwise, he delivered.

Consequently her day had been one disaster after another. For some unexplainable reason, Mrs. Hampton's auburn dye had become a Lucille Ball red. Mrs. Hampton, a longtime customer, was furious. So were the three clients Marcie kept waiting while she worked frantically to tone down Mrs. Hampton's hair color.

The problem, Marcie realized, all stemmed from what was happening between her and Johnny. She'd thought she was strong enough to resist him. She wasn't. She'd assumed that a dinner date under the pretense of "for old times' sake" was innocuous enough. It wasn't.

The measure of her desire for him could be calculated in the length of time it had taken him to convince her to go to bed with him. It distressed Marcie to admit they'd barely ordered their meal when she realized exactly what was going to happen. And damn near had. She may have called an end to their love-making, but it was the hardest thing she'd ever done. She wanted him. Loved him. Slipping back into that old mode of pleasuring a man had come effortlessly with Johnny.

Clifford's large Ford pickup rounded the corner and pulled to a stop in front of Marcie's apartment. She reached for her purse and headed out the door.

Clifford was strolling up the pathway when he saw her. He stopped, and his eyes widened the way they always did when he saw her. Widened with warmth and appreciation.

"You look pretty," he said, and leaned forward to kiss her, his movement slightly awkward. His lips grazed the edge of her mouth and part of her cheek.

He was a big man, tall and stocky, but not fat. He wore his baseball uniform, complete with cleats. *Kansas City Plumbing* was embroidered across the back of the blue-striped jersey in bold red letters.

A crop of thick, unruly hair stuck out from beneath his cap. It was time for her to give him a trim again, she noted. That was how they'd first met. Clifford had come into her shop late one Friday afternoon, looking to make an appointment. His barber had recently retired, and he hadn't gotten around to finding another. Although it was close to quitting time, Marcie had taken the appointment.

He'd seemed uneasy sitting on a chair in a beauty salon, so she'd chatted away, hoping he'd relax. She'd been surprised when he'd asked her to dinner. In retrospect she wondered if he'd surprised himself. The invitation had come in the form of a negative, tentative question. "I don't suppose you'd consider having dinner with me, would you?" He'd seemed shocked and pleased when she'd agreed.

Soon they were seeing each other on a regular basis. Clifford wasn't like other men she'd dated. He wasn't suave or sophisticated. Her experience with a blue-collar guy was limited. Clifford was a regular Joe, a nice guy without an agenda.

"How'd your dinner go with your friend?" he asked casually, sounding almost indifferent.

Marcie wasn't fooled. Clifford was worried about her date with Johnny. "Good," she said, wanting to play it down and avoid his questions. It wasn't as if she could tell him she'd been so hot for Johnny that she'd practically torn her clothes off in a rush to make love to him.

"Where'd you go?"

Marcie had hoped he wouldn't ask and sighed inwardly. The Cattleman's was one of the most expensive restaurants in town. She toyed with the idea of lying to him or claiming she didn't remember. The temptation was strong, but she'd made a promise to herself early on in their relationship that she wouldn't lie to him, nor would she stretch the truth.

The truth had an amazing elasticity. There'd been a time when she could have stretched it to the moon and back and not batted an eyelash. No more.

"The Cattleman's Place."

Clifford let out a low whistle. "This must be a rich friend."

"I assume he must be."

"How was the food?"

Marcie had foreseen Clifford's curiosity, that would be natural, but she hadn't anticipated his prosecuting-attorney list of questions.

She must have hesitated a moment too long, because he asked again. "I asked about the food. How was it?"

The truth be known, she'd barely tasted a bite. "Wonderful."

"That's what I've heard. Someone told me you can't get a cup of coffee there for under five bucks." He opened the passenger door for her, and because it was something of a hike upward, he offered his arm.

Once she was inside the cab, Clifford jogged around the front and joined her. He started the engine, his gaze trained straight ahead. Then, out of the blue, he announced, "I'm never going to be a rich man, Marcie."

"Johnny's just a friend," she murmured, and immediately felt guilty because she'd been far more than pals with Johnny. She'd said it because she didn't want to hurt Clifford, but she knew that she already had.

"Have you known him long?" he asked at the first red light.

"A couple of years. I told Johnny I was dating you now, and he said you sounded like a good person and he was pleased for me."

Clifford didn't change his expression, but she noted the way his hands tightened around the steering wheel. "Will you be seeing him again?"

That was what it all boiled down to, she realized. Would she be seeing Johnny again? Honesty was the best policy, Marcie reminded herself. "I don't know."

Clifford glanced at her, and it seemed that his eyes bored holes straight through her. "I guess what I'm really asking is if you *want* to see him again."

If she thought the first question was difficult, the second was impossible. She glanced out the side window in an effort to be truthful not only with Clifford, but with herself.

What she realized almost made her sick. She did want to see Johnny again. He was like dessert, scintillating, enticing, but ultimately unhealthy and bad for her.

Johnny whistled in and out of her life on a lark. He was always generous with her, but he wasn't the type of man who was interested in a permanent relationship, nor had he ever expressed a desire for a family. Marcie made no apologies for wanting to be a wife and mother.

"Marcie?" Clifford pressed anxiously.

"I don't know," she admitted miserably. "I just don't know."

Clifford grew quiet after that. Marcie wanted to reassure him, wanted him to know she considered him her future. But she couldn't very well tell him that when she was half crazy for Johnny, even when she knew it was a dead-end relationship.

Clifford parked the truck at the baseball field. Several other team members had already arrived and were on the grass doing stretching exercises.

He turned off the engine and kept his hand on the key. "I can't say that I'm happy knowing you want to see this other guy."

Marcie didn't imagine he would be. She wasn't particularly pleased herself.

"Would you like for me to step out of the picture completely?" he asked.

"No," she said automatically, forcefully. She didn't want to lose Clifford. On the other hand, she wanted to be fair to him, too. Although she hadn't made any specific plans to see Johnny again, he'd be back. They both knew it.

Clifford's dark eyes held hers.

"Perhaps I should leave that up to you," Marcie offered, appalled at her own lack of grit. She couldn't promise him she wouldn't see Johnny again. How he responded to that would determine the course of their relationship.

Naturally she could lie, lead him on, tell him what he wanted to hear. She could always feed him a line, one she'd swallowed a hundred times herself. But she refused to do that to the one decent, kind-hearted man she'd ever dated.

Clifford inhaled a deep breath and held it inside his chest a long time. "I'm sure all those self-help people would advise me to make a stand," he said finally. "It's either him or me, that kind of thing. But I'm afraid if I did that, you'd choose him." He paused and released his breath forcefully. "I'm probably not going to be able to afford to take you to dinner at the Cattleman's Place for another ten years or so, if then. I've got a business I'm building, a future, and that doesn't leave a lot of money for discretionary spending."

"Clifford, it isn't the fact he's rich."

"I know," he threw out crisply, "he's probably a hell of a lot better looking than I am, too." Not waiting for her to respond, he opened the truck door and hopped out.

Even though he was hurt and angry, he came around to Marcie's side and offered her his hand.

Clifford was right. Johnny was by far the better looking of the two. But there were other ways of measuring the worth of a man than his sex appeal. Now if she could only make herself do it.

21

At dawn Letty woke and discovered Murphy had built a small fire and was heating water for coffee. She sat up and stretched her arms high above her head and swallowed a yawn.

The children slept peaceably about her, innocent as lambs, exhausted from their ordeal, clinging to each other.

Her heart softened as she studied them.

Her gaze drifted to the beast of a jeep, which had decided for no apparent reason to stop running. Murphy had spent two frustrating hours attempting to find and correct the problem and had finally given up. At his best estimate they were five miles outside Questo, but it might as well have been a hundred.

Delivering the children to their grandmother had required far more time and effort than Letty had intended. She had hoped to deliver the children and be on their way long before now. Instead they'd been forced to spend the night in the jungle. Her heart pounded with dread, fearing what was happening to Luke while she was delayed.

She also had a strong desire to be rid of Murphy. She wanted him out of her life. Just looking at him, with that smug smile of his, disgusted her. The man was completely lacking in moral decency. Because of Luke she was willing to tolerate his presence, but she wouldn't for a moment longer than absolutely necessary.

The night before, when the decision was made to wait until morning to travel, Murphy had gruffly ordered her to set up camp. Then he'd promptly disappeared, leaving her to deal with all of the children alone.

To his credit, an hour after he'd abandoned her with the children, Murphy had returned with two dead iguana and announced this was to be their dinner. Letty had heard that iguanas were often referred to as tree chickens because of their taste, but she'd never actually sampled one.

The roasted meat was delicious, and after the evening meal she'd readily fallen asleep and slept like a dead woman until morning.

Taking her backpack with her, she walked away from the clearing into the protection of the woods in order to change clothes. It had been a mistake to wear the dress, one that she intended to correct.

Once she'd changed back into her pants and shirt, she returned.

"There's extra hot water if you want coffee," Murphy offered. He sat close to the small fire, holding a tin cup. He swirled the liquid around a couple of times and then raised it to his lips.

"Thank you, no," she said primly.

"Very well, Your Highness."

He was baiting her, and she knew it. So she did the only sensible thing: she ignored him. She did, however, need to discuss one small item with him, however embarrassing.

"I'm afraid," she said tentatively, "that I might have given you the wrong impression."

Unconcerned, he glanced up at her. "You probably have any number of times."

His attitude rankled, but she was woman enough to overlook that. "The other morning . . . when I . . . when we were in the lake, I . . . I guess you could say I cried on your shoulder."

"You could say that." He tipped back the tin cup and downed a swallowful of coffee.

"My fear is that you might have been misled into thinking that I'm attracted to you."

"Physically, you mean?"

"Yes," she said quickly, perhaps too quickly.

A smile edged up one side of his mouth. "That worries you, does it?"

"Not exactly. I just felt it would be best to clear the air, so to speak." This was far more difficult than she'd imagined. His attitude wasn't helping, but then she knew better than to expect any assistance from him.

"What are you afraid of, sweetheart?"

She resisted the urge to ask him to refrain from calling her by any terms of affection, especially since that wasn't the way he intended them.

"I'm sure there are plenty of women in this world who are . . . who would be strongly attracted to you, but I don't happen to be one of them. No offense meant."

He arched twin eyebrows as if to cast doubt on the sincerity of her words. The edges of his mouth quivered with the effort to suppress a smile. "None taken," he said. She had the impression he would have laughed outright if he had.

"The entire incident was an unfortunate one."

"I understand perfectly," he returned, "however . . ."

"What?" she pressed when he wasn't immediately forthcoming.

"How do you explain the night before we left Boothill?"

She stiffened. "Exactly what do you mean?"

"You want me to spell it out for you? You seemed hot enough for me then. Would you care for me to elaborate?"

Letty bristled. "I think not."

"That's what I assumed." He threw what remained of his coffee onto the fire. The water hissed against the burning wood. Murphy stood. "You'd better get the kids up. We've got a long walk ahead of us."

Letty turned to comply.

"By the way," he said, stopping her, "the top button of your blouse is fastened."

Her fingers reached automatically for the button before she realized what he'd said. Mortified, she whirled around, in such a hurry that she nearly stumbled.

It took the better part of an hour to get the children up, fed, and ready to travel.

To Letty's surprise, Murphy lifted the baby into his

own arms. The toddler didn't so much as protest. If anything, the little boy seemed deeply curious about Murphy, staring up at him in wide-eyed wonder.

They marched silently in no real order. By the time they arrived outside the Questo city limits they were tired, dirty, and hungry.

"Our grandmother lives next to the grocery store," Maria told Murphy when he stopped them a safe distance outside the city. The hill where they stood looked down into the town, which to Letty's surprise was a respectable size. Large enough to have a decent-size post office, she noted. From the number of businesses, she'd guess the population to be equal to that of Boothill, around five thousand.

Murphy handed the baby to Letty. "Wait here with the children," he instructed.

"Where are you going?" She could tell from the way his mouth tightened that he wasn't accustomed to having to answer for his actions. She didn't care. Since she was footing the bill for this little adventure, he could darn well tell her.

"First off I want to make sure the grandmother is still around to take the children."

Good point, and one Letty hadn't paused to consider.

"Secondly, it might behoove us both if I checked out the streets before either one of us goes parading down the center of them."

Another bull's-eye.

"We didn't exactly go out of our way in the last village to make friends," he reminded her.

That was true as well. Murphy never had told her what he'd blown up, but from the force of the explosion she knew it had to be something big. Something expensive that Captain Norte wouldn't easily dismiss.

"Anything else you care to know?" His eyes filled with impatience.

"No," she said, but as he turned and walked away, she changed her mind. "Murphy," she called, and stepped forward. "Please be careful."

He cast her a cocky smile and headed down the road at a half trot. "I'll be back before you know it," he promised.

He wasn't.

An hour passed and then two.

After the last episode in which she'd gone against Murphy's orders, Letty didn't dare investigate what had happened this time. Clearly something had.

All Murphy had planned on doing was checking out the town. For safety's sake.

"Your man is gone a long time," Maria commented as the sun rose steadily toward the middle of the sky.

Letty didn't correct the girl. Murphy was most definitely not her man. Nevertheless, she worried. What could possibly have gone wrong? The possibilities were endless. He could be dead, dying, wounded, unconscious, captured.

"I'll go," Vincente suggested.

"No," Letty objected.

"I'm just a boy. No one will ask questions. No one will know that I'm there," he explained with perfect logic. "I do it all the time."

"He does," Maria assured her.

Letty bit into her lower lip, undecided. If Murphy found out that she'd sent a child into town, searching for him, he'd have her hide. But what else was she to do?

All the children were looking to her for guidance. Letty felt at a loss. She closed her eyes and prayed sending Vincente was the right thing to do.

"All right," she whispered, "but please be careful."

Maria chuckled. "That's what you said to Mr. Murphy."

Letty swore the next hour claimed a year of her life. She paced and fretted and worried and stewed. The children grew restless as well, squabbling with each other, impatient and irritable. Letty knew she'd transmitted her own fears and regretted that, but she couldn't seem to help herself.

Just when she was about to give everything up for lost, Vincente appeared with a short, stocky woman at his side.

The instant the children saw her they raised their arms, cried, *"Abuela!"* and raced toward her.

The woman was breathing heavily after climbing up the steep hillside. She wore a white blouse and black skirt. Her hair was pulled back into a tight bun, and her face was red with exertion. The children's grandmother sat on a large rock to catch her breath. The youngsters all spoke at once. Even the baby took it upon himself to let out a piercing yell just then.

Abuela hugged and kissed each child in turn, then took the toddler in her arms, squeezing him protectively against her. His chubby hands clung to her neck.

Letty caught Vincente by the shoulders. "Did you find out what happened to Murphy?" she asked.

The boy's eyes went to his grandmother.

"*Abuela*," Letty said, having no other name by which to address her.

"Your man," the older woman said, struggling still to talk. She wiped the perspiration from her face with a white handkerchief. "The most unfortunate thing has happened."

Letty's heart stopped. "Unfortunate thing?"

"He came into town just as the local police received notification to be on the lookout for an American man and woman." She paused, her eyes dark and serious. "Our police chief is a conscientious man who seeks to please the new powers-that-be in our country. On receiving word that there was an American man and woman in the area, he organized a patrol." She paused to take in a deep breath. "As it happened, two officers were opposed to joining a search party without first having a cold beer. It was just bad luck that they spotted your friend in the cantina."

"Murphy went to the cantina?" Letty cried, forgetting her concern. The mercenary appeared to have a penchant for such establishments and a weakness for the women who frequented them. Just thinking about him holding and kissing another woman caused her blood to boil.

He'd done it again. He'd left her to sit and twiddle her thumbs in the hot sun with six children while he quenched his thirst and his sexual appetite.

"Where is he now?" she asked, none too gently.

"Jail."

As far as Letty was concerned, he could sit there for a good long while. She was so furious that she found it impossible to stand still.

"I've asked a friend to give me what information he could." The woman's eyes grew dark with concern. "He told me that a man by the name of Captain Norte has been notified of your man's capture."

Letty pressed her fingertips against her lips to hold back a gasp.

"The captain is said to be very pleased. He is sure to arrive before nightfall."

"Oh no," Letty whispered. She sank onto a rock and tried to think.

"There's other bad news, I fear," the older woman continued gently. "Your man put up a fight."

"How badly is he hurt?" Letty cried. She might find Murphy's behavior despicable, but she didn't want to see him suffer. Especially when he'd come to Zarcero to help her find Luke.

"This much I don't know." A soft smile touched the older woman's lips. "But from what I learned, the other two men suffered more than your friend."

"I have to break him out of jail," Letty announced, purpose making her words loud and strong, "and I have to do it before Captain Norte arrives."

The woman placed her arms around the two oldest children. "My family and I will do everything we can to help you."

Murphy spat out a mouthful of blood and worked his jaw back and forth, testing the tenderness. All in all he wasn't in bad shape. This was one exchange in which he'd given worse than he'd got. Not bad considering it was two against one, and then three. By the time he was in jail it had taken five men to hold him down.

Talk about a lack of luck. He hadn't been in town ten minutes when two local police strolled inside the cantina. He hadn't given them much concern. His fight wasn't with the local authorities, but with the rebels who'd taken control of the army. In small towns that dotted the countryside, it was difficult to detect which direction the political winds blew. It wouldn't have been unlikely to find loyalists in Questo.

With one eye on the officers, Murphy had made himself as inconspicuous as he could. Unfortunately it was too little, too late. The next thing he knew, the pair were strolling toward him. Before he knew it he was slapped around and tossed inside the city jail.

Such as it was. The building seemed to have been built by the same outfit that constructed the jail in the old television series *Mayberry RFD*. The entire adobe structure was one large room, which contained three cells divided by thick metal bars. Two desks lined one wall so that he could be kept under constant surveillance.

Murphy tried not to think about Letty, sitting in the foothills, awaiting his return. He just hoped she had the common sense not to do something stupid, like decide to come look for him herself. It would be just like her to investigate matters on her own.

The woman had no patience. That wasn't the only virtue in short supply, either. So prim and proper, she was; it had taken more restraint than he cared to admit not to kiss her senseless that very morning.

She seemed to find it important to inform him she

wasn't the least bit sexually attracted to him. And pigs flew. She wanted him, only she was too damn proud to admit it. Naive too, he realized. She didn't know what was happening to her. One thing was clear: she didn't like these feelings.

Well, she wasn't alone. Murphy wanted to make love to her again, too. He knew better than to mix business with pleasure, but nothing was ordinary when it came to this mission.

Without even trying, Letty Madden was the most alluring, enticing woman he'd ever known.

Murphy didn't like admitting that, and probably wouldn't have, if he hadn't been sitting in a jail with nothing but time and worry on his hands.

Desiring her brought out the worst in him. He'd been crude with her earlier, wanting to shock her, punish her for being so damn desirable. He didn't like being attracted to her, didn't enjoy being turned on by a prim sister of a missionary. But he was, more than by any woman in a hell of a long time.

Suddenly the front door to the jail swung open and a dumpy-looking policeman walked into the room. He was short, with a belly that looped over his belt buckle. Other than a cursory glance in Murphy's direction, he ignored him.

The two guards spoke in a rushed flurry of Spanish, most of which Murphy was able to catch. Apparently there was something important that demanded the other officer's attention. Moose-Gut had been assigned to take his place guarding the prisoner until an important man arrived. Some captain, hopefully not Norte, Murphy thought.

The first officer left, and a plan began to form in Murphy's mind. The replacement didn't look any too swift mentally, and physically a slug moved with greater speed and dexterity.

He groaned, testing the waters.

The guard ignored him.

He was about to ask for a doctor when the door opened a second time and two meal trays were delivered by a tall, thin woman. One was for the officer, and Murphy suspected the second was his.

Murphy's stomach growled. It had been a long time since he'd last eaten. To his surprise, the meal looked downright appetizing. A nice green salad with plenty of vegetables, refried beans, warm tortillas, rice, and chicken. Murphy's mouth began to water.

The guard glanced once in Murphy's direction, tucked a napkin into his shirt collar, and proceeded to eat. Murphy watched in disgust as the pig downed both dinners.

About twenty minutes passed, perhaps longer, and the outside door opened again. Lying on his back on the thin cot, Murphy stared at the ceiling with his hands tucked behind his head. More out of curiosity than any real need to know, he glanced toward the door.

His breath jammed in his lungs and he damn near fell off the cot. Poised inside the doorway was Letty. Only she wasn't dressed as when he'd left her or at any other time he'd seen her.

Letty had disguised herself as a whore.

22

Murphy didn't know what the hell kind of game Letty was playing, but whatever she was up to, he didn't like it. It required all the restraint he could muster not to stand up and demand just what the hell she was doing. As it was, he bolted upright and watched in shocked amazement as she strolled lazily inside the jailhouse.

She had on a traditional Zarcero dress, a white elastic blouse with a large ruffle. Hers, however, seemed to be a couple of sizes too big and dipped low enough to expose the top half of her magnificent breasts. The tiered skirt reached midcalf, but one side was pinned up with a red flower, revealing a healthy portion of smooth thigh. Her hair spilled down across her shoulders like a silken waterfall. Her red lips pouted perfectly as she placed her hand upon her hip and sauntered forward until she stood directly in front of the fat guard's desk.

Murphy noticed the way Letty's eyes avoided his. She wasn't looking at the guard, either; instead her gaze lingered on the two empty dinner plates. A slow, relaxed smile came over her.

"What do you want?" the officer barked.

"Everyone left you, didn't they?" she said in perfect Spanish, her tone sultry. "They always leave you with the dirty work, while the others take the credit."

"Who are you?" he asked, his voice less antagonistic.

"A friend," she said, her voice low and suggestive. "I'd like to become a very good friend."

Murphy couldn't believe she was actually naive enough to think she could walk into the jail and seduce the keys off the guard.

"I need a friend, and it seems that you've got lots of time to play." Her voice dipped seductively. "And I'm the kind of friend who'll play any game you want." She bent forward and planted her palms against the side of the desk. As she did, her breasts all but tumbled out of the blouse.

Like a lightning bolt, Murphy was off the cot. He stood with his hands biting into the steel bars. The woman was certifiable. This was a dangerous game, and he'd wager she had yet to figure out the rules.

"We could have a lot of fun," Letty continued. "Just the two of us. Just the way you like it." She straightened and planted her bare foot on the desk and slowly edged back the hem of her skirt. Her leg was long, sleek, and smooth. The guard seemed entranced by the shape and texture of her pale skin. For that matter, Murphy was equally enthralled. He'd known she was a natural beauty, but he'd forgotten just exactly how beautiful.

The guard moistened his thick lips, and Letty hastily removed her foot from the desktop.

"Later," the fat man suggested hopefully.

She whirled around so quickly she sent her hair spinning, backed her buttocks against the desk, and sighed regretfully, pouting. "I'm busy later, but I have plenty of time now."

The guard hesitated.

"Delma told me just the way you like it best."

He gave a nervous laugh and shifted uncomfortably on his chair. "You . . . you don't object."

"No," she said in a comforting sort of way, moistening her lips once more.

Murphy couldn't quite make out what she whispered next, but he understood enough. Apparently Letty claimed the guard's particular sexual deviation just happened to be her specialty. He wiped a hand down his face. He couldn't believe she was actually getting away with this.

"How much?" the guard asked suspiciously, dragging his eyes down the length of her.

Murphy's gut tightened. He didn't like that look one damn bit.

Letty named a figure. The corner of her blouse slid down her shoulder, and she nervously raised it back up. Then, as if she suddenly remembered the role she was playing, she cocked her chin and allowed the elastic to slip back down once again.

If Murphy had been watching Letty from a purely objective view, he'd have called this the worst acting job he'd ever seen. Except for one small thing. Letty had the body of a starlet—young, supple, naturally seductive. Without her inhibitions getting in the way, she was instinctively provocative. He'd noticed some of that early on when they'd first met in Boothill. Murphy had known intuitively that just beneath the surface of her self-righteous facade lay the heart of a carnal, captivating woman.

Even though it was all an act, Letty managed to have an effect on Murphy. He was as mesmerized by her sleek, enchanting body as the guard appeared to be.

Murphy's body tightened with desire as Letty maneuvered herself about the room, skillfully avoiding being fondled by the jailer. Murphy didn't know what she had in mind, and he didn't want to know, because whatever it was had to be asinine. If she thought she could overpower a man who weighed three times as much as she did, then she was about to learn a painful lesson.

Although he'd investigated every avenue of escape a thousand times, he did so again. Within minutes Letty was going to be screaming her head off, requiring help. She hadn't seemed to figure that out yet.

He glanced at the guard and saw that he'd followed her around the room a couple of times in a crazy cat-and-mouse game, then walked over to the door, where he twisted the lock.

"My oh my," Letty cooed, "you're already big and strong."

Murphy's knuckles cracked against the steel bars as his grip tightened. If the pig of a jailer so much as touched her, he swore he'd find a way to kill the man.

"Are you ready for the time of your life?" Letty whispered, leading the way into the open cell. She looked over her shoulder.

It might have been his imagination, but it seemed to him that the guard's step wavered slightly as he followed Letty into the cell.

Murphy's gaze followed them both like a hawk. He was seconds from coming unglued. The two danced around each other. Letty's skirt rustled against the guard's pants, her breasts achingly close to the fat man's chest.

The jailer lunged for her once, but she laughed and ducked. Then, by some miracle, the guard staggered, his eyes rolled back into his head, and he collapsed face first onto the cot. It seemed as if all the strength went out of him at once.

Letty closed her eyes in abject relief and clenched her hand to her breast. "Thank God," she whispered.

"What the hell happened?" Murphy demanded.

Letty pressed a finger to her lips and hurried out of the cell. Frantically she searched through the drawers until she found a set of keys. First she locked the guard inside one cell and then she unlocked Murphy's.

"We've got to get out of here," she whispered frantically. "Norte's on his way."

"Shit." Murphy grabbed her hand and half dragged her across the floor.

"Maria and Vincente are outside."

"The children?" She'd brought them into this as well. He would have thought she'd know better.

Sure enough, the two oldest children waited in the bed of a rusted-out pickup. A woman he didn't recognize sat in the driver's seat. As soon as they appeared she cast him an anxious smile and started the engine.

"Hurry," Maria urged, glancing down the street.

"The children will cover us," Letty explained, hopping onto the tailgate and slithering into the straw.

Murphy followed. As soon as they were safely concealed, he felt the additional weight of the straw, then heard the two children scramble into the front. Soon the truck took off at a leisurely pace.

"What the hell was going on back there?" Murphy demanded.

The front right tire hit a pothole and Letty was thrown against him. "I'll explain later," she promised.

"Explain now," he returned, refusing to be thwarted. They were tossed about like potatoes tumbling down a conveyer belt, but he didn't care. He wanted answers.

"We got you out, didn't we?" she reminded him.

"That had to be the craziest stunt I've ever seen. You had to dress up as a hooker. Judas Priest, you'd play the role of a nun more effectively."

"I'd think you'd be grateful instead of complaining," she muttered, sounding none to pleased with him.

Well, he wasn't exactly happy with her, either. She'd been stupid, and damn lucky she'd come out of that jail unmolested. He'd like to know what happened to the guard. As far as he could see, she hadn't slipped him anything. There were any number of ways to have broken him out of jail that didn't require her to play the role of a hussy.

The jostling continued, and Murphy inadvertently slammed against Letty once more. This time she released a yelp of pain.

Murphy cursed silently and looped his arm around her, pulling her tight against him. At least now they weren't ramming into one another. Beneath the thick load of straw the heat was stifling and the air stale; nevertheless Letty felt soft and feminine pressed up against him.

Murphy held his breath and tried not to think about the woman in his arms. Tried not to notice how soft her breasts felt against his forearm. Or how her buttocks were tucked snugly in the notch between his thighs. Complicating everything else, she smelled good. Real good. Murphy wasn't much for flowers, but the scent reminded him of lavender.

Hardly aware of what he was doing, he turned his head and nuzzled her ear with his nose. It might have been his imagination, but Letty seemed to ease her head back to him.

Imagination or not, he relaxed for the first time since he'd been arrested. He loosened his hold on her and rubbed his forearm beneath the weight of her breasts. Damn, but she felt good. Their heaviness fell against his arm, and his senses went into overdrive. It didn't do any good for him to lie to himself. He wanted her.

He pressed his lips against the back of her neck and whispered, "Thank you," close to her ear.

She sighed audibly and rolled over so that she faced him. "What did you just say?" She sounded incredulous.

"Thank you," he repeated gruffly, and because being obliged to anyone was foreign to him, he added, "You know, for breaking me out of jail." Later, when the time was right, he'd discuss her methods.

What seemed particularly right at the moment was to kiss her. Testing the waters, he lowered his mouth to hers and brushed his lips across hers. He felt her soft gasp as he stroked the width of her mouth with the tip of his tongue.

Her hand gripped hold of his shirt collar when he kissed her again, only this time he held nothing back. Groaning, he thrust his tongue deep into her mouth, probing the inside with slow, gentle forays that pitched his senses into outer space.

Letty whimpered softly and tentatively touched his tongue with her own. Murphy thought his heart was going to slam straight out of his chest at the heady excitement that filled him. He'd never been so hot for a woman. Had it been anyone else, he would have flipped them on their back and done away with any other preliminaries.

With Letty everything was different. He wanted matters to be right with her. He wanted to please her, to pleasure her. With other women he'd never felt such a keen responsibility.

Wrapping his arm securely around her, he dragged her hips against his swollen front and sighed audibly when she rotated her softness against him.

Without a lot of finesse—little was afforded him in the moving vehicle—he glided his hand up her front to her breast. Her ripe fullness overfilled his palm. It didn't surprise him that her nipple had already tightened into a bead of arousal.

"The whole time in the jail . . . ," she said between soft kisses.

"Yes?"

"I pretended . . . "

He lowered his mouth to her bared breasts, kissing, sucking, and licking her nipple. "You pretended," he prodded.

"That I was enticing you."

He chuckled softly. "Count your blessings you weren't."

"My blessings?"

"Yes." He captured her nipple between his lips and sucked greedily. She moaned and buckled beneath him. "Trust me, sweetheart, I'd have had your skirt up over your head so fast you wouldn't have had a chance to tell me about your specialty."

She stiffened. "Everytime I begin to think . . ." She hesitated, then added on a priggish note, "You're unbelievably crude, Mr. Murphy."

It seemed incredulous to him that they were practically making love and she insisted upon referring to him as "Mr. Murphy." "It's the truth, sweetheart. If you're honest with yourself, you'll admit you want me just as much."

There was no telling where their discussion or their love play would have taken them. Just then the pickup came to a rough, abrupt stop. Letty buried her face against Murphy's shoulder and exhaled sharply. They weren't given more than half a second to compose themselves, right her blouse front, and untangle their arms and legs.

"You okay?" the children's grandmother asked.

"Fine," Murphy said in a growl.

"Letty?"

"I'm . . . fine too." She sounded anything but.

"Where are we?" Murphy asked, looking around.

The old woman didn't answer. "Come. Quickly," she urged.

Murphy helped Letty down from the tailgate. He noticed that her legs weren't any too steady on the ground. His senses had taken a wallop as well, but he didn't allow it to show.

"Stay here," the woman instructed. She left them standing in the shadows and approached the house alone.

"This is the home of *Abuela*'s brother, Aldo," the youngster explained.

"He's a fisherman," Vincente added.

Several minutes later *Abuela* walked out of the house with a short, white-haired man. He looked to be well advanced in years and suffering with curvature of the spine.

"My brother, Aldo," the old woman said.

Murphy exchanged handshakes with the man.

"I understand you and your woman saved the lives of Elena's grandchildren. Our family is grateful. Now it is time to repay your kindness. Follow me."

He led them down a narrow, winding path. The only light came from the moon and stars. The dirt pathway curved a meandering trail through the dense vegetation toward the river.

"We're looking for my brother, Luke Madden," Letty said, not losing sight of the reason for this mission. "Do you know him?"

The old man paused and rubbed his chin, his look thoughtful. "What city?"

"Managna, near San Paulo."

Aldo scratched his chin a second time. "San Paulo is a large city, and I don't know any Luke from Managna."

"He's a missionary. He has a church and a school there. He's been missing ever since the coup."

"I wish you well in finding him," the old man said

when they reached the water's edge. The water slapped against the shore like a woman washing clothes by beating them against a rock.

They were going to need a lot more than luck to find Luke, Murphy mused, but he didn't want to think about the difficulties that faced them in the future when there were enough problems to deal with in the present.

"The soldiers won't think to look for you on the water," Aldo said. As he spoke he walked over to the small vessel, powered by a tiny engine. "Take my boat."

Although the offer had been made casually, Murphy was aware that in accepting the watercraft, they would be floating away with the family's source of income.

"We can't do that," Murphy protested.

"We can't?" Letty looked at him with round, pleading eyes.

"Please," Aldo insisted, directing his comments to Murphy alone. "The boat is our gift to you in appreciation for finding Elena's grandchildren. I have many friends in San Paulo who can return it to me."

Murphy didn't budge. It didn't matter how many times Aldo insisted he and Letty take the boat, it didn't change the facts. The old man was giving them his only means of livelihood. Murphy would find another way of getting Letty to San Paulo.

"You must," Elena insisted. "The roads are blocked, and the jungle is full of dangers. How far do you expect to get on foot?"

"Norte has the entire countryside searching for us," Letty added.

Murphy sighed. If he was alone, he would have handled matters differently; but he had Letty's safety to consider. "Thank you," he said, disliking indebtedness, especially where there was every likelihood that he would never be able to repay the kindness.

Letty hugged Elena and the two children.

"You forgot your pack," Vincente cried, and raced back to the pickup. He returned a moment later with her backpack and handed it to her.

"Thank you, Vincente."

"The potion worked?" Maria asked.

Immediately they were hustled inside the boat and Murphy had the motor going. Aldo and Elena insisted upon loading them down with food and other supplies. While Letty and others dealt with that, Aldo drew Murphy a detailed map of the river. With luck they could be in the capital city within a day's time.

Murphy was already several days longer than what he'd hoped to be. This was supposed to be an in-and-out mission. But he'd learned early on that missions rarely, if ever, went exactly as planned.

Not until they were making their way down the dark, silent river did Murphy have the opportunity to address his questions to Letty.

"What did Maria mean when she asked you about the potion?"

"It was nothing," she said dismissively, but she looked away—a sure sign she was uncomfortable with the inquiry.

Murphy wasn't fooled. He heard the apprehension in her voice. She sat as far away from him as she could, which seemed a bit silly after the heated kisses they'd shared earlier.

"What'd you slip that guard?" he demanded.

Her head came up, and even in the dim light he read her anxiety. "I gave him something that would make him fall into a deep sleep."

"When?"

"Ah . . . earlier."

Murphy frowned. The only thing the guard had eaten or drunk had been at dinner. "How?"

"That isn't important. It worked, didn't it?"

He wasn't going to drop this. "Tell me, Letty."

"Well . . ." She leaned forward and cradled her middle with both arms. Watching her was like watching a butterfly folding its wings, closing itself off from the world. "You might think that getting you out of that jail was just me, but there were several people involved. It wasn't easy, Murphy, and you don't seem to appreciate everything we went through for this."

"You're not answering the question." He didn't like the scenario his suspicious mind had formed. The guard had keeled over like a felled statue and was out like a dead man. When he woke, Murphy pondered, would the guard be left to wonder exactly what had transpired between him and the hooker? The way Murphy had been left to wonder about his night with Letty?

"You have to understand," she said, speaking fast and rushing her words together. "We had to get that particular guard into the jail first."

"Why?"

"Because he's stupid and weak. Delma said he'd be our best chance."

That piqued his curiosity. Delma? . . . Ah, that was the name Letty had mentioned to the guard. "How'd you get him there?"

"I left that part to Elena and her relatives. I didn't fully understand what they were doing, but apparently they feigned some kind of emergency that involved the bank. That sent the first guard out. . . ."

"Go on." He started to clench and unclench his left fist, something he did only rarely in an effort to ward off anger.

"Then Mrs. Alamos cooked up her special dinner, only you didn't eat yours the way you were supposed to."

"I didn't get a chance. Mr. Wonderful decided he deserved both dinners."

"That explains it."

"Explains what?" he demanded gruffly.

"Why . . . Never mind."

"I do mind," he snapped. "Exactly what did you put in the dinner?"

"Herbs." Her voice was so small he had to strain to hear it above the noise of the boat's engine.

"Herbs?" he shouted.

She nodded.

It didn't take him long to make the connection. "The same herbs you placed in the dinner you cooked for me the night before we left for Zarcero?"

Nibbling on her lower lip, she nodded a second time.

Murphy's fist tightened around the helm. "We never made love, did we?"

She didn't answer him.

"Did we?" he shouted.

She jumped an inch off the rough wooden seat.

"You cheated me."

"Not exactly."

"What the hell do you mean, 'not exactly'?"

"We spent the night together," she reminded him timidly. "That was what you requested, remember?"

Impotent rage filled Murphy. When he thought about the grief she'd given him over the last few days, he saw red. He should have known better than to trust a woman. Despite the fact she was the sister of a missionary, the daughter of a preacher, and holier than thou, she'd lied and cheated him.

She looked small and scared.

He didn't trust himself to say a word. Rarely had he been this close to exploding with outrage. It would serve her right if he left her right then and there—docked the boat, climbed onto the shore, and walked away from the cluster fuck she'd created. He would too, if he could figure a way to live with himself afterward.

"You owe me." He spat out the words, which sounded like sawed-off bits of steel even to his own ears.

Letty said nothing.

"I intend to collect, Letty. Don't think you're going to come out of this a virgin. You sold that right a long time ago. I fully intend to collect my due."

She raised her head, and her large, round eyes revealed her fear.

"Just remember, you owe me."

23

Luke gained strength each day. He hadn't seen Rosita since his capture. At least he didn't think he had. There'd been that one night early on when the torture had been at its worst and his mind had been fogged with pain and grief. But he couldn't trust the memory.

Nevertheless, Rosita's love was with him. He felt it as keenly as he did God's. It was his strength. What got him through each day. What gave him the courage to face the unknown.

His cell was dank and dark. Solitary confinement in hell. One thin ribbon of sunlight was all that was allowed him. He waited each day for the sun to move that precious strip of golden light to his bed, then he lay there as it washed over him, cleansing his heart, giving his soul hope. He'd come to feel that those few glorious moments in the sun was God's hand stroking him.

The days merged one into another. Luke had lost track of time, and because his memory was unreliable, he'd invented his own calendar. Today was Saturday, according to his week.

He missed his books dreadfully. His Bible most of all. He missed his life, his friends, his church. He filled his waking hours with prayer.

The sound of footsteps slapping against the concrete walkway brought him upright on the bed. He hadn't been tortured in several days and had thought the worst of it had passed.

His stomach knotted, and he tried to remind himself that God wouldn't ask him to endure anything beyond what he was able. The fear of another beating all but squeezed the oxygen from his lungs.

He couldn't bear the pain. Not again.

He slammed his eyes closed and prayed the men weren't coming for him. Immediately he felt guilty. If they didn't torture him, it would be another man. He'd heard the screams. He knew what was happening because he'd been subjected to those very atrocities himself.

The lock on the thick cell door clicked open.

Luke thought he would vomit until he saw the man who filled his doorway. It wasn't a soldier. He introduced himself as Luke's attorney.

An hour later Luke stood before a kangaroo court. His leg ached terribly, but he had no choice. The judge was the officer who'd killed his friend Ramón. A kind, elderly man who'd never hurt anyone. A saint. Luke's only comfort was knowing that Ramón had left the cruelty of this world for the glory of the next.

The room was crammed full of locals. People Luke knew from Managna and San Paulo, people he'd worked with and helped over the last two years. His gaze skimmed the crowd and he prayed for a glimpse of Rosita, his love, his heart. His disappointment was keen when he didn't see her.

"How do you plead?" asked the soldier who mocked the role of judge.

"What are the charges?" Luke asked.

The list that was read off by the prosecuting attorney was so ludicrous that Luke almost laughed aloud. He'd been charged with everything from arson to rape.

"Do you understand these charges read against you?"

The formality of the question produced a smile. "Yes." He almost added, "Your Honor," but it would have been a travesty of justice to call the man presiding over the court honorable.

"How do you plead?"

"Not guilty," Luke said without emotion.

A murmur rose from the crowd.

"Bring in the others."

Others? Luke twisted around as the door in the back of the room opened. Four boys were led into the room single file. Their faces were swollen and bloodied. It took Luke several moments to recognize them as teenagers who lived close to the mission.

"Hector." He breathed the young man's name. Emilio, Juan, and Roberto all stared with blank eyes into the distance.

Luke felt as if his heart would break. The room

started to spin as the charges against his friends were read. Their crimes, from what he could make of this mockery of a trial, stemmed from an effort they'd made to break Luke out of the jail.

"Please," Luke pleaded. "I'll tell you anything you want to know."

A sick, almost eerie smile lit up the prosecutor's face. "It is too late for confessions."

"I have nothing for which to confess," Luke cried.

"Your crimes are numerous."

"Fine. Charge me with what you wish, but let these innocents go. They're boys."

"No longer, señor."

Luke slammed his eyes closed. The weight of the world felt as if it rested solidly on his shoulders. It was real, he decided. It had actually happened. Rosita had come to him. He remembered how she told him that Hector had a plan to free him. She hadn't listened when he'd pleaded with her to let him die. As a result, these four young lives would be forever marked. The reason: their love for Luke, their desire to rescue him from this hell.

Hatred filled him, so dark and so black that it consumed him. This was what evil did. This was what greed reaped.

The prosecutor stood, his smile glib as he elaborated on the crimes Luke and the youths were said to have committed. The defense attorney sat at the table beside him and made a number of notations.

By his own estimate, Luke counted seventeen contradictions in the short testimony. Not that it would matter. This wasn't a trial. It was an excuse.

He didn't bother to listen as the defense presented its case, weak as it was.

When the time came for him to testify, Luke looked around the courtroom and viewed a sea of anger. One with a tide that swung with popular opinion. One that followed the fickle winds of who was in power and the hope of personal gain.

Disgusted as he was, discouraged and battling bitterness, Luke looked into that sorry crowd and tried to find it in his heart to forgive them.

Forgiveness and love were what he'd been preaching for the last two years. He didn't know that God would be giving him such a vivid lesson in the virtues.

"Stand."

The attorney at his side helped Luke to his feet. He wavered slightly, braced his feet apart in order to maintain his balance, and looked the judge square in the eye.

"After weighing the evidence before me, I find you guilty."

The same verdict was repeated for Hector, Emilio, Juan, and Roberto.

It came as no surprise.

"I hereby sentence you to stand before a firing squad at dawn."

Luke's eyes drifted shut as the words fell upon him like stones.

The gavel slammed against the desk, and the room erupted into applause.

24

Letty could feel the anger coming off Murphy in waves as they continued down the river. They were guided by the moon and stars and the single light of a flashlight. The heat radiated off him until the tense silence was almost more than she could bear.

She shifted painfully on the hard, wooden seat on the boat, but it wasn't the lack of comfort that caused her distress. Guilt ate at her like caterpillars chewing away on new plant growth. She had duped Murphy. Cheated him. These weren't crimes he was likely to forgive.

His accusing eyes ate holes straight through her, his look unwavering. Letty thought to speak, but she could think of nothing to say. Her excuses, which had seemed reasonable and sound back in Boothill, rang false now.

Without him saying a word, Letty knew what

Murphy was thinking. He viewed her as a hypocrite, one who spouted off her beliefs and then fell short of her own ideals when it suited her purposes. She swallowed at the tightness in her throat when she realized that was exactly what she'd done. She'd used him.

Explaining matters would be impossible, but she forced such a list in her own mind. She hadn't misled him for selfish reasons. Luke's life was at stake. Her brother was in trouble, and she couldn't sit idle and not help. Even if that meant cheating Murphy. Until he'd discovered what she'd done, he'd been content. He hadn't known the difference.

Besides, Letty felt he deserved what he got. That Murphy would demand such an outrageous payment in return for his assistance was nothing short of despicable. The only reason he'd made such an offer was because he'd assumed she'd refuse. He'd been looking for a means of salving his conscience and was furious when she'd thwarted him.

To her credit, she had followed through with the letter of the agreement and spent the night with him. She was willing to agree that she'd broken the spirit of their contract. Nevertheless, their lovemaking had progressed much farther than she'd planned.

Looking out over the dark waters, Letty vented a deep sigh, her thoughts filled with regret and doubt. It would have been better if she'd followed through with their bargain and given herself to Murphy. But she'd barely known him then, and he'd frightened her. The same way he did now. In their time together she'd come to trust him. Now and again, to her amazement, she found herself actually liking him.

After the tender kisses they'd shared earlier, she could only wonder what it would have been like if she'd followed through with their arrangement. Certainly it would have been pleasurable. If for nothing else, Letty would be grateful to Murphy for the surprising gentleness she'd found in him.

Or should she be? Murphy had proven her worst fears that she was like her mother, a slave to her own passions. A wanton. A woman with an inclination to promiscuity.

Letty's fears multiplied a hundredfold. Once she'd given herself to a man outside of marriage, she feared it would be like opening Pandora's box. There was no telling where such behavior would lead. If she married, if she gave her body to another, it would be a man she respected and admired. A man who stirred her mind. A man like Slim. The rancher wouldn't be a demanding lover. For years now he'd been satisfied with the crumbs of her affection. Murphy was dangerous, the least safe man she'd ever met.

It wasn't his soldiering ways that distressed her, but her ready and often heated response to his touch. The tender exchange of kisses was evidence of his skill to arouse her to a fever pitch. The danger seemed to heighten her desire, and that frightened her all the more.

All at once Letty couldn't bear this terrible tension any longer. "It's because of my mother," she whispered, knowing that probably confused more than helped the situation. She swallowed hard and held her chin at a proud, lofty angle, hoping he'd appreciate what it had cost her to share this.

Murphy ignored her.

"She abandoned Luke and me when we were five. My father was devastated. . . . He never remarried."

His eyes flickered once.

"She ran off with another man. Apparently this wasn't the first time she'd become involved. My father confessed that over the years there'd been several other men."

She lowered her head, afraid to look at Murphy, afraid of what he'd say if she did make eye contact with him. "My grandmother told me that my mother had a weakness for men. That she was to be pitied." Her voice trembled slightly, and she paused long enough to regain control.

"I don't think you have anything to worry about," Murphy responded gruffly.

"I don't?"

"Trust me, sweetheart, you're nothing like your mother."

In essence he was telling her what a cold fish she was, which was as great an insult as the other. Letty bristled but refused to argue with him. She couldn't very well confess how weak he made her feel. To do so would be handing him a weapon he was sure to use against her. So she held her head high, battled down the emotion, and said nothing.

"So that was what worried you?" He didn't seem to require a response. His eyes glowed in the dark night, his anger replaced with silent amusement.

"I regret having tricked you." She felt she owed him that much. "Telling you about my mother doesn't condone what I did, but I hope it explains why."

"Does it?"

"I . . . we have a long way to travel together, and I think it's important to air this once and for all. You're right, I lied and I cheated you. You have every reason for being angry. If it's any consolation, I deeply regret it. You've been more than fair with me. I can only imagine what would have happened to me alone. I am sorry, Murphy."

"Enough to give yourself to me the way we agreed?"

She glared at him. "Does everything boil down to sex with you?"

"Pretty much."

"Don't you think you're being just a little ridiculous about all this?"

"Hardly. I named my price, you agreed. What else is there to discuss?"

The man was unreasonable. "It was a contemptible thing to ask of me. You're little more than a stranger."

"You were willing to trust me with your life."

"I needed your help. I still do. How was I to know what kind of person you are?"

"Rationalize it all you want, sweetheart, but the bottom line is that you cheated me. You sold yourself to me for a price. The terms were set, and you agreed. All I'm asking is for what's due me." His anger was woven into each syllable.

"I agreed in order to save my brother's life."

"Sugarcoat this any way you want, but that doesn't change the facts."

"But I didn't cheat you, not entirely—"

"True," he interrupted, "you defrauded your way out of it. Tell me, does that make everything better?"

Letty bristled at the harshness in his voice. "All right, so you want your pound of flesh, and you'll have it." It did no good to reason this out. Not with Murphy and his one-track mind. She'd hoped that explaining her past, laying the pain of her fears at his feet, would dent his hard-ass attitude. She should have known better, should have left matters well enough alone.

"You're going to agree?"

"Yes," she all but shouted.

"When?"

"Right now." She stood, and the boat wobbled precariously from side to side. Ignoring the danger she'd be putting them in if she capsized the small vessel, she jerked the elastic-necked blouse over her head and tossed it aside.

"Letty, sit down." He hissed the words between clenched teeth.

"Not until the agreement is met. You've been terribly wronged. If you want me so damn much, take me." She started to remove the skirt, lifting it over her head the way she had the blouse. Somehow, when the material covered her face, she lost her footing. Her arms shot out in a desperate effort to maintain her balance, waving madly about. She could feel the boat rocking dangerously from side to side.

Murphy swore loudly and shouted, "Damn it, sit down!"

Before she had time to think, before she could save herself, Letty tumbled backward into the dark, cold water. As she hit the surface, the loose skirt fell over her face.

The last thing she heard before she went under was Murphy's fury.

Immediately her mouth filled with water and she started choking. Fear paralyzed her, and the current carried her, somersaulting her one way and then another, twisting the material of her skirt around her face.

When she surfaced, she screamed, terrified she would drown. Terrified she'd be lost before she saved Luke. She'd read that a drowning person's life flashed before his eyes. She felt nothing, only a crippling, horrible fear. Not even this last final rundown of her life was to be granted her. The pain in her lungs from lack of oxygen burned like nothing she'd ever known.

Seemingly out of nowhere, she felt herself being lifted out of the water. One moment she was convinced she would die, and in the next her head was above the water and she was breathing again.

She coughed and spat, then choked some more. Murphy's hand manacled her wrist. Somehow he managed to control the boat and at the same time hold on to her.

"Give me your other arm!" he shouted.

It demanded every ounce of strength she possessed to comply. His grip on the second wrist was as tight and firm as on the first.

"Come on, sweetheart," he challenged, "you've got to help me."

She heard the extreme effort it cost him to hang on to her.

The river swirled around her as if to say it had been cheated and wanted her back. The waters pulled at her from one end and Murphy from the other. She felt as if she were on a rack, being stretched apart by two opposing forces.

Once he was able to lift her shoulders above the waterline, Murphy worked on getting her back inside the motorboat. The task was incredibly difficult. The boat was in danger of flipping a number of times. Letty was able to prop one foot onto the side, but when she attempted to lift her full weight inside the vessel, she discovered she was too weak. Finally Murphy was able to fit his arms beneath hers, and with the two of them working together, he hauled her out of the murky water and back into the boat.

She fell like a dead fish into the middle of the craft, which continued to teeter precariously.

Exhausted, Murphy fell back against the helm, his breathing ragged and deep. His chest heaved with exertion.

It didn't take long for reaction to set in and for Letty to start weeping. She hated tears and the weakness she experienced when she succumbed to the emotion, but she couldn't help herself. It wasn't the first time she'd broken into sobs in front of Murphy, and each time it was more embarrassing, more difficult.

She expected him to rant and rave at her for being so incredibly stupid. She'd risked both their lives because she was hurt and angry and outraged.

She'd stripped her soul bare for him and been subjected to his sarcasm. For all the good telling him about her mother had done, she might as well not have spoken. Sitting, she draped her arms around her bent legs and hid her face in her knees. Silent sobs shook her shoulders.

The last thing Letty expected was for Murphy to take her in his arms. He sat in the bottom of the boat next to her and wrapped his arms around her nakedness.

Sobbing, she clung to him, accepting his warmth, his solace, his nearness. He repeatedly ran his hand over her wet head, saying nothing. The thunderous sound of his heart pounded into her ear. He'd been as frightened as she, perhaps more so.

She felt him press his cheek against the top of her head and then forcefully release his breath.

"Go ahead," she whispered when she was able to control her emotions.

"Go ahead and what?"

"Yell at me. I deserve it."

"I think the river said it far more eloquently than I could." Somehow in the craziness that followed her near drowning, Murphy had managed to cut the engine and steer them to the bank.

Wordlessly they clung to each other. After a long time, Murphy spoke. "You don't need to worry that you're like your mother," he said. "Any man would treasure a woman as loyal and faithful as you. It's not every sister who would risk what you have to find her brother."

She lifted her face to look up at him. He swept a wet strand of hair away from her brow. "My own mother wasn't any paragon of virtue," he admitted hoarsely. "She made her mistakes and paid dearly for them. I imagine your mother did as well. We're each our own person, we live our own lives, make our own mistakes, learn from them, and move forward."

"Does this mean you're absolving me from our agreement?" she asked hopefully.

His laugh was filled with wry amusement. "Hardly. I look forward to collecting what's due me, but all in good time. All in good time."

25

Jack had decided to ride it out a while, let Marcie cool her heels waiting to hear from him. His patience lasted all of one day. To his surprise he found himself wasting a good deal of time thinking about the beauty shop owner.

Although he wasn't thrilled with the way she'd broken off their lovemaking, he realized it had cost her plenty. When he was able to overlook his own disappointment, he felt a certain admiration for her.

Jack had experienced his share of women over the years. He loved them, was generous with them because he could afford to be, and then he left them. Not without certain regrets. Generally, when he went off on a mission, he did so on good terms with the woman of the moment. That way when the time came for his return, the lady friends in his life would welcome him back with open arms. Marcie had done exactly that a number of times.

He'd been attracted to her for the simple reason that her sexual appetite was as vigorous as his own. She was one of the few women he could spend two or three days at a time in bed with.

This was the way he'd played the game for a good many years. Women floated in and out of his life, often two or three at a time. He loved them all.

Lately, however, Jack had been giving serious consideration to a monogamous relationship.

It wasn't anything he'd voiced aloud. Certainly not to Murphy, who would have laughed himself silly. He appeared to have reached this decision in the last couple of weeks. It might be that Cain and Mallory had influenced him. When the two former mercenaries had married, it'd shocked the hell out of everyone at Deliverance Company.

This was slightly different. Jack wasn't considering marriage. No need to go overboard on this one-man, one-woman idea. It was important for him to keep his options open. But that didn't mean he'd be cheap about the arrangement. He planned to lavishly set up the woman of his choice and gift her with an abundance of his attention.

In return he'd ask for certain considerations. First and foremost was complete and absolute faithfulness. Until Marcie had broken off their lovemaking, he wasn't sure a woman was capable of such steadfast devotion. Marcie had proved otherwise. By her own words, she'd admitted that she wasn't head over heels in love with her plumber friend, yet she'd refused to betray his trust.

Jack was impressed.

He wasn't sure what had changed Marcie, but

whatever it was, he found himself liking the woman she'd become. True, he wanted her in his bed and had almost from the first moment he'd laid eyes on her. But now he wanted her in his life.

He waited until he knew she'd be home from work and then reached for the phone and dialed her number. She answered on the second ring, almost as if she'd been waiting for his call.

"It's Johnny." Sooner or later he was going to have to tell her his name, but for now he'd let that slide.

"Johnny." Her voice had that breathless, excited quality about it. She made it sound as if the highlight of her day had been hearing from him. As if he were the most special, the most wonderful thing that had ever happened to her. A man could grow accustomed to this kind of welcoming.

"I felt we needed to talk," he said.

He sensed her hesitation. "Talk? About what?"

"Anything. Everything. I don't want to lose you, Marcie."

"Johnny, don't, please."

He could see her clenching the phone, her eyes closed, her conscience fighting him as she battled down her desire for him.

"Did you tell Clifford about our date?" he asked.

"Yes."

"Did you promise him you wouldn't see me again?"

She paused, as if she didn't really want to answer him. "No. I should have, but I didn't."

Jack smiled knowingly. She hadn't promised Clifford something she wasn't sure she could deliver. Another admirable trait. Honesty. "I need to see you."

He dipped his voice to a throaty, seductive level and emphasized the word "need." It wasn't any stretch of the truth. Just hearing her voice had made him hard. He hadn't been this randy in months, and he wasn't willing to settle for second best. He wanted Marcie. The burning inside him grew hotter until it became an exotic torture to merely talk to her.

"All right," she whispered after he remained silent, "but someplace public."

"Fine. You name where." The restaurant hadn't hampered him any. Their naked hunger wasn't going to cool simply because they happened to be around other people. If anything, that could well enhance it.

"When?" She asked this with the same breathless quality as before.

"Now."

She hesitated.

"I need you, baby," he whispered into the receiver.

"Oh, Johnny, I don't think this is such a good idea."

"I do. Nothing's going to happen, I promise. Just let me see you."

Again she paused, then sighed and said, "Have you ever played putt-putt golf?"

Now he was the one who hesitated. He frowned and scratched the side of his head. "You want to play miniature golf?"

"Yes."

He heard the hint of defiance in her voice and grinned. He knew a challenge when he heard one. She seemed to think if they were involved in something silly, they'd be able to keep their minds off what they both wanted most: each other.

"Sure. Name the time and place and I'll be there."

He was waiting for her when she arrived in that rattletrap of a car she drove. Replacing her vehicle would be one of the first things he'd do for her. She'd look good in something deep blue, he decided. Ah, what the hell, he'd buy her a little red sports car.

Marcie's gaze nervously skirted his as she approached him.

"Thank you for coming," he said, and leaned forward to brush his lips across her cheek. She was wearing a sleeveless, full-length summer dress with a scooped neckline, and she smelled of roses and sunshine. It was all he could do to keep from closing his eyes and inhaling the warm, fresh scent of her.

"I should warn you, I'm good at this," she announced while he paid for their tickets.

"Do you want to place a small wager on the outcome of the match?" he suggested.

She eyed him speculatively, as though she weren't sure she'd like his terms. "Like what?"

"An ice-cream cone."

A smile lit up her face. "You're on."

What Jack didn't tell her was that he hoped she'd allow him to lick the ice cream, and when his tongue was good and cold he'd suck her breasts. It was a game they'd played in the past, one she'd apparently forgotten.

The first hole was a windmill contraption. The object was to putt in time so that the golf ball would miss the windmill blade as it circled past the hole.

Marcie went first and bent forward, holding the golf club. It may have been his imagination, but it seemed that she purposely projected her derriere toward him. Then she wiggled it in such a manner to entice him beyond endurance.

"Marcie . . ." He squeezed his eyes closed and groaned aloud.

"What?" she asked, twisting around to confront him.

"Do you have to hold the golf club like that?"

"Like what?" She batted her eyes at him in a gesture of innocence.

"Never mind," he returned brusquely. "It doesn't matter."

It didn't take Jack long to realize she'd been telling the truth. She beat him handily and enjoyed every minute of it. The surprising thing was, so did Jack.

"I suppose you're going to make me buy you that ice-cream cone?" He made it sound as though this were insult on top of injury.

"You're darn tootin' I am."

They walked next door to the small parlor, where he ordered triple-decker cones for them both. They sat across from each other at a picnic table in the shade. Jack reached for her hand, turned it upward, and drew lazy circles in her palm with his index finger.

"You said you wanted to talk," Marcie reminded him, tugging her hand free.

"Yeah." Now that the time had come, he wasn't sure where to start. "We've been good friends the last couple of years."

"Have we?" she challenged softly.

Her question caught him by surprise.

"We've been lovers and little else, Johnny. There's

more to a relationship than a two- or three-day love fest every few months."

"Okay, okay, you've got a point. But I want all that to change."

She stopped licking her cone and regarded him with large, round eyes. "How do you mean?"

His gaze held hers. "I like you, Marcie. A lot. You're one hell of a woman. I'm ashamed to admit that I took you for granted until recently."

"You mean until Clifford entered the picture."

He didn't have much ground to stand on with that argument. "You've got a point, but this time is different."

"You're right it's different. I'm not falling into bed with you the minute you snap your fingers. I'm crazy about you, Johnny, I have been for a long time, but it hasn't gotten me anywhere."

"Jack Keller," he said softly. The time had come to lay his cards on the table, expose his hand, and deal honestly and fairly with her.

"Jack Keller?" she repeated.

"My name isn't Johnny, it's Jack. I felt it was time you knew that."

She didn't say anything for the longest moment, and then, to his shock, he noted that her eyes brimmed with tears. "Marcie?" He reached into his hip pocket and produced a clean handkerchief. "What's wrong?"

She stood, walked over to the trash receptacle, and tossed her ice-cream cone inside, then folded her arms around her middle.

He'd expected a number of reactions to the truth, but tears wasn't one of them. He followed her, threw away his own cone, and then gently placed his hands against the curve of her shoulders. "You can still call me Johnny if you like," he suggested softly.

"You didn't even tell me your name."

"I did," he rushed to tell her. "But we were in a bar, remember? The music was loud, and you must have misunderstood me. I meant to tell you later."

"But you couldn't very well announce that I'd gotten your name wrong when you'd just finished screwing my brains out."

"Wrong. I didn't care what you called me as long as you let me stay with you," he whispered. He pressed his lips to her neck. "I want us to start over, Marcie. This time let's do it right."

"Why should we?" she whispered. "We both know that there's only one thing we have in common, and that's a healthy physical appetite."

"Agreed, but if we get along so famously in bed, can you imagine how well we could get along outside of it?"

Her shoulders lifted in a half laugh. She smeared the moisture across her face with the back of her hand. "Okay, let's say I agree to getting to know you better outside of bed. In other words, you want us to become friends, right?"

Jack bit his tongue. This wasn't exactly what he was suggesting, but close. He wanted her to move in with him, but he didn't intend for her to take up residence in his guest bedroom. The impatience he felt to have her back in his bed was keen, but he realized if he moved too quickly, he might lose her.

"That is what you want, isn't it?" she asked, twisting around and confronting him.

"Yes," he agreed emphatically. "Friends."

"Then what?" she pressed.

He hesitated, not sure what she wanted him to say. "Whatever you want, baby. We'll let this relationship go however you say. You're the one at the helm."

This appeared to shock her. Her eyes were wide and expectant, as if she weren't sure she should believe him. Then, as if she wanted to test the waters, she said, "Let's start with a little honesty, then. If I had your name wrong, there might well be a few other matters we should set straight."

"I agree." He raised both hands, indicating that she should ask away.

They started to walk with no real destination in mind. Because the temptation to touch her was strong and he was fairly certain she didn't want him to, Jack clenched his hands behind his back.

"Are you married?"

"No," he returned adamantly.

"Have you ever been?"

"No."

She studied him as if to gauge the truth of his response. He met her gaze boldly. "It's the truth, I swear it."

"You're away so much of the time."

"True." He didn't elaborate until he read the skeptical look in her eye and realized she was testing him and if he failed now, he could lose her. "But I'm not a salesman the way I've led you to believe."

"You're not?"

He dragged deep breaths through his lungs. The truth might be too much for her to accept. This was a gamble he had no choice but to take. "You probably won't like this. There's a danger in that, but if the truth is what you want, then I'll give it to you."

"You're an IRS agent, aren't you?"

He laughed, and because she was so damned cute, he leaned over and gently kissed her lips. "No. I work for Deliverance Company. We're a group of highly trained professional soldiers who specialize in rescue operations."

"You're a mercenary?" She sounded incredulous.

"Yes."

"Oh, God."

"Sweetheart, listen, I've been doing this for a lot of years. I'm damn good at what I do. I'm alive, aren't I?"

She nodded, but he noted that some of the shine went out of her eyes. She found a park bench and sat down.

"Say something," he said, sitting beside her.

She studied him for a long moment, then flattened her hand against the side of his face. "If I asked you to change jobs for me, would you?"

The woman went straight for the kill, he noted, and at the same time he respected her for it. No need beating around the bush if they deadlocked over an important issue.

It took him a couple of moments to compose his reply. "I don't know."

"That doesn't tell me anything."

"Let me put it like this. I'd be willing to give it a try, if you felt you couldn't live with my profession. Two men in the company were married a few years back. They both left Deliverance Company, and appear to be content. If Mallory and Cain can make the adjustment back into civilian life, then I imagine I could as well."

"They both married?"

"Yes. Happily, it seems." This didn't seem the time to announce he wasn't considering such a drastic step himself. He wanted Marcie in his life, but the legal ramifications of marriage were more than he wanted to ponder at this point.

Marcie's shoulders drooped, as if the weight of her thoughts had burdened her.

"I need to think about all this, Johnny. Jack," she said, quickly correcting herself.

"Do that, baby."

"There's Clifford to consider." She sounded worried.

"I know."

"He's been so good to me."

"I'll be good to you, too," Jack promised.

"You don't understand about Clifford."

"I'm sure I don't." Belittling the other man wouldn't be smart at this point.

"I'll need time to think this over."

"Of course you will." It would behoove Jack to be patient. He wanted Marcie. Without too much trouble he could see himself falling in love with her.

26

Luke heard the sound of the guards' footsteps outside his cell at dawn. He was ready to die. He'd had weeks to mentally prepare himself for death. That the day would come on the feast day of St. Paul, the patron saint of Zarcero's capital, was an irony of its own.

After he'd first been arrested, when the torture had been at its worst, when the unrelenting pain had kept him awake day and night, Luke had prayed for death. Later, when the agony became tolerable, he realized how very much he wanted to live. Thoughts of Rosita and their future together had lent him the strength to continue. To hope. To believe. To trust.

Now his life was about to be snatched away from him, along with the lives of four loyal youths. Innocents, whose only crime was their desire to save him from the hands of these butchers. There would be no last-minute reprieves. No dramatic rescues. This was the end.

The cell door opened, and despite the pain in his leg, Luke stood proud and tall. Soon he would be robbed of his life, but he refused to go kicking and screaming before his executioners. With his head held high and with as much dignity as he could muster, he placed two letters on top of the cot and boldly met his escorts. With one last glimpse of his cell, he prayed silently that his letters reached Rosita and Letty.

The smaller of the two guards roughly bound his hands behind his back and then shoved him forward with the butt of his rifle. Luke walked through the dark stone passageway into the light. Perhaps he was becoming fanciful in his final moments, but he felt that within minutes he would leave the ugliness of hate and vengeance and walk into the light of God's love and forgiveness.

The sun blinded him as he was led out of doors. He squinted until he saw that Hector, Emilio, Juan, and Roberto were already in place. They stood against the wall, their hands tied behind their backs. Apparently they weren't to be afforded the luxury of a blindfold.

Despite his determination to be strong, Luke experienced a painful tightening in his chest. He didn't want to die. He didn't want to leave all the things life might have held for him. He thought about Rosita and the love he felt for her and their unborn children. For the mission work he'd hoped to complete in Zarcero. For Letty, who would be completely alone now. He hoped that his death would be the catalyst that would convince her to marry Slim. The rancher had been more than patient with her.

Shoved forcefully by his captors toward the others,

Luke stumbled and his head bounced against the concrete wall. Pain shot through him, and for a moment he saw double.

When his vision cleared he noted that Juan and Roberto were both sobbing with fear. They were little more than boys. Neither one was yet sixteen. Hector looked as if he were in a state of shock and stared blindly into the distance. Sixteen-year-old Emilio had slumped to the ground, his legs no longer able to support him.

Background noise filtered toward Luke. The sound of women sobbing and pleading for mercy rose from outside the compound. The boys' families, he guessed sadly. Luke knew that Rosita would be there, and his last thought before the firing squad raised their rifles was of her. He closed his eyes and prayed that God would take the love he felt for Rosita and place it in the heart of another man. One who would cherish her the way Luke would have had he been allowed to live.

He closed his eyes, prepared to meet the God he served.

"Wait."

Luke's eyes flew open as an officer marched across the compound with wide, purpose-filled steps. His gaze centered on Luke as he spoke to the soldier in charge of the execution. Luke didn't know what was happening, but he noticed the way hope lit up his friends' eyes. They stopped and looked to Luke as if he might be able to explain these strange happenings.

"Faith, my friends," he whispered, wanting to encourage them.

During his captivity, Luke had met many of the army's leaders, but he didn't recognize this latest addition.

The two officers held a short conference. Soon a soldier marched forward and grabbed Luke by the upper arm and dragged him away from the others.

"Proceed." The order was issued by the officer in charge of the firing squad.

"No," Luke shouted, struggling. "No!"

His scream was obliterated by the sound of firing rifles. The shots echoed into the early morning, mingling with screams of terror. Luke twisted around to see the bloody, lifeless bodies of the four youths slumped against the wall. The scent of sulfur and death hung in the air.

His grief and horror, his sense of loss, were so keen that his knees gave out on him and he fell to the dirt. His stomach rioted and the contents surged up his throat. He gagged and vomited. He was no longer in Zarcero, he was in hell, in the very hands of Satan himself.

When he'd finished heaving, Luke was lugged into the commander's headquarters and slammed onto a chair. He looked at the faces of the two men and felt nothing. No fear. No pain. Nothing.

The compound commander and the second man spoke quietly, but Luke paid them no mind. He felt as if his mind had isolated itself from the inhumanity of what he'd just witnessed, from the travesty committed against his friends. He dared not think about the lives of these innocents or he would go mad, so he sat completely numb.

"I've come to ask you about your family," announced the officer who'd stopped the execution.

Luke glanced briefly in the rebel's direction.

"Answer Captain Norte," Captain Faqueza, the camp commander, shouted when Luke wasn't immediately forthcoming.

"My family," Luke repeated, still numb, still dazed.

"Tell me about your family," the captain pressed.

"I belong to the family of God."

His response warranted him a slap across the face.

"You have a wife?"

"No," he whispered.

"A sister, then?"

Luke said nothing.

"These were found on his cot," Commander Faqueza said, and placed the two letters Luke had left inside his cell on top of the desk. The other man reached for the first note.

"Letty."

Luke's head snapped up and he narrowed his gaze. "What's my sister got to do with this?"

"Letty Madden," Captain Norte repeated, having trouble pronouncing the English name. "I believe that was what the woman said her name was."

"Letty's here?" Adrenaline shot through Luke's bloodstream, and he bolted upright and out of the chair.

He was forcefully shoved back down as Captain Norte paced in front of him. "I've met your sister and her friend."

Her friend? Luke hadn't a clue who that would be. Not Slim. Luke couldn't imagine the rancher in Zarcero. Not now. Letty's man friend would be completely out of his element in Central America at the best of times.

"What have you done with her?" Luke demanded.

"Nothing," Norte said, and then added with a soft, demented laugh, "Yet, that is. Your sister has proven to be something of a nuisance. With the help of her troublesome friend, she's managed to destroy a fuel dump, kill two of my men, and steal a jeep."

"Letty?" Luke was incredulous. "You must be mistaken. My sister works for the United States Postal Service."

Norte snickered.

"It's true."

"We had word of her friend's capture recently, but unfortunately before we were able to question the man, he escaped. We believe your sister was behind that as well."

"Letty?"

"Apparently she managed to drug the guard."

"You have the wrong woman," Luke said without emotion. He didn't know what Letty was doing in Zarcero, but he prayed she'd leave while she could.

"I have a score to settle with your sister."

Luke said nothing.

"And it seems to me that the way to get to her is through you."

"He was sentenced to death," Commander Faqueza complained, apparently upset that Luke hadn't been shot with the others.

"He will die," Norte replied confidently, "you have my word on that. But first I will use him as bait to trap two enemies of our people."

27

Letty woke with a start and bolted upright. She exhaled slowly and glanced around, finding her bearings. Yellow-cheeked parrots, egrets, and frigate-birds chirped a cheery greeting. She saw the boat and realized they were still on the river, but Murphy had secured it so they could both catch a few hours of badly needed sleep.

She wasn't entirely sure what had woken her. For several moments her groggy mind refused to function. Then all at once a terrible sadness, a deep, soul-wrenching grief, pressed heavily against her chest. Alarmed, she flattened her hand over her heart, wondering at the strong, powerful sensation. It was Luke, she realized with a start. He was feeling this pain, and it was almost more than he could take.

"What's wrong?" Apparently she'd inadvertently woken Murphy. He propped himself up on one elbow and studied her.

"I don't know," she whispered, battling back the waves of mind-bending sorrow. "All I know is that it has something to do with Luke. Something's happened, something terrible. I feel his agony, his grief." She didn't look at Murphy, knowing he was skeptical of the emotional link she shared with her twin brother. "Murphy, we have to find him soon. Something really awful has happened. . . . Whatever it is has broken his heart."

"We'll be in San Paulo by afternoon," Murphy said.

"We have to hurry," she whispered, and buried her face in her hands until the sensation dwindled and faded.

"Take it easy, sweetheart, we'll get there all in good time."

"I'm worried." She straightened and looked down the river, eager to be on the way.

He sat upright, yawned, and rubbed a hand over the side of his jaw. He hadn't shaved in a couple of days, she noted, resisting the temptation to reach out and stroke his face. The desire surprised her. They'd shared a number of small intimacies since beginning this trip. Letty felt comfortable with him in ways she hadn't with any other man, save her father and brother. Even Slim, the man she'd once felt she would marry.

"You've got that look," Murphy muttered, and frowned at her as if he weren't sure what to expect next.

"What look?" she asked, reaching for her backpack and running a brush through her tangled hair.

"I don't know, but I don't like it."

Letty pinched her lips together. "You don't need to worry. We'll find Luke and be out of here soon enough, so you say. Then I won't harass you with unpleasant looks."

"I didn't say it was unpleasant," he snapped, reaching for his weapon. He leaped from the bow of the boat to the shoreline. "All I said was that I didn't like it." With that he disappeared into the bush.

Letty continued brushing her hair, convinced Murphy was by far the most disagreeable human being she'd ever had the misfortune of meeting.

She didn't understand him. One minute he was snapping at her like a cantankerous turtle and another time he was holding her, comforting her, reassuring her that she wasn't responsible for the sins of her mother.

At one point she'd offered him her friendship, which he'd soundly rejected, yet he was quite possibly the best friend she'd ever had. In the past week Letty had shared more confidences with this soldier of fortune than she had with her closest, dearest childhood friends.

Letty realized Murphy wasn't interested in listening to her worries. He probably would rather she'd left them unspoken. Her concerns must have embarrassed him. She knew they did her and vowed that whatever was to follow, she would no longer burden him with her past.

Within half an hour they were chugging down the river once again. Letty sat at the far end of the boat, her back straight, fervently avoiding him. If Murphy had any complaints about her attitude, he left them unsaid.

They must have traveled two hours or more without speaking. Letty swore she'd swallow her tongue before she'd be the first one to speak. This too appeared to suit Murphy's purposes. He had never seemed more content. He leaned back and whistled merrily, as if they were on a Caribbean cruise rather than a rescue mission to save her brother's life.

"That's the look I detest the most," he said, stretching his long legs out in front of him. He leaned against the side of the craft with one hand on the engine.

"What look?" she flared, immediately angry with herself for reacting.

"That uptight prude look of yours."

"I'm not a prude!"

Murphy laughed.

Letty folded her arms and glared at him. "Isn't there anything you like about me?"

"Sure," he returned lazily. "You've got one of the finest pairs of tits I've ever seen."

Letty closed her eyes. "You are by far the most vulgar, crude man I've ever known."

"Sweetheart, that's a compliment."

"Then kindly keep your *compliments* to yourself. You disgust me."

Murphy grinned broadly, apparently well pleased with himself. "Yup," he announced, "this is the way I like it best. You madder than a firecracker and me enjoying it. It doesn't get any better than this."

"Well, far be it from me to raise your level of consciousness out of the gutter. Not when you seem to enjoy it there so much."

Murphy chuckled. "Don't be so quick to dismiss the gutter, sweetheart. You meet lots of interesting people."

"I can just imagine."

"You know, it's downright pleasurable baiting you."
He chuckled softly. "I don't know what I'm going to
do for fun once we're finished with this mission."

"I imagine you'll find some other form of sordid
entertainment."

"I'm sure I will," he said, continuing to be amused
with himself, "but I have the feeling it won't be nearly
as enjoyable as my time with you."

The long stretch of silence between them had
seemed intolerable, but this conversation was worse.
"How long before we reach San Paulo?" she asked,
more as an effort to funnel the topic away from herself and to the matters at hand.

"An hour, possibly two."

She sighed expressively. "Are you going to abandon
me again?"

"Abandon you?"

"Yes," she said sternly. "Twice now you've insisted
that I stay outside the city while you go on alone to
investigate. I'd like to remind you that both times
have turned into unmitigated disasters."

"Is that a fact?"

"Yes," she returned emphatically. "You left me for
ten hours outside of Siguierres. When I felt I had no
choice but to check up on you, I discovered you making love with a whore in some sleazy cantina."

"Just to set the record straight, I was gathering
information."

Letty rolled her eyes. "I can only wonder what you
learned. When I found you, it was more than apparent that you were talking to her bosom."

Murphy snickered loudly. "Don't worry, your breasts win hands down over hers. She didn't have near enough to satisfy me."

"Would you kindly shut up?" He chuckled, and she knew he was baiting her, but she couldn't help herself. "You know what your problem is?" she flared, unable to keep silent.

"No, but I bet you're about to tell me."

"First off, you don't know how to talk to a woman—"

"I beg to differ. I can sweet-talk the best of them."

"Hookers, you mean. But when it comes to dealing with a real woman, a lady of refinement and culture, you're at a complete loss."

He didn't disagree with her, she noted.

"And so you do what you've always done," she continued, "what has become, I would say, your expertise. You insult and berate what you don't understand."

He arched his eyebrows as if impressed with her insight. "From listening to you," Letty went on primly, "I strongly suspect that you don't have a clue of what it really means to make love."

"Now just a minute—"

"You think of sex as a bodily function, sort of like shaving or brushing your teeth. Something mildly enjoyable when the mood strikes you. I sincerely doubt that you've ever really been in love. You're absolutely ignorant of what it means to make love to a woman on an emotional level. The only plane that exists for you is the physical. You might well be the greatest lover in the world, or assume you are, but in reality, I pity you."

The amusement faded from his eyes and he

clamped his mouth closed. Letty had said far more than she'd intended. Well, it would do him good to sample his own brand of medicine.

The rest of the morning they traveled the river, communicating only when it was necessary.

When they passed a fishing boat, Letty knew they must be nearing San Paulo. Her heart slammed against her chest with excitement. Soon they'd find Luke. And once Luke was safe, she'd be rid of this obnoxious, ill-tempered, unreasonable mercenary.

Unless, of course, he insisted on claiming his fee.

Murphy's mood had turned foul after his discussion with Letty. She'd proved to be an easy mark. He enjoyed provoking her, indulging himself. This time, however, she gave as good as she got. What surprised him was how accurate she'd been.

What she'd said hit home. He didn't know how to talk to a woman. His dealings with the opposite sex were generally linked to women of the night. He'd avoided relationships. The most meaningful time he'd spent with the opposite sex generally didn't last longer than a pleasure-filled hour or two.

As for what she'd said about making love . . . there, too, he suspected she was right on. He'd been having sex for years, but he'd never really made love. Not that it plagued him, but he was left to wonder at the difference.

It was just past noon when Murphy found a safe spot to dock the boat. He considered leaving Letty while he ventured into the city, but he dared not. The woman had a penchant for finding trouble, and the city would be a prime spot. He wanted her near so he could protect her if necessary.

They carried everything with them. Murphy found an honest-looking laborer who, for a fee, promised to return the boat to Aldo. The man agreed, claiming he had relatives in Questo, and personally guaranteed its safe return.

Following that, Murphy led the way into the city, taking the back streets, keeping Letty close to his side. It wasn't long before he realized they'd walked into some sort of religious holiday. The streets were decorated, and an air of festivity floated about them. The natives were dressed in their best attire. Musicians played their instruments on every major street corner.

"What's going on?" Letty asked.

"Hell if I know. It looks like a celebration." All the better, Murphy felt. This was the first piece of good luck they'd had.

"We're going to buy ourselves some clothes and join in," he said, steering her toward an open-air shop.

The entire inventory hung from the shop's ceiling. Blouses, shirts, dresses in a variety of sizes and colors, swayed in the gentle breeze.

Murphy wandered around, checking out the merchandise, hoping he'd find something to fit his bulky build. If he didn't change out of the fatigues, he'd stand out like a pumpkin in a rice field.

No need announcing to the rebel troops that he'd arrived. With a fresh set of clothes, he'd be able to manipulate his way around town and blend in with the crowds.

He left Letty while he tried on a shirt and a pair of pants. There wasn't a mirror inside the dressing room, but the transformation must have impressed her because she took one look at him and burst into giggles.

When Murphy saw his reflection, he understood why. The white cotton pants and shirt with multicolored embroidery on the wide pockets made him look something like a karate expert. The shop owner added a colorful cloth belt, insisting it was a necessary addition because of the feast day. The wide sombrero completed the transformation.

Luckily Letty already wore the traditional Zarcero dress. On impulse, Murphy bought her a lace shawl and a new pair of shoes. He paid for their purchases with cash.

"Where to now?" she asked once they were back on the street.

He grinned. "To the celebration, where else?"

"But—"

"Trust me, I know what I'm doing."

The center of town was a madhouse. The city square was jammed with citizens who were badly in need of an excuse to celebrate.

Soon after they'd made their way into the town square, a religious procession moved past. An altar boy carrying a large gold cross led the way, followed by the priest, dressed in full orthodox regalia. Behind him was another boy carting a three-foot statue of the Blessed Virgin. Following up the rear, in perfectly matched rows, were twenty other young altar boys.

As the priest walked past, those gathered in the city square blessed themselves. The priest waved a pot of

incense. Behind the religious procession came a pla-
toon of marching soldiers. The gaiety fizzled, and a
somber mood took root as the uniformed men filed
past.

Letty edged closer to Murphy, and he could feel
her fear. He placed his arm around her shoulder.
"Don't worry," he whispered for her ears alone. "They
don't see us."

As soon as the small parade continued down the
street and out of sight, the music started up once
again. Men played guitars and sang, children raced
across the lawn, and women congregated.

"Let's get something to eat," Murphy suggested. He
was famished and knew Letty must be, too.

She nodded.

Taking her hand in his, Murphy led the way. If they
were to get separated in this crowd, it would be close
to impossible to find each other again.

He found a vendor and purchased a meal that consisted of a mixture of rice and meat, tasty and filling.

"Don't talk," he instructed as they sat on the grass.

"My accent is perfect," she insisted, sounding
downright insulted that he should suggest otherwise.

"I want to listen."

"Listen?"

He nodded.

"Just what are we supposed to be doing?"

This woman was driving him nuts. "Pretend we're
lovers."

Predictably, Letty blushed.

"We only have eyes for each other, understand?"

She nodded.

It wasn't difficult to feign an infatuation for Letty, Murphy discovered somewhat to his chagrin. In fact, the role came far more naturally than he would have liked.

Every now and again he'd lean forward, brush the hair from her shoulder, and kiss her neck. Soon his head was nestled in her lap as he lay in the cool grass and stared up at the bright blue sky as though he hadn't a care in the world.

Within an hour he'd learned the whereabouts of the military compound and the commander's name. News of the execution of four teenage boys was rampant. A day meant for joy had been tainted with grief.

As the two women who strolled past talked about the execution, Letty's eyes met his. "They executed children?"

"So it seems." Murphy stood and helped Letty to her feet. "Let's mingle."

As he edged the way outside of the town square, he found two well-armed soldiers advancing in his direction.

"Let's dance," he said, taking Letty's hand firmly in his.

"Dance?"

It was close to evening, cooler. A row of Japanese lanterns was strung between trees, defining the area meant for dancing. Murphy turned Letty into his arms. He wasn't exactly light on his feet, but he did a fair job of faking waltzlike steps.

It had been one thing to sit with Letty, but it was another to hold her in his arms. She moved against him as naturally as if they were long-standing partners.

Her warm breath tickled the base of his neck. The need to close his eyes and soak in her gentle softness was strong, but he resisted. Lordy, she tempted him.

He found her staring up at him, and her eyes smiled into his. They continued to sway to the music. What information they might have learned in those moments was lost on him. Murphy all but drowned in the depths of her eyes.

Unable to resist, he lowered his head and his mouth touched hers, tasting the softness of her lips, outlining their shape with the tip of his tongue. Letty moaned softly, and her arms crept about his neck.

"We have to find Luke," she whispered huskily, and hid her face in his throat.

"We will," he promised. He closed his eyes momentarily and breathed in the fresh, womanly scent of her. An educated guess told him the army held Luke Madden at the military compound with the other political prisoners. If the executions had already begun, there was no time to lose. He sincerely hoped, for Letty's sake, that it wasn't already too late.

Murphy wished he could protect her from what they might discover, but he could see no way. Her brother was all the family she had.

When the music ended, he led her off the dance floor. What they needed now was a vehicle. However, because of the festivities, the streets were barred from traffic. There didn't appear to be a single car in sight.

His idea about blending in became increasingly difficult as the soldiers filtered into the crowd. They appeared to be on a quest, searching for someone.

"We have to get out of here," Murphy whispered. "Come on."

They hadn't gone far before he instructed her to cover her head with the shawl. She readily complied.

Pretending an absorption with her, he managed to hide his face. Another pair of soldiers advanced toward them, and Murphy turned Letty into an alley.

"Kiss me," he instructed.

"I beg your pardon?"

"Just do it, and pretend you've wanted nothing more for hours on end. Understand?"

She nodded. He had his back to the wall, and Letty slanted her mouth over his. She didn't possess a lot of finesse, but to her credit, she gave it all she had.

With one eye open, Murphy watched as the soldiers walked past. He closed his eyes and took control of the kiss, deftly switching positions so that she was the one with her back against the wall.

His mouth was hard on hers. She whimpered softly and then parted her lips to admit his tongue. Her arms slid around his neck, and she was fully involved in the exchange.

Both were breathing hard and heavy before he ended the kiss.

"Are they gone?" she asked.

"They were gone a long time ago," he whispered.

Letty muttered disparagingly under her breath, then asked, "Is everything a game to you?"

"No. I just wanted to see how much you wanted me. Now I know. You're crazy for me."

"Don't be ridiculous. All I want is to find my brother and get the hell out of here." She wrapped the shawl around her shoulders as if it were a plate of armor, her dignity sagging and badly ruffled.

"Don't worry, we'll get Luke out," Murphy said with a confidence he wasn't feeling. He slipped her hand around his arm. Night was just beginning to settle in. The real celebrating would begin soon, and passage through the streets of San Paulo would become impossible. They'd best make their escape now while they could.

They'd gone a short ways when Letty stopped, staring. "Look," she whispered, awed.

Murphy caught a glimpse of two men on stilts, dressed in outlandishly colorful outfits. Each carried a flaming baton, and at intervals they would stick the batons down their throats and then blow flames into the sky.

"I've never seen anything like that."

"I did once in Rio during Mardi Gras."

Suddenly her arm slipped from his. "What is it?" he asked.

"I think I see someone I know."

Before he could stop her, she slipped into the crowd. Murphy attempted to follow her, but it was impossible.

"Letty," he shouted, uncaring who heard him. "Stop."

He skirted his way between, around, in and out, but it was useless. Within seconds he had lost her completely.

28

Marcie picked up her polished pink bowling ball and enthusiastically approached the pins. She studied the shiny hardwood alley and stepped forward, swinging her arm back and then releasing the ball.

It rolled off her fingertips and coursed down the middle of the lane, zeroing in on the head pin. Then, at the last possible moment, just before the ball slammed into the pins, it veered sharply to the left, knocking down three out of the ten pins.

Her shoulders sagged with disappointment. She'd done everything exactly the way she should. The ball had zeroed in on the head pin, then had chosen a path of its own. All she'd managed to knock down were three lousy pins.

"It's all right, honey," Clifford called from behind her.

Marcie pushed down the sleeves of her thin knit sweater. The air-conditioning in the bowling alley had always been too cold for her.

"I was cheated," she cried.

"You can get a spare."

Clifford spoke with the utmost confidence. His smiling eyes reached out to her, and Marcie did her best to smile back, but it was difficult.

If her bowling was off, then she blamed Johnny . . . Jack Keller for that. Their meeting the night before had stunned her. He'd been so open, so sincere, so forthright. When she'd discovered that all this time she hadn't even known his name, she'd been hurt and angry. Only later did she appreciate the risk he'd taken to set the record straight.

"You can do it," Clifford called when the ball return spat out her pink ball. "Here."

He joined her and, gripping her by the shoulders, gently eased her two shorts steps to the right. "You should be fine now."

Marcie poised the ball in front of her and stared at the remaining pins, determined to pick them up. She wasn't going to let a little thing like Jack's proposition unsettle her from the really important matters in life, like bowling.

Smiling to herself, she started down the alley, putting some energy into her swing and delivery. This time when the ball left her fingertips it headed straight as a bullet down the right-hand side of the alley. The way it looked, she would leave the six middle pins standing.

Disappointed she turned around, not wanting to watch.

"That's it, that's it!" Clifford shouted. He waved his hand to the right as if that would influence the direction of the bowling ball.

Marcie turned around, and to her surprise she noticed that just as it'd happened before, the ball took another dramatic sweep to the left. Only this time it solidly hit the head pin. The remaining pins exploded as if they'd been hit by a blast of dynamite.

"I did it, I did it," Marcie cried, jumping up and down as if she were on a pogo stick.

Clifford joined her, wrapped his burly arms around her waist, and lifted her over his head. "That's my girl," he said, grinning up at her, his face filled with pride and happiness.

Marcie returned to the bench as proud of this one small accomplishment as she was of anything she'd ever done. It was as simple as mind over matter.

Clifford walked up to the ball return and reached for his own bowling ball. The smile on Marcie's face faded as she studied him. The plumber would never be poster boy-toy material, but he was gentle and charming.

Marcie knew how difficult it must be for him not to question her about what was happening between her and Jack. He'd asked about Jack only once, and then just to inquire if she'd be seeing him again. When Marcie had admitted that she didn't know what she'd be doing, he'd praised her honesty and hadn't pressed the issue again.

If the situation had been reversed, not knowing would have eaten Marcie alive.

Clifford threw the bowling ball and scored a strike.

She applauded wildly, reached for her beer, and saluted him. He bowed eloquently and marked the score sheet.

Marcie couldn't imagine what it would be like to bowl with Jack. They'd never so much as attended a movie or a football game together. She didn't even know if he liked sports or cheered for the Kansas City Chiefs.

Other than their lone dinner date, their entire relationship had revolved around their time in bed. Not that she hadn't enjoyed herself. The sex had been incredible, but there was more to everyday life than a quick tumble in the sack.

Now Jack claimed he wanted her on a permanent basis. Marcie noted that the word "marriage" had never come up. At least not in regard to their relationship.

True, Jack had said something about two of his friends having recently married, but she'd noticed how he had carefully avoided the topic when it came to the two of them.

Men generally avoided the M word when it came to her, Marcie realized. A small pain stabbed her heart, and she shoved thoughts of Jack from her mind. It wasn't fair to Clifford to spend time with him and stew about another man.

"How about catching something to eat?" Clifford asked when they'd finished with the game.

"That sounds great." She feigned enthusiasm, although she wasn't hungry.

Clifford carried both their bowling balls out to the car. He seemed a bit edgy, Marcie noticed, but she suspected his uneasiness had to do with the uncertainty of what was happening with them.

They pulled into an all-night diner, one of his favorite spots. The waitress motioned them to the booth in the corner, and Marcie slid across the red vinyl seat.

Clifford reached for the menus tucked behind the sugar canister and handed her one. "I'm in the mood for a cheeseburger," he announced. "How about you?"

Marcie shook her head. "I'm not that hungry," she murmured absently. "I think I'll just have a piece of lemon meringue pie."

The gum-chewing waitress stopped for their order a couple of minutes later.

"So," Clifford said, holding on to his water glass with both hands, "how's life treating you this week?"

"Good," she said.

He cleared his throat and briefly met her eyes before lowering them once more to his water glass. "I got to thinking this afternoon about you and this other friend of yours."

"You want to know if I've seen him again, is that what this is all about?"

Clifford shook his head. "No," he said with emphasis. "It's probably better if you don't tell me, and not because I'm burying my head in the sand, either. If you are seeing him, which you certainly have every right to do, I'd dwell on it more than I should and risk screwing up Mr. Wallace's remodeling project." He smiled tightly and focused his concentration on the tabletop once more.

"Clifford, maybe—"

"I don't mean to interrupt you, but if you'd let me finish what I have to say, it would be easier. Okay?"

"Sure." He was so adorable that Marcie had to work not to slip out of her seat and join him on the other side of the table. Instead she reached across the table and squeezed his hand.

"When I left it up to you to date this old friend of yours, I got to thinking that maybe you assumed I didn't really care if you did date this other guy."

"Oh, Clifford, I know better."

"I'm not much to look at, I realize that. There's grease under my fingernails, and I could stand to lose a few pounds."

Marcie had never seen anything but a gentle, kind man who was good for her and to her. Clifford would never pretend to be something he wasn't. He'd never lied to her. He was thoughtful, sweet, and generous.

"You're my teddy bear."

A smile quirked one edge of his mouth upward. "No one's called me a pet name before. At least none that they were willing to say to my face." He sat up straight and rubbed his hand along the backside of his neck.

"When I met you I'd given up the hope that I'd meet someone special," he continued. "Hell, I'm close to thirty-five now. My younger brother's got four kids. His oldest is going into junior high in September."

"Bobby?"

Clifford nodded. "I've never been good with women, talking with 'em and stuff like that. It seemed every time I was around an attractive woman my tongue would get all tied up and I'd say something stupid that would sound like an insult. Then I met you." He chanced a look at her.

"You came into my life at just the right moment as well," Marcie said. She'd never mentioned her past. Never told him about the mistakes she'd made. The time, energy, and esteem she'd squandered on users and losers. For all Clifford knew, she was as white and pure as lambs' wool.

"I did?"

"I'd given up on finding a decent man."

"You?" He seemed incredulous. "But, Marcie, you're beautiful. There must have been a hundred men who wanted to make you their wife."

She hadn't the heart to tell him the truth. Men didn't marry a good-time girl. They'd had their fun and their kinky sex with her and then gone home to their wives and girlfriends.

Clifford lowered his head once again, then arched his back and stuck his hand inside his pants' pocket. He brought out a diamond ring, which he held between his thumb and index finger. The stone was small and glittered in the light.

He cleared his throat and looked skeptically at her. "I've been trying for the better part of a month to find the nerve to ask you to marry me, Marcie. This here diamond's been in my pocket all this time."

"A month?"

"Everytime I'd try to come up with the words, my tongue would stick to the roof of my mouth. I must have rehearsed what I wanted to say a thousand times. Then your rich friend came in the picture and, well . . . I decided I'd wait to see what happened with him."

"But—"

"I know, I know. This guy's still in town, and I figure you're probably seeing him. I called you last night and there wasn't any answer."

"You didn't leave a message on the answering machine?"

"No," he admitted reluctantly, "I figured I was going to lose you to this fancy guy even before I had a chance to propose."

"Clifford, please." Her throat was closing up on her at the unexpectedness of the proposal. She didn't know what to say.

"I know this is probably the worst thing I could possibly do to you now. The truth is, Marcie, I was afraid this diamond would be burning a hole in my pocket when you told me you were going back to your old boyfriend."

"Oh, Clifford."

"I love you, Marcie. I have from the day I first walked into your shop and you gave me a haircut. It was the first time a woman had ever cut my hair. You were so friendly and nice and chatted away like I was someone special. Women generally treat me like a husky Forrest Gump. I suppose that's because sometimes I don't make a whole lot of sense."

"Clifford, you're smart and kind. . . ."

"Yeah, but I don't fit the image of the tall, dark, handsome hero, and so . . . Never mind, none of that is important. What is important is that I love you. I want to marry you, and if you agree, I promise I'll do everything within my power to make you happy."

Marcie covered her mouth with both hands as tears blinded her eyes. "There's so much you don't know about me."

"I know everything that's important."

Marcie wiped the moisture from her face as she saw the waitress arrive with their order. She sniffled and smiled at Clifford.

"Would you mind very much if I took a day or two to think it over?"

He grinned and nodded. "I thought that was what you'd say. Take as long as you need. I'm not going anywhere."

Then, with barely a pause, he reached for his cheeseburger and ate it like a man on the brink of starvation.

29

Hopelessly lost, Letty wandered aimlessly through the streets of San Paulo. She'd gotten separated from Murphy when she'd thought she'd recognized a young woman from Luke's mission. Letty couldn't remember her name. Rosa. No, Rosita. Something along those lines.

Letty had met Rosita the previous summer. She remembered her specifically because the lovely young woman was so clearly infatuated with Luke. Her twin, being obtuse and completely blind to matters of the heart, seemed blithely unaware of this woman's devotion.

Letty had caught a fleeting glimpse of her. There was every likelihood Rosita could tell Letty what had happened to Luke. In her excitement Letty had broken away from Murphy, then twisted and curled her way though the throng, calling to Rosita.

There'd been so many people. Soon Letty had become caught up in the crowd, trapped in a sea of moving humanity. The last look she'd had of Rosita, Letty had found herself steered in the opposite direction.

In that brief glance, Rosita had looked pale and drawn. The deep shadows beneath her eyes spoke of pain and fear. It looked as though the beautiful young woman hadn't slept in a week.

Once Letty realized she'd lost sight of Luke's friend, she'd wanted to weep with frustration. Then she'd remembered Murphy.

"Oh, shit." She'd actually said the words aloud.

By this time he was nowhere in sight. The very least he could have done was keep up with her, she thought, exhausted and alone. She wrapped the shawl he'd purchased for her more tightly around her shoulders. Not because she was chilled, but for the security it afforded her. Which was pitifully little, she realized.

Again and again, as the evening progressed to night and the night to morning, Letty had tried to think of where he would be. Where he would think to look for her or meet her.

Every logical place had turned up empty. She'd gone back to the apparel store and waited outside the locked doors, certain Murphy would think to check for her there.

She'd even traipsed all the way back to the river where they'd docked the boat. That had been a big mistake. Not only was there no sign of Murphy or the fishing vessel Aldo had lent them, but she'd run headlong into a group of drunken soldiers.

Luckily she'd escaped their interest and slipped away. Even more fortunate was that not one of them was in any condition to chase after her.

The city square had also turned into a dead end. She'd lingered around there for hours, hoping she was inconspicuous, knowing she wasn't.

As the sun crept over the horizon, Letty realized she had nowhere else to go. Nowhere else to look. They'd lost one another irrevocably, and it was her fault. The only thing for her to do now was look for someone else to help her locate Luke.

That little shit, Murphy mused as he stalked through the dark alleyways. One minute Letty had been within his grasp and the next thing he knew she was gone.

The frustration was worse than heartburn. He'd been up and down the streets of San Paulo without so much as a trace of her.

Of all the stupid, idiotic things for her to do, this topped everything. As best he could figure, she'd chased after someone she'd *thought* she recognized. Someone she recognized from where?

He should have known better than to get involved in this fiasco. Women like Letty Madden lay awake nights thinking up ways to ruin men's lives.

When Letty had first approached him, he'd recently returned from a mission and was in no mood to take on another. In the few days he'd been home, he'd actually started to enjoy the role of the gentleman rancher. Not that he was tempted to make anything permanent of it.

The sedate life wasn't for him. Then again, he'd thought the same of Cain and Mallory when they'd retired from soldiering. His two friends were as high on adventure as he was himself, and he'd been sure they wouldn't last long in civilian life. But he'd been wrong.

Mallory perhaps he could understand. The hulk of a man had stepped on a land mine and nearly lost his leg and his life. When he'd returned to Deliverance Company, whatever element had made him a good soldier was gone. Sometime between the accident and his recovery he'd lost his thrill for adventure. Murphy suspected the injury coupled with meeting Francine were what had led to Mallory's retirement.

Cain was an entirely different story. Cain had been their leader, the most fearless, intrepid man Murphy had ever met. It was difficult to believe that a woman was solely responsible for Cain's unexpected retirement, but it was the truth.

A lovely San Francisco widow had turned his friend's life upside down. Before Murphy could account for what happened, Cain had set up house in Montana and was raising cattle with the best of them. More shocking to Murphy was the fact that Cain was happy.

Unlike Mallory, who'd taken to raising llamas and children on a Washington State island, and Cain the rancher, Murphy didn't know anything but soldiering.

Why such thoughts would come to him while he traipsed through the rebel-controlled streets of San Paulo on a wild-goose chase seeking Letty, Murphy didn't know. Frankly, he didn't want to know.

At this point, he promised himself, if he ever found the pest, she'd be fortunate to escape with just a good tongue-lashing.

He'd looked everywhere. The streets. The city square. The river. He'd even walked into a women's rest room, thinking she might be there.

His patience, limited in the best of times, was gone. It'd evaporated in the time he'd spent searching for her. The only thing left now was to locate Luke Madden. Her brother was the best chance Murphy had of finding Letty.

If the little shit was still alive.

Letty surrendered all hope of ever finding Murphy. She simply couldn't waste any more time looking. In her search, she'd kept an eye out for Rosita or anyone else she might recognize from the mission in Managna.

At nine the evening of the second day, she found herself standing in front of a Catholic church. Earlier, in Siguierres, she'd walked willy-nilly into just such a church, thinking she'd be safe. Instead she'd stumbled into a rebel command post. To say she'd learned her lesson was an understatement.

The large wooden door creaked as she gently pushed it open to peek inside. Her relief was palatable when she realized this was no military headquarters.

She stepped inside quietly. The church's interior was lit with several candles. Rows of thin pews with bare wood kneelers formed uneven lines down both sides of the sanctuary.

The altar was an ornate wooden structure, painted

white and trimmed in gold, that stretched two floors to brush against the ceiling. As she stared at the front, at the floor level, she realized that a body lay adorned in a white robe.

Letty remembered Luke telling her that many people believed that the cathedral in San Paulo possessed the actual remains of St. Paul. Not the original St. Paul, the one popularly known as the thirteenth apostle, but another one who had followed several centuries later. The practice of displaying the decayed bodies of dearly beloved saints was common in Central America.

Holding her breath, Letty carefully moved forward and slipped into the last pew. Seeing that the kneeler was down, she knelt and bowed her head for prayer.

If ever she needed divine intervention, it was now. Everything was a mess. Even if Murphy did happen to find her, he'd be so furious that he'd never feel he could trust her again. Then there was Luke and the time she'd wasted looking for Murphy.

Letty didn't know how long she prayed. She was exhausted, hungry, afraid. And that was only the tip of the iceberg.

She heard a movement, a creak of a shoe, a *whoosh* of air, a fragmented sigh. Even if it had been a soldier, she wouldn't have cared. Emotionally she was ready to collapse. Physically she'd gone past the point of no return.

Letty opened her eyes and raised her head. Her dark eyes met those of a white-haired priest she guessed to be about sixty. He blinked. So did she.

"My dear," he whispered in stilted English, "these are dangerous times for a woman alone."

"Yes, I know," she whispered in Spanish, knowing the language was safer for them both.

"I'm Father Alfaro. Is there anything I can do to help you?"

Letty hesitated. "I don't think so." She stood, certain he would ask her to leave, but her legs were shaky and she fell back into the pew.

"You're ill?"

"No, I'm fine," she said, dismissing his concern. "Really."

"Where are you staying?" He entered the pew and sat next to her, took hold of her fingers, and gently patted the back of her hand.

Her hesitation was answer enough, she suspected. Squaring her shoulders, she looked him directly in the eye. She had to trust him; there was no one else. "Have you heard of the mission in Managna?"

"Yes, of course."

Hope sent a shot of adrenaline into Letty's bloodstream. "Then you must know my brother, Luke Madden. He's the missionary in charge of the Managna mission." She leaned forward and gripped the priest's frail arm. "Do you know what happened to him? Have you heard anything about him? I feel certain he must have been arrested, but—"

"My dear, you mean to say that you've come all this way hoping to find your brother?"

She nodded. "Can you tell me anything about what's happened in Managna?"

The priest's eyes saddened. "Unfortunately, no. I've heard of your brother, yes, and the work he's done among the people. He's spoken of with great love."

"He's been arrested?"

The priest studied her for a long moment before answering. "Yes, I believe so."

"Then he's alive." Her spirits soared. Luke was alive. Alive. The music of relief made for a lovely song.

"My dear, I'm sorry, I can't say. I simply don't know."

Her shoulders slouched with the weight of her dashed hopes.

"It was for your brother that you were praying just now?" he asked gently.

Luke, yes, but her heart had been filled with Murphy as well. He'd come to Zarcero because she'd needed him. Despite knowing she'd tricked him, he'd continued with the mission. She wouldn't have blamed him had he dumped her then and there. Although he struggled to depict himself as a scoundrel, Murphy was an honorable man. In this instance he'd behaved more ethically than she. She'd tricked him. Duped him. All for her own purposes.

"My dear," Father Alfaro whispered, "are you alone?"

"Alone?" She glanced over her shoulder, uncertain what he was asking. That no one else was with her was obvious.

"Is there another traveling with you, perhaps a man?" he continued, his voice barely above a whisper.

"We were separated," she answered, making sure her own voice contained only a hint of sound. "How did you know?"

The faintest hint of a smile touched the corners of the elderly priest's eyes. "It is better that I don't answer."

"A friend helped me cross from Hojancha into Zarcero."

"And your friend? You say you were separated? How long ago?"

"Two days. I thought I saw someone who knew Luke, and when I turned around . . . my friend wasn't there. I've spent every minute since searching for him."

The priest frowned.

"Have you heard anything about . . . my friend?" Letty felt as though a vital part of herself were missing. Without Murphy she was lost and confused. Uncertain where to go or what to do next. All the while, Luke's life hung in the balance.

"No, nothing," Father Alfaro whispered.

"And nothing about Luke?"

"I cannot help you with your brother."

"Please," Letty pleaded, squeezing his hand. "I must find my brother."

"I'm sorry, my child."

"But surely there's someone who can help me." She had nowhere else to turn. Nowhere else to go. If Father Alfaro refused her, she might as well surrender herself to the authorities. If ever she'd been aware of her own powerlessness, it had been in the last two days without Murphy. He'd become more than her guide and protector. Much more. He'd lent her the confidence she'd needed. The courage to face the future.

Father Alfaro stared at her with unflinching regard, as if seeing her for the first time. It was the look of a man who was being asked to risk his life for a stranger on the strength of his intuition. The strength of his ability to gauge her character.

"I know a man who can get us information about your brother." Again the words were whispered so low that there was almost no sound. His breath brushed past her ear.

"Please, oh, please," she said eagerly, doing her best to constrain herself. "I'll do anything. Pay anything. Can you take me to meet him? But we must hurry. I fear Luke's in grave danger."

"No. You must not see this man, or talk to him."

"But—"

"You heard of the four boys who were executed?"

She nodded. The streets had been filled with news of the horror.

"They were all from Managna."

"No," Letty gasped.

Father Alfaro nodded sadly. "So it is said."

"Could it be that my brother was shot with them?" Letty asked, barely able to think past the anxiety she felt for her twin.

"I can't answer your questions," the priest answered gently. "But I will do what I can to help you find the information you need. In my heart, I feel God will answer your prayers and you'll find both these men you love so much."

Letty sucked in her breath. Both men she loved so much. . . .

The old priest was right, she realized with a shock. She had fallen in love with Murphy. It wasn't anything she'd expected to happen. Certainly nothing she'd planned. She wasn't even sure she was pleased about it. In the two days they'd been apart, she'd felt as if a giant hole had opened up in the area of her heart.

"Oh no," she said aloud.

"No?" The priest regarded her quizzically.

"Not Murphy," she whined, barely realizing what she was saying. Life would be so much more predictable with Slim. Safe, kind-hearted Slim. Even if she did love Murphy, that didn't mean he wanted anything to do with her.

The door behind them creaked. Letty tensed, as did Father Alfaro.

"You must go," he whispered, "and quickly. Return to the church tomorrow morning. I will find out what I can about your brother."

"Thank you," she whispered. She turned to retreat from the pew at the far end.

"Judas H. Priest. Letty."

A harsh male voice echoed like a pistol shot through the church.

"Murphy." She scrambled onto the polished wooden pew, leaped over the back, and raced toward him. He looked like hell warmed over. As bad as she felt.

He held his arms open, and laughing and crying, she flew into his embrace.

His arms closed over her and held her with such strength that she couldn't breathe. Letty didn't care. Her lungs might not be able to function, but her heart was in fine shape.

"Where the bloody hell have you been for the last two days?"

"Me?" she gasped. "Where were you?"

He didn't answer. "You try this kind of stupid stunt again and I'll—"

"Yes. Yes."

Slanting his mouth over hers, he kissed her with an urgency and hunger that robbed her of what little breath remained in her.

"I should kill you after what I've been through the last two days."

"This hasn't exactly been a picnic for me."

He didn't stop kissing her. Again and again his mouth roughly claimed hers. His teeth ground against hers, and when she sighed, his tongue swept the moist interior until they were both panting and breathless.

She twined her arms around his neck and stepped onto her tiptoes. "I didn't know what to do."

"I couldn't make myself stop looking for you," he murmured between kisses.

"I was so afraid."

Murphy chuckled. "You? I don't believe it for a moment."

Father Alfaro cleared his throat pointedly. "Perhaps you should introduce me to your friend, my dear."

30

Keeping his arm around Letty, Murphy turned to face the man of the cloth. He wasn't going to let Letty out of his sight unless he could be certain exactly where he could find her again. In the last two days he'd turned San Paulo upside down looking for her, worrying about her damn fool neck and risking his own in the process.

"Murphy, this is Father Alfaro." Letty gestured toward the priest.

"Pleased to meet you, Father," Murphy muttered, leaned forward, and offered the older man his hand.

"Father has a friend, someone who might be able to find out what's happened to Luke."

Murphy studied the priest, wondering exactly how much they should trust this man. His instincts were generally good, and it seemed to him the priest could be counted as an ally.

While Murphy had roamed the city, he'd made a few subtle inquiries of his own and learned that Commander Faqueza, the man in charge of the military complex, was a real bad-ass. Faqueza had a reputation for torturing his prisoners and enjoying the process of crippling them mentally. If by some miracle Letty's brother was alive, Faqueza might well have broken him. Letty could be risking her life for a brother gone mad with pain.

"I'll learn what I can," Father Alfaro assured Luke, "but I can't make any promises."

The priest's gaze held his a second or two longer than necessary, as if to say he didn't personally hold out much hope Luke was alive.

"I can't tell you how much we appreciate this," Letty responded for them both.

Murphy's hand tightened around her shoulder. The relief he'd experienced when he'd walked into the church and found her was beyond description. He'd given up, convinced himself the only way he'd connect with her again was through Luke.

For two solid days the uneasy restless sensation in the pit of his stomach had persisted. Try as he might, he couldn't shake the feeling he should be able to find Letty.

Not until the sun had set and night had blanketed the capital city had Murphy recalled that when they'd separated briefly in Siguierres, the first place Letty had gone to had been the local church. As soon as he'd remembered that, he'd quickly stalked from one house of worship to another, looking for any trace of her.

"We've got another problem," Murphy told her

grimly. Now that he knew Norte was in town, the sooner they found Luke the better. Murphy was smart enough to recognize that Norte's presence was no coincidence.

"What?" Her anxious eyes met his.

"Norte's in town."

"You know Captain Norte?" Father Alfaro's voice dipped with tension as he mentioned the other man's name.

Murphy nodded.

"I don't think you'd say we were two of his favorite people," Letty said, and Murphy felt the tension tighten her shoulders.

The priest shook his head sadly. "Captain Norte does not make a good enemy."

Murphy had already determined as much.

"You must not be seen together." Father Alfaro rubbed his hands together nervously. He shot them a look and seemed to come to some sort of decision. "Come," he ordered. "You'll be safe with me. Hopefully by morning I'll have some news of your brother."

Murphy knew the priest was taking a substantial risk on their behalf and hesitated to place the other man in danger. If not for Letty, he would have refused.

Father Alfaro seemed aware of Murphy's concern. "You needn't worry. I've placed my life in God's hands many times." Expecting them to follow obediently, the priest led the way out of the sanctuary.

Once outside, Father Alfaro walked in the shadows around the side of the church to the two-story structure next door. They entered the back of the building and made their way through the kitchen and down a long hallway.

Murphy noticed that Father Alfaro moved as silently as possible and didn't turn on any lights. He paused at the bottom of the stairs and glanced upward, waited a moment, then escorted them into what looked to be a library. Once inside, he closed the door softly. The moonlight that filtered in from the windows was minimal.

Murphy smelled lemon oil and old books, not an unpleasant combination. The priest flattened his hand against the fireplace mantel and appeared to be searching for something. After a moment Murphy heard a soft clicking sound and then watched in amazement as a bookcase swung open like a door inviting them into a magical, fictional world. Only all that was inside the compact space was a cot and nightstand.

"You'll be safe here for the time being," the old priest told them. "I'll come for you in the morning as soon as I can. Until then I must ask you to be as silent as possible."

Murphy nodded, and with Letty at his side the two entered the secret room. Letty sat on the side of the bed, and from the way her shoulders slumped forward, Murphy could see that she was exhausted. He wasn't in much better physical shape himself. The emotional and physical demands of the last two days had taken their toll on him as well.

"Rest well, my friends," Father Alfaro whispered before the bookshelf silently slid back into place.

The space was instantly dark and smelled of old

books, dust, and mildew. The little light afforded them came through narrow cracks in the bookcase.

Murphy stood for a moment and found his bearings. Locked inside a secret room in a priest's home wasn't something handled in any military handbook. It sure as hell wasn't anything he'd run into in all his years of soldiering. But his main concern was Letty's safety, and he figured they'd be secure enough.

He heard her stretch out on the narrow cot and half expected her to insist that since there was only one bed, he should take the floor. Unwilling to argue with her, he was about to do exactly that when she whispered, "There's room enough for you, too." Her voice was reed thin and inviting.

Something was definitely wrong. Murphy resisted the urge to slam his palm against his ear and clear his head. He actually hesitated, unsure if it was a good idea for them to be that close. Tired as he was, it would be damn difficult to resist making love to Letty. This, he decided, was a symptom of utter exhaustion.

This woman owed him. She'd promised him. He wanted to make love to her more than he'd ever desired any woman. And yet . . .

"Murphy?"

Silently he moved toward the cot. She'd scooted as far as possible to one side and still remained on the bed. Murphy removed his gun and set it on the nightstand within easy reach.

"How is it," he couldn't resist asking, "that of all the churches in San Paulo you stumble upon the one priest involved in covert activities?" He wasn't accustomed to dealing with this kind of incredible luck. Talk about a needle in a haystack.

Letty took an elongated moment to answer him. "I believe God sent me to Father Alfaro."

Had there been more light, Letty would have seen him scowl. Murphy wasn't comfortable with her response. If God was willing to allot favors, there were a number of more important ones he wanted. Then again, it would be just like this God of Letty's to see fit to place them both in the path of temptation. If having them sleep together was God's idea of a joke, Murphy wasn't laughing.

He reluctantly eased himself down on the cot. Although she'd insisted there was plenty of room for them both, there wasn't. He twisted, rolled from one side to the other. Together they discovered the most comfortable position was for him to lie on his back and for her to sleep on her side with her head tucked against his chest.

Murphy's eyes drifted closed as he hugged Letty to him. Her arm came around his waist and she released a soft, feminine sigh of contentment. This was about as close to heaven that Murphy intended to get. This woman felt incredibly good in his arms. The kind of good that had as much to do with the emotional as it did the physical. The kind of good a man like Murphy feared most, because it meant he cared.

Caring was an expensive emotion for a mercenary. It had cost the life of more than one good man. He'd seen Cain take a bullet because his thinking was muddled with thoughts of Linette. He was determined not to let the same thing happen to him.

"Father Alfaro knew about you," Letty said, cutting into his thoughts.

"What do you mean?"

"He asked if I was traveling with a man."

"When?"

"Early on, when we first started talking."

Murphy had to give the matter some thought. He suspected the priest had connections with the CIA, which was good news as far as Murphy was concerned. He might well be in need of those alliances.

"I'm so tired," Letty whispered, and nestled deeper into his embrace.

"I know, sweetheart."

"I'm not sure what I would have done if I hadn't found you." She yawned a second time.

"Me either," he admitted. He could feel himself giving in to the demands of his body. Before he fell completely asleep, he cupped her shoulder and lowered his chin just enough to touch the top of her head. Dropping his guard completely, he wallowed in the rightness of having her in his arms. He might as well own up to the truth. He cared deeply for Letty.

31

"Luke."

His name came to him on the faintest breath of sound. He rolled his head to one side and opened his eyes. Rosita's face was framed in the small square box of his metal cell door.

"Rosita?" Was it possible that she could be real? His heart slammed against his ribs as he carefully eased himself off the cot, trying to ignore the pain. He moaned with the effort it cost him to move. The agony went deep, but he would have suffered far worse for the chance to see Rosita.

"I'm here."

Little more than her beautiful dark eyes showed through the box. But it was enough to send joy crashing through him. This gift, this wonder of seeing the woman he loved, brought him incredible happiness.

"How is it you're here when—"

"Don't ask. They won't let me inside your cell. Not again."

"Then you *were* here before?"

"Yes." She blinked back tears. "Please, let me touch you." The only part of her hand that she could get past the steel bars were two fingers. Luke pressed his lips against the pad of one and nearly wept. Her fingers worked against his face, caressing his unshaven cheek. He closed his eyes, savoring the simple pleasure of her touch.

"I'll always love you," he told her, choking on emotion. He paused, fearing if he spoke again, he wouldn't be able to keep from sobbing.

"And I'll always love you."

For the longest moment they did nothing but cherish this unguarded gift of being together. The thick metal door couldn't bar the love he felt for Rosita or hold hers back from him.

"Are they beating you?" Rosita asked in a voice that said she feared the truth.

He couldn't lie to her. "Some. Not as bad as in the beginning."

He watched as the tears crowded her eyes, making them bright and clear; then the moisture spilled down the side of her face.

"Hector and the others?" he asked.

"They were given a decent burial." Her voice cracked slightly.

He was almost afraid to mention his sister's name. "Have you heard from Letty?"

"Letty, no. Is she here? In Zarcero? How is that possible?"

"I don't know, but I'm afraid she must be. It was the reason I wasn't killed with the others."

"That explains why—" Rosita stopped abruptly, as if she'd already said more than she intended.

"Tell me," he ordered.

"My uncle . . . the reason he let me in to see you was to tell you good-bye. Commander Faqueza has ordered a public execution in two days' time."

"It's a trap. You have to find my sister and tell her."

"But how? Where?"

Luke pressed his forehead against the door. It felt cool against his skin. Cool and hard. He needed to think and couldn't. His mind clouded with concerns and worries. Anyone he knew who might have helped Letty into the country was either dead or already in prison.

"I'll try to find her, Luke," Rosita promised, "I just don't know where to start looking."

"Do what you can." He couldn't worry about Letty now. Later, when he was alone, he'd dwell on his twin sister and pray God would keep her safe. These moments with Rosita, quite possibly his last, were too precious to waste.

He kissed her fingertips once more. "After I'm dead, Rosita, you must—"

"No," she cried. "It was a miracle you were saved. You aren't going to die, my love."

"We don't have time for denials. We have to face the truth now, while we can." If he wasn't gunned down by a firing squad or hanged, as some of the other political prisoners had been, there was every likelihood that the beatings would kill him.

"How can a God let this happen to us?" She wept openly. Her voice trembled with the force of her sobs.

"How could He allow Hector and the others to die such a horrible death?"

Luke had repeatedly asked these same questions himself. "God isn't the one responsible for the hate in this world," he assured her, wanting more than anything to hold Rosita one last time. He would die a happy man if he could feel her softness against him. If he were allowed one last opportunity to touch her sweet face and feel her heartbeat against his own.

She glanced over her shoulder, and he saw a flicker of fear. "I must go." Wiping the moisture from her face, she offered him a brave smile, turned abruptly, and was gone.

Luke heard the gentle fall of her footsteps as she sped away. The physical effort it cost him to stand caused him to tremble violently. He barely made it back to the bed before he collapsed.

He was suffocating with the weight of his worries. Norte was going to use him to trap Letty.

Luke knew his sister well. She'd do anything to rescue him, including placing herself at incredible risk. He couldn't allow that to happen, but he didn't know any way to prevent it.

Letty would come racing in on a white charger, believing she could save him, and in the process sacrifice her own life. His sister hadn't a clue what these men were like. She'd never seen evil on this level. Neither had Luke until he'd been taken captive.

The only way he could thwart Captain Norte was to die before the public execution could take place. With his eyes open and raised to the heavens, Luke looked to God.

"Let me die," he pleaded, "before it's too late."

32

"*As of two days ago your* brother was alive."

Her heart in her throat, Letty whirled around to face Father Alfaro. "He's alive?" The priest had come for them bright and early that morning and led them to the home of a friend, someone he trusted. Murphy had disappeared with Father Alfaro shortly after their arrival. She wasn't keen on their being separated so soon after finding each other, but she wasn't given any choice.

Murphy looked to Father Alfaro and then to Letty.

"What is it?" she asked. She was beginning to know Murphy, and there was something he wasn't telling her.

Neither one seemed eager to elaborate. "Luke's hurt," she cried, certain the news was bad. "How seriously? Can we move him? Does he need a physician?"

"Letty," Murphy said, and gently wrapped his hand around her forearm. "It isn't that."

"My source wasn't able to learn of your brother's physical condition," Father Alfaro continued. "All he could tell me was that your brother is alive."

"There's more," she insisted, unwilling to be protected from the truth. Murphy should know her well enough by now to recognize that. "Tell me," she insisted. "I need to know."

Once again the two men exchanged looks.

Murphy was the one who spoke next. His eyes held hers and his words were low and even, without emotion. "Luke's been sentenced to death."

Letty closed her eyes and held her breath until her chest tightened and her lungs ached.

"His execution is to be held publicly at noon in two days' time."

"Two days," she repeated. The blood seemed to rush from her head, and the world started to spin. For an instant she feared she was about to faint. The need to sit down became urgent; she reached out blindly and lowered herself onto a rough wooden chair.

"Letty?"

"I'm okay." But she wasn't. She hadn't felt right all morning. Although she'd slept better in Murphy's arms than she had in weeks, she'd awakened exhausted, weary to the bone.

The ill feeling had intensified as the morning had progressed. She probably should have said something, but she'd been fairly certain the feeling would pass. It hadn't.

"We've got to save him," she said, looking to Murphy. She'd found herself doing that more and more often. Along with her heart, she'd given him her trust. In her eyes, he was capable of the impossible. As obstacles in saving Luke became more and more insurmountable, she relied heavily on Murphy's talents.

"I gave you my word I'd find your brother, Letty, and I will." His jaw was clenched with grim determination.

The need to touch him was strong. To flatten her palm against his cheek and thank him. Those two days wandering about the city without him had taught her valuable lessons. As much as she wanted to find and free Luke, she could do nothing without Murphy.

The priest cast the mercenary a worried glance. The atmosphere in the small adobe house reeked of tension. Not understanding, Letty looked to Father Alfaro.

"We fear the execution might be a trap," the priest explained.

Murphy chuckled. "Norte wants us. And really, can you blame him? We made him look like the fool he is. What he doesn't realize is that he hasn't got a prayer. Not only are we going to escape his clutches, but we're going to steal Luke right from under his nose."

"The word on the street is that Commander Norte will richly reward the person who captures either of you."

"I see." And Letty did. As Father Alfaro had told them the night before, Captain Norte didn't make for a good enemy.

"You should be prepared for the worst," the priest told her gently. "We'll do everything within our power, but it's possible we won't be able to save your brother."

"You must," she cried. Her heart desperately wanted to believe it was possible to rescue Luke. Her brother deserved so much better than this. He'd given his heart to the people of Zarcero, dedicated his life. Without Luke, she'd be completely alone and lost. Without him, her anchor would be missing.

"You have my word that I'll do everything I can to free Luke," Murphy said, the intent look back in his eyes.

"I can't ask for anything more than that," she returned.

The rest of the morning was spent with Murphy and Father Alfaro talking and making plans. The two appeared to come to some form of agreement, and soon afterward Murphy left. He didn't tell her where he was going or how long he'd be away.

Letty sat in the shade of a tree, trying to analyze what was wrong with her. The achy, restless sensation persisted into the afternoon. She attempted to put some name to what she felt. The physical symptoms resembled a low-grade case of the flu, but she knew it was more than that. In some ways it seemed as if this queasiness were connected with her twin.

Letty waited impatiently for Murphy's return. Several matters needed to be discussed and decided. Her mind was so occupied with that, she wasn't aware of the subtle changes going on about her.

At first.

It came to her all at once that she was being watched. She wasn't sure how she knew, but she trusted this sixth sense. For a long time she remained motionless, afraid to move, fearful of attracting attention to herself. The same sixth sense that told her she and Father Alfaro were no longer alone warned her that if she did move, she'd be a dead woman.

As soon as the thought went through her mind, fear drifted in like a thick fog, the haze of it making it difficult to reason out exactly what was happening.

With her breath held tight within her chest, she glanced across the yard. Father Alfaro sat inside the house at a table. He appeared to be reading.

A vision flashed into her mind of a jail cell, of torture and death. For one single instant she could smell the filth, taste the horror, and feel the pain. Then it was gone.

The next moment, a picture of Murphy hell-bent for leather surged like gangbusters into her mind. She seized the image and held on to it, needing him just then. If he were here, he'd know what to do. She had the pistol with her—he'd insisted she carry it at all times—but reaching for it now would be useless. She'd be dead before she could even point it. And even if she could get her weapon without drawing attention, she wasn't sure about firing it. She'd done so the one time, and only because Murphy had insisted. She wished she'd paid more attention now.

Maybe it was because she was thinking of Murphy and the gun that she was prepared for what happened next. His voice, soft and urgent, drifted from behind her.

"Letty, when I shout I want you to drop to the ground and cover your head. Have you got that?"

She gave a small, imperceptible nod. Every muscle in her body went tense.

Soon after Murphy whispered, Letty saw three soldiers hiding in the vegetation close to the house. Two of them had pointed their rifles directly at her. The other man had his trained on Father Alfaro, through a window.

Dressed in camouflage, they blended in perfectly with the scenery. It was a wonder she'd been able to pick them out at all.

The taste of fear filled her mouth, attacked her senses. A humming sound roared in her ear, and the scent of anticipation, the choking swell of the afternoon heat, settled over her like concrete blocks. Her throat felt as dry as a crusted, empty lake bed.

"Do it!" Murphy's cry cut through the hot, still afternoon air like a razor-sharp scissors through paper. Swallowing a scream, Letty fell face first into the dirt. Remembering what he'd said about covering her head, she brought her arms up to protect herself.

The quick, staccato bursts of Murphy's weapon roared over her. Letty froze with fear, unable to scramble to safety even if he asked it of her.

Three soldiers lay dead outside the adobe structure. Three good men, downed by their own sloppy work, Murphy mused. Letty and the priest had been sitting ducks. The guerrillas could have had them any time, but Norte's men had been overly confident and forgotten one small thing. Him.

When Murphy had arrived on the scene, he'd recognized instantly that Letty had sensed the soldiers' presence. Their interest had seemed to be focused on the priest. Not until later had they realized Father Alfaro wasn't alone.

Murphy thanked the powers above that Letty had had the presence of mind to remain silent and still. He was convinced it had saved her life.

When he'd happened upon the scene, he'd been scared spitless. Letty in grave danger. He'd strongly suspected his feelings for her had changed. Little by little she'd chipped away at the wall of his defenses until he'd fallen hopelessly in love with her. The moment he'd recognized he could lose her to a guerrilla's bullet had removed all doubt of the sentiment he felt for her.

Murphy wasn't being immodest by claiming he was a good soldier. Furthermore, he understood the reasons that made him good. Death had never been any big threat to him. It held no terror. His world consisted of a few carefully chosen friends and Deliverance Company. And that was it. The full extent of his existence. He was a man with little to lose.

His life to this point had been devoid of contentment, of joy, and, most profoundly of all, of love.

He wasn't particularly happy to own up to the fact he loved Letty. It wasn't an emotion he was comfortable with. He feared loving her might mean he'd need to surrender a part of himself, and frankly that worried him. He'd die for her in a heartbeat. Stop a bullet in order to save her life. But he wasn't sure he should let her know how much he cared.

The silence that followed the blast of gunfire was louder than a cannon burst. He stepped out from behind Letty and walked over to where the guerrillas lay. With the boot of one foot, he turned them over and checked to be sure each one was dead. They were.

He experienced no emotion, no sense of regret, no sense of loss. This was what he did. He found no pleasure in killing, no thrill.

"Murphy . . ." His name was a weak cry from Letty's lips as she raced toward him and into his arms. He scooped her up and held her against him. She trembled violently, her arms holding his neck so tightly that it was close to becoming a stranglehold.

"It's all right, sweetheart."

He derived such a simple enjoyment from holding her that he momentarily forgot about the priest.

Father Alfaro looked pale and drawn as he walked outside the adobe house. Murphy noted that the other man's steps weren't any too steady. The priest removed a white kerchief from his pocket and mopped his brow.

"Mother of Jesus," he whispered, staring at the dead men.

"You all right, Father?" Murphy asked, releasing Letty.

"Fine. Fine." He glanced over at the dead soldiers again. "They're Norte's men."

"Then he knows where we are."

The priest closed his eyes. "Alphonse," he said as though in deep pain. "He would never have betrayed me without first being tortured."

"We've got to get out of here," Murphy said, in a hurry to get Letty to a safe place. Only he wasn't sure where.

"Letty," he called. Only seconds earlier she'd been

in his arms. Now he caught a glimpse of her inside the house, sitting with her face in her hands as if the scene outside the door were more than she could bear to view.

He wanted to comfort her, explain that he would have spared her this if it had been within his power.

"Letty, we've got to get out of here," he called again. He knew he sounded gruff and impatient, but it couldn't be helped. She was in danger, and he'd die before he'd let anything more happen to her.

Suddenly he caught a movement out of the corner of his eye. He threw the priest to the ground and fell for cover himself, but he couldn't reach Letty.

Rolling in the dirt, firing as he went, Murphy counted two other guerrillas. He heard one muffled shout of pain, then silence. The eerie, unnatural silence that often followed gunfire and death.

"Let's get the hell out of here!" he shouted, eager to get Letty and the priest to safety. His steady gaze scanned the jungle, his senses on full alert.

Letty's scream caught him off guard. The sound of a single gunshot filled him with a crippling terror. Dear God in heaven, not Letty. *Please, don't let them have Letty.* He bargained with everything he had. His life. His heart. His soul.

He roared to his feet with a cry of outrage and raced into the house. He was ready to kill or die, whatever the situation demanded. He discovered Letty standing with a .45, the one he'd given her at the start of the mission. The pistol dangled from her hand.

A soldier lay dead no more than five feet from her.

She looked to be in a state of shock. Deathly pale, she stared sightlessly at the dead man on the floor. He lay in a pool of blood, his eyes open. The rebel was dead, but even then Murphy could feel his hate.

He walked over to where she stood and gently pried the pistol free from her fingers.

"You all right?" he asked gently.

She shook her head, walked outside, and promptly vomited.

33

Rosita walked into the dimly lit room and looked at the body of the man stretched out on the table. A piercing pain cut through her heart as she realized what her uncle had told her was true.

Luke was dead.

A sob wrenched itself from her throat, and she covered her mouth in an effort to hold back a cry of bitter anguish. It wasn't supposed to have happened like this. They should have been married, she should have borne his children, and they should have spent many long, happy years together. He'd loved her, and she'd loved him more than any man she'd ever known. More than she would ever allow herself to love again.

"Quiet," came the husky voice of her uncle. "If anyone finds you here, I'll be in trouble."

She answered him with a strangled sob of grief. "What happened?" she asked, needing to know.

"The guard told me he died in his sleep."

"His sleep?" Rosita didn't believe him, although he was her uncle and the one who'd helped her see Luke two other times before.

"No one knows the exact cause of his death. He was alive when the lights went out, and then in the morning he was dead. Commander Faqueza questioned the guards, and no one went into your friend's cell all night."

Gently, in a gesture of farewell, Rosita touched Luke's face. He looked serene, at peace. Beautiful in a way that words could never describe.

"Captain Norte is said to be very angry," her uncle informed her. "He'd planned to use your friend to trap the others."

Rosita studied Luke and realized this was what he'd prayed would happen. It was the only way he could save his sister and spare them both the terror of witnessing a public execution. He'd always put the concerns of others first.

Luke Madden had stolen her heart the first year he'd arrived in Zarcero. For months Rosita had kept her feelings to herself, afraid to let him know how much she cared.

Later, when Luke came to love her, her heart sang with joy. As deliriously happy as she'd been then, she suffered now. The pendulum of love swung in both directions, she realized. The depth of her love was equal to the deep, emotional agony she suffered at his death.

"We must go," her uncle warned.

"A minute more," she pleaded. She wanted to look

at him a bit longer, memorize the peaceful look on his face, sear it into her heart for the long, lonely years she would have without him.

"Are you ready?"

She nodded, and the hot tears continued to stream down her face.

"I could do nothing more to save him," her uncle said sadly. "I tried."

"I know you did." She pressed a gentle hand to his arm. "Thank you for the risk you took to bring me here."

"Your friend was a good man."

Rosita wiped the tears from her face. "I wish you could have known him."

"I did in some small ways. He did not curse when they tortured him. He had only love. If any man is with God, it is your friend."

34

Letty knew that Murphy was worried about her. She'd killed a man. She hadn't wanted to do it, and she would live with the agony of regret the rest of her life.

The guerrilla had given her no choice. It had come down to a simple equation: him or her. The shock came for Letty when she realized how desperately she wanted to live.

She hadn't so much as hesitated, and it was that quick thinking, that pure instinctual desire to live, that had saved her.

Father Alfaro had hurriedly ushered them to another house of a friend he could trust. This night they were in a space under the floor of a barn. The room was only slightly larger than the space afforded them in the priest's secret room in the rectory library.

Murphy sat across from her, eating the dinner that

had been provided them. He used the tortilla to scrape up the beans, downing the food hungrily. He'd almost completely finished before he noticed she hadn't touched her meal.

"Letty, eat."

She shook her head. "I can't. I'm not hungry."

He set aside the tin plate and moved so that he was sitting next to her on the mattress. "Honey, listen, it was self-defense."

She closed her eyes, willing him to stop talking. The strange sick sensation that had been with her since morning returned.

" . . . probably saved my sorry ass as well," Murphy continued. "He wouldn't have stopped after killing you."

"Murphy." Blindly she reached out and gripped his arm.

"Are you going to be sick again?"

"No. Oh, Murphy . . . no, please, no."

"Honey, what is it? Don't go soft on me now, kid."

"He's dead."

"Sweetheart, you didn't have any choice."

"Not that soldier," she said sobbing. "Luke." She bent forward and pressed her forehead to her knee. That was what was wrong. All day she'd felt it. All day she'd struggled with this horrible sick feeling in the pit of her stomach.

"But Father Alfaro assured us that as of two days ago he was alive."

The grief she felt overwhelmed her. It felt as if she'd been weighed down with bricks and then thrown over the side of a boat. She was going down, deeper and deeper and powerless to stop, powerless to help herself.

Not until Murphy wrapped his arms around her did Letty realize that she was clinging to him. The sobs went so deep they produced a physical pain. She rocked back and forth, sobbing, gasping for breath, mourning for the twin brother she'd lost.

"Letty, honey, don't cry like this. We don't know what's happened to Luke."

"I know. My heart knows."

"But Father Alfaro said—"

"He's dead. My brother is dead. We're too late. We can't save him."

Murphy held her until she had no more tears to shed. She clung to him, her fingers pinching his flesh in her grief, in her desperation. Still he held her, still he comforted her.

When Letty's tears were spent, he gently laid her down on the mattress and sat with her. He whispered reassurances, but Letty couldn't hear them. Couldn't. Her heart felt as if it would melt inside her chest with the overwhelming weight of her sorrow.

At some point she must have fallen asleep because the next thing she knew it was dark. The room hidden below the barn was pitch black.

She knew Murphy was beside her because she heard the even rhythm of his breathing. Then she remembered her brother, and the anguish and pain returned.

"Letty . . ."

She rolled over and buried her face in his neck. "Make love to me," she whispered. "I feel so alone, so empty. I need you. Please, Murphy, please, make love to me."

Murphy closed his eyes and prayed for strength. Letty in his arms was temptation enough, but for her to plead with him to make love to her was more than any man should have to refuse.

"Honey," he whispered gently, brushing back the hair from her face, "you don't know what you're asking."

"I want you. I need you, Murphy, please." She moved against him, rubbing the tips of her nipples against his chest, their hot tips searing him until he felt as though he'd been branded. He gritted his teeth and willed her to be still.

He needed her, too. His body had been telling him so in punishing ways for weeks. But not now. Not like this, with her heart heavy and out of her mind with grief, certain she'd lost her brother.

Murphy didn't know what to make of this mental link she shared with her twin. He was far more comfortable dealing with hard, cold facts. The two-day-old information given them that morning claimed Luke Madden was alive. He preferred to put stock in that and not some intuitive notion Letty had come up with that her brother was dead.

Earlier, Murphy had promised her he'd find Luke, and he wasn't giving up until he had the evidence he required. Dead or alive, he was determined to locate Letty's brother.

She continued kissing his neck, her moist lips sliding across his skin in instinctively sensual ways. Murphy closed his eyes and battled down the desire that had begun to throb through his body.

"Letty, please . . . "

"I feel so alone."

"You aren't alone. We don't know Luke's fate. Not yet."

"I know what's happened," she whispered, and sobbed softly. "He's dead. I feel it in my head and in my heart." Her hands roamed his chest, spreading moist kisses down his abdomen. He gripped hold of the blanket, clenching it with both hands as he struggled to resist her.

"You don't know what you're asking." His voice rumbled with the effort it took to reject her. If there was a God in heaven, Murphy sincerely hoped his sacrifice would be richly rewarded. This was far and above the most noble deed he'd ever done.

Only Letty was capable of raising him to this level of do-goodness. He'd known she was trouble the minute he'd met her, but he didn't know she would affect his heart.

Unable to restrain from touching her any longer, he rubbed his hand down the length of her spine, stopping short of her buttocks, savoring the warm, smooth feel of her.

He needed her. His mind and his body had been telling him the same thing from the beginning. But the strength of his desire was more profound than the evidence straining against his fatigues. She was like sunshine in a closed-up room, revealing the dust and neglect. Without warning she'd stormed into his life and with her prim and proper ways exposed him to what he really was. Exposing his heart to what he'd become.

Her gentleness was an absolution to the cruel, often severe world of soldiering. He hadn't understood why Cain wanted Linette in his life. Why he'd given up so much of himself for the chance to marry the widow. It all made an ironic kind of sense now.

Cain needed Linette for the same reasons Murphy needed Letty.

Letty's love helped cancel out the things he'd done, the horrors he'd seen. The cruel hate of man's inhumanity to man. It helped absolve the things he'd been forced to do. What he would do again come morning if necessary.

"Don't you want me?" Letty asked.

"Want you? Honey, you have no idea."

"Then why won't you make love to me?" She snuggled closer to his side, torturing him more than if he were trapped in the hands of a sadist. She was so damned sexy and was too naive to know it. So damned innocent she took his breath away.

"Don't make me say it," she whispered, burying her face in his shoulder.

"Say what?" He was completely perplexed.

"Damn you, Murphy." She slammed her fist against his chest.

"What is it you don't want to tell me?" He flipped her onto her backside and gazed down at her, not understanding. Her eyes, bright with tears, stared up at him with more than a hint of defiance. Her rebellion was short-lived, and she looped her arms around his neck and raised herself enough to kiss him.

He'd taught her well, he realized as her mouth settled over his. Her tongue stroked his, renewing the battle of wills in which he was willingly conquered.

"Letty, say it," he breathed, forcefully breaking off the kiss.

"I love you," she whispered.

His heart went berserk. "Oh, honey." He rolled away from her and onto his back.

"That's exactly why I didn't want to tell you. You don't want my love, don't need it. Having me say it only embarrasses you. I didn't want you to know, didn't want to tell you."

He swore once and hauled her back into his arms, hugging her tight against him. But when they kissed this time, he was the one in control, he was the one directing her mouth to his.

"Oh, Letty," he muttered against her lips. "Don't you know how much I love you?" His tongue met hers, and he pressed her body intimately to his, flattening her breasts against the hard wall of his chest. She felt so damn good. Too good. What strength he possessed to resist her was fast dwindling.

With a reluctance that drained him, he pushed himself away from her. He threaded his fingers through her hair. Just looking into her beautiful eyes made him realize how much he cared. Enough to hold off making love to her because the time wasn't right.

Hers were filled with surprise, with question. "You love me?"

"More than my own life."

"When did you know?"

Leave it to a woman to ask a question like that. "This afternoon."

"With the guerrillas?" she asked.

"Yeah. Probably sooner, but I didn't want to own up to it."

He kissed her then for the sheer pleasure of it. Because denying himself what he wanted most was the purest form of hell he'd ever known.

"You love me." She repeated it with an incredulousness that he found amusing.

"Is that so difficult to believe?"

"Yes. . . . I thought, I assumed you saw me as a damned nuisance."

"I do. But I love you more. When this is over, I want us to marry." He couldn't believe he'd suggested marriage, hadn't known it was coming until the proposal slipped out.

"You want to marry me?" This too came in a manner that suggested she wasn't sure she should believe him.

"I love you so damn much." He kissed her again, greedy for her mouth, showing her in the physical what he felt in his heart. "So much that I'm going to wait until we're married to make love."

"You want to wait?"

"All right, all right, that was a rash statement. We'll wait until we get back to Boothill." He sat up and removed the silver chain from around his neck. "Here, this is your engagement ring." The tiny gold angel made a clanking sound against his dog tags as he slipped it over her head.

Letty fingered it.

"The angel belonged to my grandmother. It's the only thing of hers I own. I've thought of it as my good-luck charm—now it's yours."

"You're giving me your good-luck charm?"

"I'm giving you my heart. You're going to be my wife, Letty."

"What about Deliverance Company?"

"I don't know," he answered. "We'll figure all that out later." He hadn't stopped to consider that she might not want him. When it came to husband material he wasn't much, but he loved her.

"Good idea."

"Can you go to sleep now?" he asked brusquely.

She didn't say anything for a long moment, then nodded. "Can I call you Shaun after we're married?"

He grinned. "I suppose you'll have to. It wouldn't be seemly for a wife to call her husband by his surname."

She nestled into his arms as if they'd spent half a lifetime sleeping together. He'd just started to drift off to sleep, happier than he could remember being at any other point in his life, when Letty spoke again.

"I want children."

"Children," he repeated. That was another aspect of this marriage business that he hadn't stopped to consider. "Can we discuss that later?"

"No. I won't sleep unless I know you want the same things as me."

"Children," he repeated, thinking of his married friends. Both had become fathers and revealed no regrets. "Why not? Before I know it you're going to have me completely domesticated."

"I hope so." He heard the smile in her voice.

Murphy closed his eyes and drifted off to sleep. He kept Letty close to his side all night. She woke him once and whispered something about being thirsty. He found her some water, which she drank greedily, and then they both returned to sleep.

In the morning Murphy knew something was terribly wrong with Letty. Her eyelids fluttered open and she stared up at him sightlessly.

"Letty?" He pressed the back of his hand against her forehead. She was burning up with fever.

He roused Father Alfaro, who contacted a doctor friend of his he could trust. By the time the physician arrived, Letty was delirious. She recognized Murphy but no one else, and she clung to him.

"What's wrong with her?" he demanded when the doctor had completed his examination.

"I don't know, but it doesn't look good. Her fever is very high. I have seen such a fever and rash one time."

"Yes?"

He didn't respond right away. "We must get her to a hospital."

A hospital. The man was asking for the moon.

The doctor's eyes were grave. "Otherwise she will not live more than two days."

35

"*Marcie, did you order* the Apple-Smith perm?"

Marcie stopped counting the money in the till to think. The beauty supplier had stopped in earlier that afternoon, and she'd ordered an extensive list of items. "I can't remember."

"I specifically asked for the Apple-Smith perm, don't you remember? You know Gladys Williams insists on it, with her thin hair." Samantha sounded justifiably upset.

Marcie vented a deep sigh. "I'm sorry, I can't recall what I asked Vickie to send us. I'll give her a jingle in the morning and check to be sure I ordered the perm."

"I've got to take care of my LOLs."

"I know." Samantha was a whiz with the little old ladies, and a large section of her clientele consisted of the over seventy crowd.

Her friend hesitated. "You sure you're all right, Marcie? You've been in never-never land all day. What's bugging you?"

"I'm fine." She managed to scrounge up a smile.

"It isn't just today, either. You've been preoccupied for days now."

Marcie set aside the stack of one-dollar bills. She'd tried counting them three times and each time had come up with a different number. "I have, haven't I?"

"Are you sure this isn't something you want to talk about?" Samantha set aside her purse and leaned against the glass counter, crossing her arms. "I got the time. It used to be that we'd talk for hours on end, remember?"

That was true enough, but those had been during Marcie's bar-hopping days. The two had often gone out together after work and then traded war stories in the morning. But times had changed. Marcie had abandoned that lifestyle, and Samantha was a single mother with a kid to support.

"Clifford proposed," Marcie confessed.

"Clifford! All I can say is that it's about time. I was ready to hog-tie that man and ask him when he was going to pop the question."

Marcie laughed, but it was forced.

"Gee, honey, aren't you happy?"

"Sure," Marcie said, and meant it. She was ecstatic. She'd waited the better part of her life for a man to ask her to be his wife. This was a dream come true.

"Oh." The happiness drained from Samantha's face. "You're in love with Johnny, though, aren't you?"

"Yes . . . no. Oh, Sam, I don't know anymore."

"Have the two of you been . . . you know?" Her voice lifted slightly with insinuation.

"You want to know if I'm sleeping with him, right?"

"Listen, honey, if you don't want to say, that's fine, because it isn't any of my business."

Marcie stuck the money back inside the till and slammed the drawer shut. "No, not that I haven't been tempted. Johnny always did have a way about him that made my knees go weak."

"You mean to say you *haven't* slept with him lately?" Samantha sounded incredulous.

"How could I, and look Clifford in the eye?"

"I suppose you're right." Samantha plunked herself down on one of the padded chairs by the washbowl and crossed her long, slender legs. "Johnny's the one you're crazy about, but it's Clifford who proposed."

"Actually, Johnny mentioned something about the two of us setting up housekeeping."

Samantha's head snapped up, her eyes wide. "He did?"

Marcie was sorry she'd told her friend this part because she knew exactly what Samantha would say, and she was right.

"Then what's the problem? There's no contest, is there? I mean, Clifford's sweet and everything, but, honey, Johnny's the kind of man who'll make your blood run hot just looking at him."

"I know, but . . ." Marcie let the rest fade. Clifford was the Rock of Gibraltar, while Jack Keller was like shifting sands. Intellectually she knew this, but emotionally she struggled. She panted after Jack, but she cared about Clifford.

"Uh-oh," Samantha whispered. "Speaking of the devil. Look who just pulled up."

Marcie didn't want to look. It could only be Jack, and she didn't want to see him. When she was with him she couldn't think clearly, couldn't trust herself to do what she knew was right. He knew that too and used it against her. Little by little, bit by bit, he was chipping away at her defenses.

She'd told him she needed to think about moving in with him, the same way she'd told Clifford she needed time to consider his marriage proposal. It'd been several days now, and Jack had obviously grown impatient.

"I'm out of here," Samantha whispered, winked at Marcie, grabbed her purse, and was out the door.

"Howdy, Sam," Marcie heard Jack greet her friend, his voice husky and deep.

Marcie didn't turn around. She closed her eyes and summoned her defenses.

Jack stood behind her. She could feel his presence as keenly as if he were touching her.

"Marcie."

"Hello, Jack." Her fingers dug into the glass counter.

"How's my girl?" he asked next, and cupped her shoulders. His hot breath warmed her as he bent forward and kissed the side of her neck. He sucked gently and ran his tongue brazenly over her smooth skin.

Marcie curled her toes at the fiery sensation that shot through her.

"I've been thinking about you day and night," Jack confessed, "wondering if I was going to ever hear from you again."

"I . . . I said I'd call."

His lips continued to nibble away at her. "I couldn't wait any longer. I had to know."

Marcie's eyes drifted shut, and she drooped her head to one side, exposing her neck to him. The desire to turn around and bury herself in his arms made her weak when she desperately needed to be strong.

"I haven't come to a decision yet," she told him, struggling to keep her voice even. "I have to think of every aspect. This is important, very important."

"It's what I told you, isn't it?"

"No," she denied, and the breathless quality was back in her voice. "It's everything."

"Let me help you make up your mind," he whispered.

"That's not a good idea." Although her lips said one thing, her body said another. Her head was lolling back, and she rocked it gently from side to side to give him greater access to her skin.

"Baby, I'm going crazy wanting you." He slipped his arm around her waist and fitted her backside to his hard, masculine front.

"Jack—"

"I know I shouldn't be here." His hands were busy with the front of her uniform. Before she could find the strength to stop him, he'd unfastened her blouse and eased his hand inside, cupping her breast. Her nipples turned traitor and beaded instantly. She couldn't keep herself from trembling and rotating her buttocks against his throbbing erection.

"Easy now, baby, easy." A wealth of satisfaction

echoed in his dark whisper. His free hand cupped her crotch, rubbing the junction between her legs.

Marcie couldn't believe she had allowed him to do this to her. She'd lowered the venetian blinds at closing time, but the slats remained open. Anyone passing on the sidewalk could look in and see what they were doing.

It was hard to believe that any man was capable of reducing her to this level, and she sobbed softly, willing herself to find the strength to resist him.

Jack misunderstood her cry of distress as one of need. "The couch is still in the back room?" he asked urgently. His hot breath branded her ear.

"Yes, but I don't think—"

"That's been our problem," he countered huskily, "we both been thinking too damn much. It's time to recapture the fire we once shared."

"Oh God."

Marcie never intended for them to end up on the couch in her back room. She wasn't entirely sure how he got her there. One moment she was in front of her shop, battling back her own treacherous body. The next thing she knew, she was in her back room, lying across the sofa. Within seconds Jack had her blouse peeled open and her breasts exposed. He knelt on the floor and buried his face in her bounty, cupping her fullness in his palms. His mouth locked on to a nipple and he sucked greedily.

The instant his mouth closed over her nipple, the pulse throbbing between her legs intensified and she lifted her hips from the sofa.

"That's good, baby, real good. Let me see how ready you are." His voice was hoarse with need.

No sooner had the words parted his lips than he stuck his hand up her skirt and swept aside the crotch of her panties.

Marcie stiffened in his arms. It'd been so long since she'd made love, so long since a man had touched her this intimately. Her body reacted and she gave a strained cry at the unexpected burst of pleasure. She was stunned, dizzy, almost delirious as he began to work his fingers inside her, stretching her, readying her for him.

"No—"

He cut off her cry of protest by kissing her. His tongue echoed the stroking movements of his fingers, the rhythm fast and hard.

The sensation he created was like fire, spiraling into a tighter and tighter coil. It threatened to break through and take control any moment.

Marcie knew what he was doing, what he'd intended from the first. He was using her body against her, bringing her to climax, pleasuring her first. She also knew that afterward he would expect the same relief. This was more than heavy petting, it was an unspoken agreement to have sex with him.

"Jack, no." Her voice was a weak wail of anguish as she broke off the kiss and struggled to a semisitting position. Breathing heavily, she leaned on one elbow.

Jack's breathing was equally ragged. His head drooped forward as if her words hadn't fully broken through the fog of his desire.

"You don't mean it. Tell me you don't mean it?" he pleaded.

It took her several moments to compose herself to where she could look him in the eye again, let alone speak. "I'm sorry, truly I am. I never intended for matters to progress to that point."

Jack leveled himself off the floor and sat at the end of the couch, his elbows on his knees. He glanced at her and exhaled sharply. "I'm the one who needs a cigarette this time. You got one?"

She shook her head. "Not with me."

He rubbed his face.

"How about a shower?"

She wasn't much help with that, either. "I could stick your head in the washbasin."

He chuckled. "I'll pass."

She sat up and took a couple of minutes to catch her breath. Her fingers refused to cooperate as she fastened the small white buttons in the front of her blouse. "I can't think straight when you touch me."

Jack laughed. "I disagree. You seem to find a means to thwart me without much of a problem. Don't misunderstand me, I'm frustrated as hell, but at the same time I'm a little in awe of this newfound control of yours. You've changed, Marcie."

He couldn't have paid her a better compliment. "I'm not the same Marcie anymore. I haven't been in quite some time."

"Live with me, Marcie," he said, reaching for her hands. "Baby, we're good together."

"In bed, you mean."

"Within six months we'll know each other like only married people do," he countered.

"But we might not even like each other."

He captured her face between his hands. "I've always liked you. You're sweet and gentle and good."

Marcie bit into her lower lip.

"What is it?" he asked gently. "Tell me and I'll do anything within my power to fix it."

"I want children, a home, a family." Her eyes held his. "I want a husband."

"You're looking for me to marry you, aren't you?"

"Yes," she whispered, unwilling to take second best. She didn't tell him Clifford had proposed. This was not a contest to see which one could buy her the biggest diamond.

"Marriage," he repeated as if it were a dirty word.

The bell above the door chimed, and Jack looked to her. The CLOSED sign was in the window, but she hadn't locked the door.

"Marcie?"

Clifford. She bolted off the couch so fast, she nearly tripped over her own two feet.

"Clifford, hello." Her cheerful greeting sounded false even to her own ears. She was sure her cheeks were flame red and that he must know she had another man in her back room.

"I hope you don't mind my stopping in unexpectedly like this." He removed his baseball cap and held it in both hands. His gaze drifted toward the back room.

"No, of course not." She leaned against the glass counter and avoided looking him in the eye.

"I realize I haven't given you much time . . . "

"You want to know if I've reached a decision yet?"

"Yeah." Again he looked past her toward the back of the shop and the drapes that separated the two main parts of the business. "I don't mean to pressure you," he added.

"I know that."

His gaze focused on the front of her uniform, and he edged his way backward toward the front door. "I can see that I've come at a bad time. . . ."

"I'll call you," she promised, "okay?"

"Sure." His eyes filled with an incredible sadness. "Sure," he repeated. "Whatever you say." Having said that, he turned hurriedly and walked out the door.

Marcie had the incredible urge to cry. She'd seen the look in Clifford's eyes and recognized it all too well. It was the same look of disappointment and hurt she'd felt a number of times in her dating career. It generally came when she learned the man she'd been seeing for three months was married. Or how she felt when a guy asked her for a small loan for his ailing mother and she knew damn well it was for booze.

She returned to the back room and slumped onto the couch.

Jack stood above her. "All right," he said impatiently. "Let's get married."

36

Letty was only vaguely aware of what was happening to her. She felt herself walking down a long narrow corridor. Doors opened from each side of the hallway, and each one seemed to beckon to her.

She stopped and read the nameplate and was tempted at each door to enter, would have if not for Murphy, who stood at the end of the hallway, calling to her. He sounded angry and desperate. When she hesitated, he commanded her attention. He refused to allow her to rest or to stop. His demands on her became relentless.

Once she reached him, he didn't seem satisfied. He wanted something from her, but she couldn't figure out what it was. Because she loved him, she tried to give him whatever he asked, but he made no sense to her befuddled mind. He seemed to think it was terribly important for her to drink something bitter tasting.

Later his voice became gentle as he spoke to her. His hands cooled her face and washed her face and neck. She couldn't remember being so dirty. With everyone else he sounded urgent and impatient, but with her he was uncharacteristically tender.

She slept and had trouble waking. A discordant noise interrupted her rest. It sounded like the roar of an engine. Like that of an aircraft. She felt the sun on her face and the force of the wind. It felt cool when she was so terribly, uncomfortably hot.

Then he held her against him and told her again how much he loved her. He promised to find Luke for her.

Luke. A sob obstructed her throat at the mention of her brother. He was forever gone to her. Forever lost. She'd found him too late. The intense grief was mingled with the memory of an unexpected gift. Murphy's love. Her hand closed over the tiny gold angel.

"Remember, I love you," Murphy whispered.

Letty wouldn't soon forget.

She was wrenched out of his arms and set inside a seat. But this wasn't like any car she'd ever known. She realized as she gazed at a row of panels that she was inside a plane and Father Alfaro was with her.

The sound of guns and angry shouts interrupted their farewells. Murphy reacted immediately, leaped back, and slammed the door closed.

"Go, go, go!" he cried, but he wasn't speaking to her. "Get the hell out of here!"

Letty's head lolled to one side, and she saw Murphy racing across a grass field. She gasped with alarm when she saw a band of guerrillas surround him. Her gasp became a cry of frustration and anguish as red tips of fire exploded from the end of a machine gun and she watched, helpless, as Murphy fell.

"No . . . no, not Murphy . . . must go back."

"We can't," Father Alfaro said, his words marked with sadness.

"He didn't have a chance," the pilot said in a strong American accent. Letty tried to focus, tried to think clearly, but everything was cloudy, obscured from her as if she were trapped inside a deep fog.

"Why didn't he come with us?" So little of this made sense to her.

"He made himself the target instead. He saved our lives," Father Alfaro told her, gripping her hand. "No greater love has a man than he who lays down his life for his friends."

Soft sounds drifted toward Letty. The distinct click of a clock, counting off the seconds. The padded footsteps against a tile floor, the scrape of metal rings against a rail. The scent was that of disinfectant and something else she couldn't name.

It cost her a surprising amount of energy to lift her eyelids and look around. The first thing she saw was a round clock on the wall, then a television mounted in the corner. A railing, like that for a shower, looped around her bed.

If she didn't know better, she would think she was in a hospital. The view outside her window looked decidedly like that of Texas. But that didn't seem possible.

The last thing she remembered was being in

Zarcero and of Murphy holding her. She remembered something else. A small, worrisome fear niggled at her conscious. A plane and gunshots and Murphy putting his own life on the line for her.

Murphy. She smiled, closed her eyes, and reached for the chain around her neck.

It was missing.

Frantic now, she forced herself to sit up. Stretching awkwardly, she reached for the button that rang for the nurse. A disembodied voice responded.

"Miss Madden, you're awake. That's wonderful. I'll be right in. You've got an anxious gentleman here, waiting to see you."

Murphy. It had all been so confusing. Murphy wouldn't abandon her. Not after giving her an engagement necklace. The whole episode with the airplane had been part of some terrible nightmare. She closed her eyes and whispered a prayer of thanksgiving.

The nurse arrived moments later. Her wide, friendly smile put Letty at ease. Then, when she least expected it, she thrust a thermometer in Letty's mouth and took her blood pressure.

"You said my friend . . . ," she asked the minute the temperature gauge was out of her mouth.

"In a minute, dear." The nurse smiled graciously and reached for Letty's wrist to check her pulse. It was all Letty could do not to mention that her heart was in fine working order. She wanted her necklace and to see Murphy, in that order.

The friendly nurse retrieved the dog tags and seemed surprised when Letty kissed the angel and placed the set over her head. It wasn't much of an engagement ring to anyone else, but it was worth more than any diamond to her because it had come from his heart.

"Would you like me to send in your friend now?"

She nodded enthusiastically, then changed her mind. "No, wait. I must look a sight."

"You look a thousand times better than when they brought you in, dear. For two days we didn't know if you were going to live or die. You've been very ill."

The kindly nurse ran a brush through Letty's hair. "Are you ready for your friend now?"

"Please." Letty was so eager to talk to Murphy. So eager to learn what he'd discovered about Luke in Zarcero. Eager to show him how much she loved him.

She heard the heavy footsteps before he entered her room and closed her eyes briefly in anticipation of seeing him again.

But it wasn't Murphy who entered her hospital room, grinning from ear to ear. It was Slim.

"Welcome home, Letty," he greeted her, his ever-present Stetson in his hand. "My, but you're a sight for sore eyes. I can't tell you how glad I am to see you."

"Slim," she murmured, unable to disguise her disappointment.

"From what I understand, we're lucky to have you."

"Hello." Hiding the devastating disappointment was more than she could manage. "Do you know anything about Murphy?"

"He didn't come back with you?"

"No. I don't know." She lay back against the pillow, overwhelmingly tired and broken and alone. Slim was her friend, but Murphy was her heart. Her very reason for being alive.

Jack loved her. He hadn't realized his feelings for Marcie until after he'd proposed. Then he wondered why it had taken him so long to recognize the truth. Contacting her after a nine-month silence had been a fluke. But once he saw her again, he'd been completely taken by the changes he'd seen in her. Their intermittent love fests were based on something more than sexual satisfaction. True, it had taken her refusal to bed him again for him to see the light. In the weeks since, he'd enjoyed spending time with her. He found Marcie to be intelligent, well read, and well versed in political affairs. Not only did she have a decent head on her shoulders, but she was warm, witty, and fun.

What Marcie did for him sexually was something else. If ever there was a woman who equaled him sexually, it was Marcie Alexander. Now she was about to become his wife.

He resisted the urge to phone Cain and let his friend know he would soon join the ranks of the married himself. He might even ask for a little maritial advice from his former boss—although the way he felt right then, he didn't need anyone or anything but Marcie.

She'd let it be known she wanted kids. He hadn't actually given any thought to the matter of a family. There was no reason he should. But now that the subject had been introduced, he was excited at the prospect of becoming a daddy.

Jack had visited Cain not long ago and been amazed at how well his friend had adjusted to fatherhood. Fact was, Jack had never seen more startling changes in anyone.

Cain fussing with dirty diapers was as much of a shock as Cain herding cattle. Now *that* was a sight to behold.

Apparently Mallory was into this baby thing in a big way. The last Jack heard, Mallory and his wife, Francine, were already planning a second addition to their family.

Now he was next. Damn, but it felt right. In retrospect he didn't know why he'd taken so long to take the plunge. He guessed he'd been waiting for the right woman. Well, he'd found her in Marcie.

He walked into the kitchen, opened the refrigerator, and popped a green olive in his mouth. She was due to stop off at the apartment at any time.

Earlier that afternoon he'd picked out a diamond that had set him back ten thousand. Jack never thought he'd spend that much money on a wedding band, but he wanted Marcie to know he loved her. He was proud of her, of the person she'd become in the last several months. Proud that she hadn't fallen into bed with him the minute he'd showed up at her beauty shop.

If she insisted, he'd wait until after the wedding ceremony, he was that crazy about her. He sincerely hoped she wasn't going to put him off again, but he'd cross that bridge when the time came.

The doorbell chimed, and he did a quick visual on the apartment. Marcie was early, but that was a good sign. Very good. She was eager to see him, too.

To his surprise, it wasn't Marcie standing on the other side of the door, but another woman. She wasn't bad looking, either. A little on the thin side and pale, as if she'd recently recovered from a bad case of the flu.

"Are you Jack Keller?"

He leaned against the doorjamb. "Depends on who's asking."

"Letty Madden."

Madden. Madden. The name rang a bell, only he couldn't remember from where.

"Do you have a minute to talk?" she asked. From the look in her eyes she wasn't going to be easily turned away.

He hesitated. It wouldn't do well to have Marcie arrive and find him with another woman. Well, she needn't worry; she was the only woman for him, and he'd take a great deal of pleasure in proving that to her.

"I've come a very long way to find you, Mr. Keller," Letty Madden announced primly. "It has to do with Murphy."

That was where he'd heard the name. Letty Madden was the name of the irritating postmistress who'd hired Murphy to find her brother in some hellhole Central American country.

"Come on in," he said, gesturing toward the living room.

She hadn't gone more than a couple of steps when she faltered. Jack feared she would have collapsed right then and there if he hadn't caught her. He gripped hold of her elbow and then slipped an arm around her waist.

"Easy now," he said gently, and guided her to a chair.

"Sorry. I was released from the hospital yesterday. They didn't advise me to travel, but I had to talk to you."

"You know about me?"

"Murphy mentioned you frequently."

This was interesting, since he'd always known his friend to be closemouthed.

"Have you heard from him lately?" she asked eagerly.

"Not in some time."

It was pathetic to see the light fade from her eyes. "I thought, I'd hoped he'd be in contact with you."

"He mentioned you as well," Jack announced. "You're the one who wanted to hire him to take you to Zarcero. Right?"

She nodded, and a hint of a smile touched her mouth. "I don't suspect he mentioned me with any real affection."

Jack didn't answer right away. Murphy had considered the woman to be a thorn in his side. "Did you find your brother?"

She swallowed tightly and looked away. "We were too late, he'd been killed."

"I'm sorry."

"So am I. Luke was a decent, God fearing man." Her hand went to her neck and she fingered what looked to be dogtags and a small gold angel. Jack had seen only one such angel in his life. It had belonged to Murphy. His friend had called it his good-luck charm.

"Where'd you get that?" he demanded.

Her eyes widened, as though she weren't sure what he meant. It seemed to take her a moment to realize he was referring to the necklace.

"Murphy gave it to me." Her eyes held his. "I haven't heard from him. Not a word. Nor will anyone tell me what's happened to him. I've lost my brother, I can't bear to lose Murphy, too."

Jack frowned. These were the words of a woman in love. Her hand closed around the dogtags as though she were clutching a lifeline, the only thing that kept her from losing control of her emotions.

"I'm afraid he's dead," she whispered, and her voice cracked.

"Murphy dead?"

"I didn't know where else to turn."

"Tell me what happened." He sat across from her and listened as she related the details of their adventure in Zarcero, pausing only when he asked questions. She stopped at an incredible point, explaining that she'd been half crazed with fever and Murphy had gotten her and a priest friend to an airstrip, then held off rebel troops himself while they'd escaped to safety.

"The priest?"

"I never saw him again," she murmured sadly.

"He was in the plane with you?"

"Yes, I think so. I don't remember anything after that. The next thing I knew, I woke up in a Texas hospital. A family friend had been notified and was waiting to speak to me. As soon as I was released from the hospital, I came to find you."

"You haven't a clue where the plane landed?"

"None. I'm sorry. I was too sick. Apparently I'd been bitten by a particularly dangerous spider, but I'm fine now." She brushed the hair away from her face, a gesture of nervous anticipation. "Will you locate Murphy for me?"

Jack didn't need to weigh the decision. There'd been a time a couple of years back when he'd been captured and tortured. It'd been Murphy who'd led the team of men who broke him out of prison. He wouldn't hesitate to repay the favor now.

"I'll be on a plane as soon as it can be arranged." He'd need to talk to Marcie first, explain everything. But she was sure to understand.

Letty's eyes drifted closed with supreme gratitude. "Thank you," she whispered.

"Hey, I owe Murphy big time."

"So do I." But she didn't elaborate.

Jack couldn't help wondering exactly what had happened between those two in that jungle.

Letty left, and not five minutes passed before Marcie arrived.

"Hello, Jack," she said softly.

He looped his arms about her waist and dragged her inside the apartment, ready to kiss her good and proper, show her how crazy he was about her. He would have, too, if she hadn't turned her head aside at the last minute.

"Baby?"

Not until then did he notice that her eyes were bright with tears. "Marcie, what is it?"

"I'm so sorry," she whispered.

"Sorry?"

She clenched her hands together and lowered her head. "I can't marry you, Jack."

He almost laughed. The woman had to be joking. Marriage was what she'd said she'd wanted. He'd gone out and purchased a diamond. Something was very wrong with this picture, and he had yet to figure out what it was.

"Not going to marry me?"

"I decided," she said, her voice low and breathy, "to accept Clifford's proposal, if he'll have me."

37

Marcie closed her eyes briefly in an effort to calm herself before she rang Clifford's doorbell. She'd been to his house only one other time, and that had been for a short visit.

He lived in a two-story house close to Olathe, a suburb of Kansas City, in a house that had once belonged to his parents. He'd moved in after he'd been forced to put his father into a nursing home. It was a solid old house with flower beds out front and space for a small garden in the back.

No one answered, and Marcie had begun to fear she'd made the trip for nothing when the door abruptly opened.

To say that Clifford was surprised to see her would be an understatement. He stared at her as if seeing a ghost.

"Marcie, what are you doing here?"

Good question. "I thought we should talk."

He held open the screen door for her. "Sure."

The house was dark and cool on the inside. The furniture was large and bulky, sturdy, like the man himself. An old upright piano that probably hadn't been played in years stood against one wall. Framed photographs were arranged across the top.

It caught Marcie's attention because she'd always wanted to learn how to play the piano as a girl. There'd never been money for that sort of thing. Her father tended to drink up more than he contributed to the family's income. By the time she was thirteen her parents had divorced and she'd seen her father only intermittently since.

"You want something to drink? I got a pot of coffee on, if you're interested."

She was nervous enough as it was without having to hold on to a coffee cup. "No thanks."

Clifford gestured toward the overstuffed sofa. He was still in his work clothes but had removed his boots. His white socks were a stark contrast with his black short-sleeved shirt and jeans.

Marcie figured he must have come home, started reading the newspaper, and fallen asleep on his chair. That was what probably had taken him so long to answer the door.

"I figure I know why you're here," he said, sitting across from her. He sat close to the edge of the chair and leaned forward. Something on his hands demanded his attention because he couldn't seem to make himself look at her.

Clifford knew? Marcie sincerely doubted that.

"I apologize about the other day. I should never have dropped by the shop, but I was anxious for your answer," he murmured sadly.

Marcie almost smiled. "Is it the ring that's bothering you or the marriage proposal?"

"Both, I suspect. In retrospect, I imagine that little diamond isn't much of an incentive for you to marry a guy like me. Forgive me, Marcie, I gave it to you for all the wrong reasons."

"I hope that's not true. I came here to tell you something," she said, hurrying her words in an effort to say what she must.

"I know you were with that other guy, if that's what's worrying you."

Marcie shifted uncomfortably. "You're right, I was." She couldn't lie. Not to Clifford, who'd only been kind and honest with her.

"I could see when I came that I'd arrived at an inconvenient moment." His voice was heavy with sarcasm.

Marcie inhaled deeply, regret tightening her voice. She clenched her hands nervously. Having him find her with Jack made everything she had to say so much more difficult. "We didn't make love. I swear to you, Clifford, we didn't."

"But you were tempted."

"Yes." Her voice was small and wobbly.

Clifford leaped off the sofa with a dexterity that surprised her. He walked over to the window and rammed five fingers through his hair. "That seems to be answer enough for me. You can keep the diamond, Marcie. I bought it for you. I don't know how this other guy will feel about you keeping it, but I hope you will."

"He won't like it."

Clifford's shoulders tensed. "No, I don't suspect he will. I sure as hell wouldn't want my wife wearing a ring another man gave her."

"Don't misunderstand me, I fully intend to wear that diamond ring."

One shoulder lifted in a jerky laugh. "You always were a stubborn woman." He turned to face her, and his eyes held hers for a long moment, as though he intended to memorize her features. "I love you, Marcie. I knew from the first that I was probably going to lose you. You're too good for me. You loving this other guy doesn't come as any shock."

"It doesn't come as any great shock?" she repeated softly. Marcie hadn't expected to cry. When the tears clustered in her eyes and dribbled onto her cheeks, she was taken by complete surprise.

"Marcie?"

"You're an idiot, Clifford Cramden," she shouted, "an idiot. Don't you know the kind of woman I am? Men don't give women like me diamond rings."

He looked like a man in shock.

She was on her feet and not sure why. She didn't want to leave, so she started pacing in front of the old upright piano. "Don't you dare tell me you're not good enough for me. It's the other way around." Her arms cradled her middle. "There've been more men in my life than I can count. I made love with so many men that eventually I stopped loving myself."

Wordlessly, Clifford continued to stare at her.

"For years I was convinced that all men really

needed to change was the love of a good woman. Only I wasn't smart enough to realize that when I dove into the ocean to save a drowning man, I risked going down with him." She sniffled and angled her head toward the ceiling. She rubbed the moisture from her cheeks and sat on the piano bench, curving her hands over the smooth polished-wood edge.

"It took me a long time to realize that when a man slapped me around, then claimed he didn't know why I put up with him, that he knew what he was talking about."

"A man beat you?"

"Men, sweetie, more than one. I'm a slow learner."

"This guy you were with tonight? Has he ever laid a hand on you?" he demanded, his fists clenched.

"Jack? No, never."

Clifford relaxed. "Good."

"Don't you see, Clifford?" she cried, having trouble keeping her emotions in check.

"See what? What type of person you are? I saw that right off, Marcie."

She stared at him, uncertain she understood what he was saying.

"You're a warm, generous, loving woman."

She sniffled. "Didn't you hear a word I said? I have a history with men, Clifford. An endless, boring history with a number of users."

"Yeah, well, we all have a history, don't we? I knew about yours a long time ago."

"You did?"

He glanced away from her and lifted his shoulders in a half shrug. "There were any number of so-called friends who felt it was their duty to let me know you had something of a reputation."

Marcie closed her eyes at the sick feeling that attacked the pit of her stomach. "Other than that one time, you never once tried to get me to bed."

"Do you know why, Marcie? Because with me you were always a lady. You never gave me reason to suspect anything else. I was proud to be with you. You're warm and funny, and you made me laugh. Some of the best times of my life are the ones I've shared with you."

"You're an idiot."

"For loving you? Hardly. It means a great deal that you'd come here to personally tell me you were going with this other guy. I don't blame you. He can give you a hell of a lot more than I ever could."

She couldn't believe what he was saying.

"You see, loving you means that I want whatever you do."

"Clifford Cramden, I love you. It's you I want to marry, not Jack Keller. You."

"Me?" He narrowed his gaze, as if he weren't sure he should believe her. "You came here because you want to tell me you're marrying me?"

She walked over and stood directly in front of him and leveled a threatening look directly at him. "Don't even think about changing your mind."

"Changing my mind. I . . . you're sure?"

"I'm more positive about this than I've been about anything else in my life."

"But—"

"Don't be making up excuses to talk yourself out of it, either. Understand?"

"Yes, but—" His eyes lit up like lampposts.

"I've been waiting all my life for a man as good as you."

With an infectious grin on his lips, he pulled her down and into his lap. "I'm crazy about you, Marcie. You don't have a clue how damned difficult it's been not to make love to you."

"We've got plenty of time for that," she said, slipping her arms around his neck.

"A lifetime," he said, kissing her with a hunger that left her breathless and clinging.

She smiled up at him and knew they were both going to be very, very happy.

38

The week that passed was the longest one of Letty's life. She sat by the phone, leaped on it the minute it rang, waited breathless for word about Murphy. She didn't care who delivered it. Jack Keller. Father Alfaro. Even Captain Norte himself.

Not knowing was driving her mad. She didn't sleep, and she had absolutely no appetite. No news wasn't good news; it was no news—and she was desperate to learn Murphy's fate.

When she couldn't bear the silence any longer, she took matters into her own hands. This time she went directly to where she was sure to get information: the Central Intelligence Agency in Washington, D.C.

It took her the better part of two days to work her way through the bureaucracy. She had to shout before anyone heard her; now she suspected they would tell her everything just to get her off their backs. On the third morning she was ushered into the office of Agent Ken Kemper.

"Ms. Madden." He escorted her into his office, moved behind his desk, and gestured for her to take a seat.

Sitting down himself, he reached for a file. "You're inquiring about Reverend Luke Madden and a mercenary by the name of Shaun Murphy."

"That's correct." She clasped her hands together and waited. Early on, she'd learned that the less information she volunteered, the better.

"Reverend Madden is your brother?"

"Yes."

"A missionary in Zarcero?"

"That's correct."

"What is the basis of your interest in Mr. Murphy?"

"He's the man I hired to find my brother," she stated matter-of-factly.

"I see."

His mouth thinned with evident disapproval. Letty said nothing. She made no excuses for hiring Murphy. The federal government had given her no choice. She'd done everything within her power to get some kind of government intervention. Her pleas had been ignored, so she'd had to take matters into her own hands.

"Was hiring Mr. Murphy wise?"

"What else was I to do?" she cried, losing her patience. "I begged and screamed for our government to help me find Luke."

"Surely you understand that would have been impossible."

"So I was repeatedly told. That's the reason I hired Mr. Murphy." She angled her chin proudly, refusing to give one inch.

"Then you located your brother?"

Letty's throat was in danger of closing up on her. "I'm fairly confident he was killed." Just saying the words was difficult. "I don't have any solid proof of that, but nevertheless I'm afraid there's no hope for Luke."

The agent lowered his gaze. "It's our understanding as well that your brother was murdered."

She didn't speak until the emotion dissolved in her throat. "Since you have information regarding my brother's fate, then you must also know what's happened to Mr. Murphy. You people have ways of learning the truth, of finding out what you want to know." She tightened her jaw. "You have my word that if you don't tell me, I'll make the biggest pest of myself you've ever seen."

"Bigger than you have already this week?"

"Yes," she returned furiously. "I don't know if you're aware that I'm a federal postal employee."

"I believe that was in the letter you wrote."

Letty, who rarely raised her voice, did so now in frustration and anger. "Don't you know it's a dangerous thing to irritate a disgruntled postal employee?"

"Ah . . ."

"Tell me what you know about Murphy!" she shouted.

A stark silence fell between them. "If you'll excuse me a moment . . ."

"No. Tell me."

He hesitated, then pushed a button on his intercom. "Send in Agent Moser."

Within five minutes a second agent arrived. He walked into the room, shook hands with Letty, and sat on the chair next to hers.

"What we're about to tell you can never leave this room," Agent Kemper said in warning.

"It would put innocent people's lives in danger," Agent Moser added. "Is that understood?"

Letty nodded.

The two men exchanged looks, as if they were deciding which one would deliver the information.

"We had word about your mercenary friend."

"Yes," she whispered. Her throat went dry with anticipation.

"I'm afraid it isn't good." The second man pushed up the glasses that had scooted down the bridge of his nose.

She hadn't expected it would be. She would have heard from him otherwise. "Is he dead?" she asked starkly. "That's all I want to know."

"I'm afraid so."

Letty closed her eyes, and it felt as though her heart had stopped completely.

"We're very sorry, Ms. Madden," Kemper said gently.

"Apparently he was captured on an airfield?" Agent Moser made the statement a question.

She nodded. So that part had been real and not some fever-induced dream.

"He was taken prisoner and executed the following day. I believe he was hanged."

39

Letty sat in the cool evening shade on her porch and shelled peas, watching thick clouds drift effortlessly across the deep blue Texas sky. It had been a month since she'd returned from Washington, D.C. Longer since she'd contacted Jack Keller. She hadn't heard from him, but she had the answer now. There was no reason to hope. Her brother was gone. And she'd lost Murphy as well.

In time she'd be able to look at a sunset and not feel crippling emotional pain. In time she'd rebound. Time was the great healer, the great comforter.

Because he was worried about her, and because in his own way he loved her, Slim had stopped off to visit every night for two weeks. Although she appreciated his concern and friendship, she'd finally, gently, asked him to stay away.

She hadn't returned to the post office yet. Hadn't

decided if she'd ever go back. She'd found a certain solace puttering around her garden, living from one day to the next without demands, without a schedule. This leave of absence from responsibility would aid the healing process, Letty decided. She needed it.

Evenings were her favorite time, when she sat here and soaked in the beauty of the sunset and relived memories of the days spent with Murphy, traipsing through a Central American jungle. In years to come she fully expected to experience the joy of having loved him instead of the maiming sorrow of his death.

A fragile peace had come regarding the loss of her brother. The pain cut deep, deeper than any grief she had yet to experience. She'd lost so many loved ones. For all intents and purposes, her mother had been out of her life when she was five; her grandmother had died when Letty was eleven; and her father's death had come when she was a young adult. But her brother, her twin . . . that was by far the greatest loss.

She accepted Luke's passing. She'd done everything humanly possible to help him, to reach him in time. Even before she'd gone in search of Luke, she'd been warned to prepare herself for the worst. But she'd refused to give up hope.

What others didn't seem to realize was that no amount of mental preparedness would have equipped her to deal with the death of her twin.

She believed Luke had asked God to take him for some greater purpose. His death, like so much of his life, had been a direct answer to prayer. Try as she might, she couldn't begrudge her brother that.

It was for Murphy she grieved. Murphy she would

miss. Loving him had brought her such unexpected joy. It had been the surprise of her life.

Falling in love had caught them both unaware. At first she'd found him vulgar and offensive. He'd gone out of his way to shock and incense her, but it had all been an act. Inside he was one of the most compassionate and thoughtful men she was ever likely to meet.

She treasured the memories of him playing with the children in Questo. Her only regret was that he'd never have the opportunity to tease and laugh with their children.

His gentle side had revealed itself when he'd held and comforted her after her near rape in Siguierres. Those moments in his arms were ones she'd hold in her heart through the years. She'd been so foolish and idiotic to have fired him after seeing him with the woman in the cantina. She recognized now that the real reason was that she'd been jealous. Her heart must have known even then.

A smile played over her lips. Murphy had taught her so much about herself, lessons she wouldn't soon forget.

In the distance she saw an approaching plume of dust, and she sighed. Slim again, she suspected. Keeping a vigil over her wouldn't help the way she felt about him, but the rancher hadn't seemed to realize that.

But it wasn't Slim's pickup that made its way down the long dirt driveway that stretched between her house and the road.

Setting the bowl of peas aside, Letty stood and looped her arm around the porch column. She blinked, and her heart quickened as the silhouette of a man became visible. Soon the man, one lovingly familiar, became recognizable. A man she loved more than her own life.

Murphy.

Her heart refused to stop banging against her ribs, like sticks against a tin drum. He remained in her thoughts so much of the time, it was understandable for her mind to conjure him up. Perhaps she was hallucinating.

The pickup pulled to a stop, and the dream continued. The driver's door opened, and he climbed out of the cab.

Letty's arm around the post served as a desperately needed anchor.

She didn't know if she dared believe what her eyes were telling her. Greedy for the sight of him, her gaze roved from his dark, thick, military-style cut hair to his cowboy-booted feet.

He stood at the bottom of the steps, and a slow, lazy smile eased up the edges of his mouth. His gaze slid longingly to hers, and the love she read there convinced her this was no dream, no aberration. This was Murphy, and he was real and alive.

A strangled cry escaped her throat, and she literally sailed from the top porch step and into his arms.

He caught her and threw back his head and released a deep-throated laugh. "For a minute there I was wondering if you remembered who I was."

"Murphy . . . oh, Murphy." She directed her mouth to his, not giving him time to explain or respond while she roughly planted wet kisses over his face, not caring where her lips landed. All that mattered in those moments was holding him, kissing him, and glorying in the truth that he lived.

"Letty, sweet Letty." He growled her name and wrapped his arms about her waist, then lifted her several inches off the ground. He buried his head in the delicate curve of her neck and exhaled sharply.

"I love you so much, so much, so much," she chanted again and again, unable to say it enough times.

"I love you," he insisted. Cupping her face with his hands, he made love to her with his mouth and tongue until they both trembled and clung to each other.

Letty felt the reluctance with which he ended the kiss, inching his lips from hers. He smiled down on her and brushed his thumbs across her cheeks, moist with tears she hadn't realized she'd shed.

"I was told you were dead," she said when she could.

Still clinging to each other, they sat on the top step. Tucked in his arms, Letty pressed her head against his shoulder.

"Who told you that?" he demanded.

"The CIA."

His soft laughter stirred the hair close to her temple. "One thing you need to learn, sweetheart, is never to believe the government."

"But I saw you shot down . . . at least I think I did."

"You were in no shape to remember much of anything."

"Were you . . . shot, that is?"

He hesitated. "Yeah, a couple of times."

She gasped and would have anxiously investigated his injuries, but he stopped her.

"I'm fine."

"I know, but—"

"Hey, I'm here, aren't I? Thanks to Jack and a few other of my closest friends."

"Jack Keller did find you?" She would be forever grateful to Murphy's friend. Somehow, all in good time, she'd come up with a way of repaying him personally for bringing Murphy home to her. "Tell me everything. I need to know it all. What did you learn about Luke? Don't hide anything from me."

He kissed her, his mouth lingering over hers as if he needed to feel and taste her once more before he continued.

"After you were shot they took you to Norte, didn't they?"

He tensed, then nodded. "Yeah."

"Did they . . . torture you?"

"Let's just say Norte was very pleased to see me, but furious that I'd been shot. You see, he'd been so eager to do the deed himself. Now it seemed I was to die and deny him the sadistic pleasure. He didn't want to simply finish me off, he wanted me to suffer for the error of my ways first."

Letty tensed, knowing he must have been in terrible pain.

"The two shoulder wounds quite possibly saved my life."

"How?"

"I was thrown in prison."

"Without medical attention?" That was criminal, inhumane . . . but exactly what she would have expected from Norte.

"A woman by the name of Rosita saved my life."

Luke's friend, the woman she'd thought she'd seen in San Paulo.

"Apparently she had someone on the inside willing to assist her on a limited basis. She came to me seeking information about you." He hesitated and planted his hands on either side of her face as his gaze delved into hers. "You were right. Luke is dead. I'm sorry, honey, I would have done anything to spare you that."

"How?" The word had a difficult time making its way out of her throat.

"She believed he went peaceably in his sleep, but she doesn't know for sure."

Murphy's arms tightened about her. "Apparently, before he died, he'd learned that the two of us were in Zarcero, and he asked her to do whatever she could to locate you and get you out of the country."

Tears welled in her eyes. Even with his own life about to end, Luke's thoughts had been for her.

"She loved your brother."

"I know." Her voice came out frail and trembling. Although Luke had never mentioned his feelings for Rosita, Letty knew in her heart that he'd come to love her as well.

Murphy gathered her close.

"I probably would have died if Jack and company hadn't arrived when they did. I don't suppose you'll feel any sadness when I tell you Norte's dead. I would have taken a great deal of pleasure in doing him in myself, but Jack beat me to it. As it happened, I wasn't in any condition to manage it."

Murphy was right, she didn't feel the least bit of

regret. The world was a better place without his hate.

All these long, lonely weeks she'd been left in the dark, believing the worst, suffering. "Why did you wait so long to come to me?"

"I couldn't, love. I was in pretty bad shape by the time Deliverance Company got me out of San Paulo." He brushed the hair aside from her neck and kissed her there. Raising his eyes to meet hers, he encountered the chain. "You're still wearing the necklace."

"It's my engagement ring, remember?"

"Engagement? We're engaged?"

"You proposed," she reminded him, not taking kindly to the fact that he'd apparently forgotten.

"I proposed marriage? Me? You've got to be joking." His look was skeptical. "I sincerely hope you didn't take me seriously."

"I most certainly did. Listen here, Shaun Murphy, you may think you suffered in Zarcero, but that's nothing compared to what I'll do to you if you've changed your mind about us."

Laughing, he wove his fingers into her hair, his eyes smiling into hers. "Unlike certain people I know, I keep my word."

"Are you suggesting I don't?" she grumbled, infuriated that he'd imply such a thing. She stopped abruptly. "Are . . . you're talking about our agreement."

"I fully intend to collect my due."

She wrapped her arms around his neck, sighed deeply, and pressed her head to his chest. "And I intend to deliver."

Epilogue

Letty stood on the porch with her hands braced against the wood railing. Her gaze traveled to the night sky, ablaze with a million blinking stars. A full moon stood guard over the earth.

Letty would have liked to believe Luke was looking down on her and smiling from one of those stars. She hadn't been able to sleep for thoughts of her brother.

Out of the blue, Luke's letter had arrived a month earlier. It had come as a shock to receive something penned almost a year ago. Rosita had enclosed it with a note to explain that the envelope had been found in Commander Faqueza's office shortly after the legal government of Zarcero had been restored.

Letty had read it countless times, so often she'd committed it to memory.

My dearest Letty,

It grieves me to write and tell you that by the time you read this letter, I'll be dead. A few days ago I stood trial and was condemned for crimes committed against the people of Zarcero. The trial and all that has befallen this country deeply distress me, but I can do nothing.

Don't weep for me, Letty. I leave this world confident that I've completed the work God set out for me, but I don't go without regrets. There's such irony in all this. You see, for the first time in my life I'm truly, deeply in love. My hopes for the future are but ashes now, for God has called me for a greater purpose.

I know you, Letty, almost as well as I do myself. Please, don't be bitter. Forgive my killers. I am leaving, but I promise that you will never be alone. My love will always be with you. In your darkest hours, and in your greatest joys, I'll be there. The military can take my life and all that I have, but nothing could destroy the closeness we have always shared.

Do you remember when we were kids and you sometimes claimed you could feel if something was wrong with me? I was never sure what to make of that "feeling" of yours. I'm ashamed to tell you I didn't believe you. Now I understand, because I've felt it too. For you. God has such wonderful plans for you, Letty. Such grand adventures. I can leave you now, because in my heart I know that you'll find happiness. I'm no prophet, but it wouldn't surprise me if you mar-

ried within the next few months. How I wish I could see you as a wife and mother.

You were always smarter than me. At least you liked to think so! For the first time I'll know something before you do. Heaven. The next time you look up in a night sky, look for me, Letty. I'll be up there smiling down on you.

I remain . . .
Your brother

The child moved within her womb, and Letty pressed her hand against her abdomen and smiled softly to herself. She'd learned so much about herself this last year without Luke. She missed him dreadfully, but it was as he'd always said. God closed one door and quickly opened another. She was a wife now and soon to be a mother. The fears that had crippled her about her own mother had long been laid to rest. It was as Murphy had assured her in the jungle. She was nothing like her parent, but it had taken his love to prove what she should have recognized long before.

The screen door opened. "Letty?"

"I'm here." She glanced over her shoulder at her husband.

Murphy joined her. "You couldn't sleep?"

"I was just thinking about Luke."

He stood behind her, slipped his arms about her waist, and flattened his palm against her rounded tummy. "Although we never met, I would have been proud to call him friend."

"Luke would have shook his head in wonder over

the two of us." And marveled at the changes love had wrought in them both.

"Hey, from what I read, your brother seemed to know about me."

Letty sighed softly. "I think he did." Luke had been right, too. She was truly happy. Despite her concern, Murphy seemed to find contentment outside of Deliverance Company. The security company he'd formed had more business than he could handle.

"What about Jack?" she asked, thinking of the company and Murphy's proposal. "Will he come to work for you?"

Murphy kissed the side of her neck. "It doesn't look that way." He levied a deep sigh that rumbled inside his chest. "If I didn't know better, I'd say Jack fell in love."

"What's so odd about that? You did too."

"Yes, but I have a wife and Jack doesn't. He's been in a foul mood for months. From my experience, when a man goes around self-destructing there's generally a woman at the heart of the problem."

Letty didn't disagree with her husband's assessment of Jack's troubles because she suspected he was right. "Jack's going to be fine."

"Oh?" Murphy chuckled. "And how would you know that?"

"I don't, for certain, but I wish him well." She owed Murphy's friend a great deal and wanted him to be happy.

"You ready to come back to bed?" Her husband yawned loudly.

"Yeah." She turned, and together, arm in arm, they walked back inside the house.

As they turned away, a shooting star blazed a fiery trail across the black satin night.